Of Wizards and Wolves

Of Wizards and Wolves

Tales of Transformation

Edited by
Lisa Mangum

WFP

Contents

Of Wizards and
Wolves ... and Dave
Kevin J. Anderson

Writers draw inspiration from the world around them, from their experiences ... even from grief.

This anthology is for our friend and mentor Dave Wolverton, who also wrote as David Farland. He was many things: a brilliant author, close colleague, and an unparalleled and inspirational writing instructor.

Dave passed away unexpectedly in January 2022, just before he would have appeared as a featured speaker and instructor at the twelfth Superstars Writing Seminar. Dave was one of the founders of Superstars in 2010, along with Brandon Sanderson, Eric Flint, Rebecca Moesta, and me. He was passionate about helping new writers, guiding them in their careers and their creativity.

The loss of Dave stunned all attendees of the conference—even as his passing inspired them. We had already established a practice of creating anthologies to raise money to fund scholarships named after another beloved Superstars member, Don Hodge, and editor Lisa Mangum proposed this anthology specifically as a memorial to Dave. *Of Wizards and Wolves.* For those familiar with Dave's writing, it was a perfect summation.

And to cap it off, we even have a story by Dave, "Barbarians," set in his incredible Runelords universe. What could be a better tribute?

But we felt we could do more. We also wanted to expand the scholarship program to create the granddaddy of them all, the David Farland Writing Endowment. The proceeds from this book will fund a special scholarship for an aspiring author to attend the Superstars conference by covering registration, travel, hotel, and food expenses so the recipient can get the full experience of the event.

It was the least we could do for Dave's memory.

Dave and I grew up together as writers, and we bootstrapped each other's careers from the very beginning. I first met him shortly after he'd won the grand prize in the Writers of the Future contest in 1987 for his exceptional "On My Way to Paradise," which he expanded into an equally exceptional novel, published by Bantam Books.

We were two of the first "young Turk" authors selected for the new Star Wars novel line, with my own Jedi Academy trilogy and Dave's *Courtship of Princess Leia*, which catapulted our midlist careers onto the *New York Times* bestseller list. He changed his writing name to David Farland for a fresh start when he launched his imaginative Runelords series, and that was how he became known to another generation of readers.

I learned so much from Dave. Early on, we were both part of a small, somewhat secret group of writers at the same level, eager to learn from one another, exchanging inside information, passing along tips, reviewing contracts. Dave and I were on countless panels at science fiction conventions around the country; we taught workshops together, and we kept teaching each other. I made several career breakthroughs thanks to vital advice Dave gave me.

Every year or two, we would get together with a few like-minded authors to spend days on the Oregon coast or Las Vegas, trying to decode the publishing business. We wanted to know how we could get better, how we could push the envelope and rise higher.

In 2009, Dave stayed with Rebecca and me at our house in Colorado, along with Eric Flint and Brandon Sanderson. We spent days brainstorming the intricacies and vagaries of a writing career. At that time, each one of us was a *New York Times* bestselling author, and we shared our knowledge and perspectives. After that weekend, realizing that others might want to learn the business side of writing, we all founded the Superstars Writing Seminars. That's only one of his legacies.

Not just an amazing writer, Dave was also a tireless teacher and mentor. In addition to co-founding Superstars, he served as the Coordinating Judge for the Writers of the Future contest. He created the Apex Writers Group with a burgeoning membership of ambitious, professionally minded writers. He was a guest lecturer at my graduate program in publishing at Western Colorado University. His writing books, especially *Million Dollar Outlines*, are truly foundational works for anyone who wants to become a successful writer.

He was more than Obi-Wan, more than Yoda. He was Dave, a Jedi Master whose pen was mightier than a lightsaber. Most of all, to me he was a friend.

He was gracious, humble, witty, kind, and absolutely generous with his time, knowledge, and imagination. The extent of his influence was like the gravitational pull of a giant star, while the depth and impact of his loss is like a black hole.

Dave was only sixty-four years old, and we should have had decades more time with him, dozens more books, and hundreds more new students who would forever feel the influence of his heart and mind.

We hope you enjoy these stories inspired by Dave's legacy.

Magic Hands
Storm Humbert

For David Farland

I could have snapped my fingers, but instead I chose to fly from LAX to Detroit, rent a car, and drive to my parents' house northeast of Webberville—a total travel time of eight hours. I was sure that told Mom how little I wanted to be there to see my father die, but I was coming—didn't really have a choice. A wizard's death is always a major event. It changes the world.

Webberville's Main Street was unchanged other than an uncomfortably modern facade for the post office. There was still the Panther Barber Shop and the Happy Home Salon. Nothing named for people, so the names could stay the same even when ownership changed. There was comfort in that familiarity that somehow compensated for the excitement a young magician like me got from LA or Vegas—something appealing about knowing my home hadn't left me behind because it wasn't going anywhere.

It was as if my father had frozen everything with a time

charm until I returned. He hadn't, but that would have at least explained why he was dying so young—he was only sixty-one. I'd thought I'd have more time to forgive him for Maggie. I wasn't sure I was ready, but this was my last chance to do it— his last chance to ask.

When I pulled into my parents' drive, Mom walked out a little slower than I remembered, gave me a long hug, and said how happy she was that I was home. Once we'd gotten into the kitchen, she said, "He's back in our room."

I didn't respond. I'd hoped there would be more talking— maybe she'd ask about work or if I was seeing anyone—before she asked me to go in.

"You can do this," Mom said, as if I'd been there only yesterday—as if it hadn't been years.

She had this way of smiling that was like a dare. Her eyes locked onto mine, and she held the stare as if she thought she could will her confidence, joy, laughter—whatever she wanted me to have—directly into me.

That was a kind of magic neither my father nor I could imitate. I always thought that if I held that eye contact, maybe it would work, but I never could.

I left my bags in the kitchen and took the long, short walk down the hall. The closer I got to the room, the more the magical flux of my father's passing pressed on me like a desperate humidity.

The smells of his favorite foods suffused the air: an acrid sweetness with a hint of grill marks. I was consumed with a confusion of fear and happiness—of everything at once. There was a charm of Dad's own making on the door—one stronger than I could ever craft—designed to contain the energies that were spilling from him. I hadn't opened the door yet, and the shadow of his waiting presence already overwhelmed me. *What will it be like inside?* I took a breath and turned the knob. The first vision hit as soon as I entered the room, and it was all I could do to close the door behind me.

"You're doing great, sweetie," Dad said. He was clean-shaven, his hair short and dark. In all my life, I'd never seen Dad without some kind of facial hair. He looked barely a boy.

Mom breathed, "He, he, hoooo," as she lay in what seemed to be an adjustable medical bed complete with stirrups, but it wasn't metal or plastic. It was twisted bark covered in pillowy moss. The branches had grown from beneath two sets of floorboards and burst into the center of what would eventually be my room.

It was a southern magnolia, Mom's favorite, and the smell of the yellow flowers clung to everything like a too-sweet film. Mom's light-brown hair was matted with sweat, and the bags under her eyes were full of undreamt dreams.

I was in the doorway with a clear view of the red-and-purple sunset out the window over Dad's shoulder, but I was higher than I should've been—as if I were floating.

"All right," Dad said. "One big push."

As Mom inhaled, all the charms I'd failed to notice came alive. They covered the walls, ceiling, and floor—rippling with light. I'd never seen so many in one place, packed so close together. I was sure the swelling edges would merge at any moment and swallow us all in a blink of unbound, chaotic magic. I tried to decode the charms, but it was like trying to read a sentence written in three dimensions while standing inside a single letter.

Then Mom sighed, and a baby cried. The charms leapt from the walls and shrunk down to motes of light that rushed to cover the baby. The child glowed in a way that made the sunset in the window seem drab, and this light reflected in Dad's sea-green gaze.

I now looked up at him through my own infant eyes instead of down upon the scene itself, and there was love in him that shamed magic with its power.

"Hello, little Liam," he said, but as he spoke, my vision darkened, and he faded away. But his voice echoed after me as if it sought, with all its baritone might, to pull me back.

"I was afraid you wouldn't come," Dad's elderly voice finished from the bed where he lay dying. It took me a moment to connect the ends of the two sentences split across time.

I staggered into the chair at his bedside. "Mom asked me to." It was the truth, but not all of it.

Dad smiled, and the lights glowed a little brighter. A breeze full of lilac and dogwood blew through the closed windows even though it was the middle of fall. The entire room bent to Dad's whims.

"You say that like she hasn't asked you before," Dad said.

His eyes were identical to the ones that had looked at me when I'd been born just moments ago, and that made me sad for all the time I'd missed. That wasn't only on me, though, and he knew it.

"Dad, I just—"

He shook his head, and my mouth slammed shut. I wasn't sure if it was magic or obedience, but I was too scared to check.

Dad flipped his hand over on the bed. The hand was as thick and strong as ever, wrinkled by age but not withered or shrunken. I knew he wanted me to take it. The gesture wasn't conciliatory. It was neither forgiving nor asking forgiveness. It was instructional. It was my father leading me through a process, as he always had. I didn't want to take it, but if I didn't, I'd come for nothing.

Once I did, he squeezed and said, "We have work to do."

"Dad, why do we have to do this?" I said in a small voice as I lugged a belly-sized boulder to the loader's bucket. "You could snap your fingers and make all the rocks disappear."

It was the middle of May—an especially hot, muggy May—and Dad and I were walking lines up and down the field, pulling up rocks so they didn't damage the planter. We'd been at it since early morning when it was a cool sixty-five degrees. By eleven o'clock, it was ninety with a stiff, thick wind, and cicadas squealed the heat from the nearby woods.

"I don't use magic for work," Dad said without a trace of labor in his voice, despite carrying four stones the size of the one I'd just struggled with.

After he clacked them all down into the bucket, I said, "It's not like I'm saying do a magic show or anything."

Dad was already walking away to get the next load of rocks, but he glanced back over his shoulder to let me know he was still listening.

"I'm just saying you wouldn't have to work so much if you used magic sometimes."

Dad bent down and palmed another big stone out of the dirt, then walked back to the loader. He carried it like a weightless rubber ball, and I stared. I was always a little obsessed with my father's hands. They were so thick and strong, like my grandfather's and great-grandfather's—so much different than mine.

Even years later, when I hit puberty and started working out and playing sports, my fingers remained spindly little things with narrow joints and small nails. No matter how often I helped Dad on the farm over the years, my hands never got more like his. Of course, I didn't know that then, so I often wondered what I'd do when I had my father's hands—what sort of miracles I'd make.

"If I use magic to grow the crops, then magic gets to be a job. It gets to be that I'm selling magic," he said. "Trust me, squirt, you don't want to sell your magic. It never feels right. Better off if you learn to love your work."

Somehow, I yanked my real hand from his, and the memory blinked out like an unplugged TV. *Cheap shot.*

"Really, Dad?" I said. "That's what you want to say? Trust me. I get it. You don't like what I do."

"I love what you do," he said.

His face was so earnest—almost surprised—and that threw me. I didn't know what to say.

"I didn't like it at first," he said. "But then I figured out *why* you do it." He was calm as he looked into my eyes. "We've seen all your magic shows. Even the pay-per-views."

I hated how he looked at me—like I was still a boy—so I said, "You don't get to say that. You haven't known me for twelve years. You don't know why I do it."

"Liam, you just want me to hate it so you can do it to spite me."

"It's not like you wouldn't deserve it."

My father looked calm, but the room's temperature dropped, and a window cracked from the change. By the time my eyes found the noise, it had been repaired. My breath misted in front of me, and my hand shot back into my father's as if drawn by an invisible cord.

It was over ninety degrees—typical for June—but it felt at least a hundred as Dad and I carried my and Maggie's winter stuff to the barn.

"She's gonna flip," I said as we set the snowsuits inside the door.

"That's the plan," Dad said. "You know what they say, you only turn eight once."

I was fifteen, so it was hard for me to admit that I was as excited for Maggie's surprise as she would be. I tried to play it cool because I was getting to be a man and that seemed like the thing to do. I'd grown four inches in a year, and Dad had just taught me how to shave. On my next birthday, he'd start my magic lessons so I could be a wizard, like him.

I tried to watch—to learn—as Dad cast glowing charms into the barn rafters, but the changes around me were distracting.

The first thing was the winter smell. It was the crisp, empty-air scent that's left after the pollen is long gone and the sweet aromas of summer aren't even a memory. Dad's breath misted first, maybe because he was in the haymow, but soon mine did too. It wasn't like normal breath mist, though, because it didn't go away. Instead, the fog drifted up into the peak of the barn, and a small cloud began to form.

That cloud grew from a spinning twist of my father's breath into a giant, fluffy mass that filled the entire peak of the barn and reached all the way down to about five feet above the haymow. The barn walls transmuted the heavy summer breeze that blew in from outside into a howling winter wind, and a couple minutes after our breaths stopped being drawn into the cloud, it started to snow.

It took about twenty minutes to get a few inches of snow on everything, during which time Dad and I put our jackets on and threw a couple snowballs back and forth to test it out. Dad had barely finished making a fifteen-foot snowdrift from the haymow to the barn floor when Mom led Maggie in.

Maggie dropped the lunchbox she'd taken to basketball camp right in the small side doorway. She squealed as she ran in her sandals and shorts through shin-deep summer snow to jump into Dad's arms.

"Oh my gosh! Oh my gosh! Oh my gosh! Thank you, Daddy!"

"Liam helped too," Dad said as he put her back on the ground.

Maggie jumped and hugged me just as hard—as if I were the one who'd made a cloud inside or conjured a snowstorm in the middle of June. She always hugged me like that—like I was magic just because I was her big brother. I missed it.

"Put your snow stuff on, sweetie," Dad said. "Then we can build a snowman."

"Okay." Maggie let go and bounded away.

I nearly fell over—as if I'd been leaning on her.

While Maggie, Mom, and Dad were rolling the balls for a snowman, I climbed into the haymow and stuck my hand into the cloud. Pinprick motes of cold danced on my skin, and I spun snow through my fingers like cotton candy.

Dad stared up at me with a deep smile. It wasn't extra broad or toothy, but deep—something in the eyes—and that was when I understood he'd made that miracle just to see the looks on our faces.

I slid my hand from Dad's and took a deep breath to steady myself. I wasn't going to let him sneak under my guard with some sweet memory of Maggie.

"Why that one?" I asked.

"Because that was what I thought of the first time your mom talked me into watching one of your shows," he said. "That look on your face—wonder. That's why you do it." Then he rolled his head to look at me. "And because you weren't the only one who loved her."

I had so much I wanted to say—so much I'd wanted to say for years—but I couldn't even look at him. I wanted to tell him that in all my study of magic since I'd stolen his books and left home, that I'd never found another mention of an indoor weather charm—that he might have been the greatest wizard ever.

I also wanted to tell him that he loved his magic more than he'd loved his daughter—that he hadn't done enough to make her better—but I didn't get the chance because Dad squeezed my hand, and we were off again.

"You're getting close, Liam," Dad said from across the cherrywood kitchen table. "The form of the charm is perfect, but you've got to let the magic flow into the shape."

Dad traced the figure of the simple luck charm he'd been trying to teach me into the air again, and it glowed a soft cerulean. Then he balanced the coin on the knuckle of his thumb for at least the twentieth time.

"What do you want to bet this time?" he said with a sly smile.

"I don't want to bet anymore," I said. "I want you to tell me what I'm doing wrong." I slammed my fists on the table. "Why doesn't my magic work?"

As the thunder of the blow rolled out of the room, the click of my father's thumbnail sent the coin spinning.

"Better call it," he said.

"Heads, I win. Tails, you lose," I said as quickly as I could. "Loser mows the lawn until I'm eighteen."

"Deal," Dad said as the coin thunked onto the table. It bounced a few times, then twirled as coins do before they fall one way or the other, but it didn't fall. It spun slower and slower until it stopped stock-still on its edge.

Dad stroked his beard in faux befuddlement. "Huh," he said. "That's so weird. Don't you think that's weird, Liam? It's not heads, so you don't win. And it's not tails, so I don't lose."

I rolled my eyes and slouched into my chair.

"If you don't win, and I don't lose, guess that means I have to win, right?" Dad said.

"Guess so. Gee-whiz, I'm learning so much, Dad." I clenched my fist under the table. All I'd ever wanted was to be a wizard like him, but my magic wouldn't work, and all he did was tease. *What if I didn't have it?*

"You would if you relaxed and focused," he said.

"Yeah, it's my fault," I said. "Sorry I can't focus on studying magic while Maggie is in the hospital and my all-powerful wizard dad isn't doing anything to help her."

Dad's face tightened so hard, so fast, that his forehead seemed about to split right down the crease between his furrowed eyebrows. He put his pointer finger against his forehead and scorched a symbol into it.

The smell of charred skin filled the room, but he didn't wince.

"Come here," he said.

When I didn't move immediately, he stepped out of himself —like a ghost dispossessing a body—and walked through the table to stand in front of me. His translucent nose hovered about an inch from mine, and I could see through his scowling, astral eyes to the serene, closed ones of his body slouched in the chair.

I screamed when he touched his smoking finger to my forehead, but it didn't hurt—didn't feel like anything, actually.

He snapped his fingers in my face, and I blinked. When my eyes opened, we were in the middle of Maggie's crowded hospital floor.

"They can't see us," Dad said.

He didn't wait for me to respond before stalking toward her room and through the closed door. I ran to catch up. He walked through her curtain and stood over Maggie, who was sleeping. I went to the other side of the bed.

By then, Maggie looked healthiest while she slept—like the doctors would release her as soon as she was awake—so I was glad we'd come at night.

"Magic isn't about making things out of nothing," Dad said. "Magic doesn't *make* anything—at least not anything you can touch, taste, or smell. Magic lets us move things from one place to another."

Dad looked at me for the first time since the kitchen, and I felt I should understand something that I still didn't.

"When we make fire, we pull heat from somewhere else. When we freeze things, we move their heat elsewhere. Even now, all I've done is move our consciousnesses from the house to here."

He ran his fingers through Maggie's hair. It didn't move.

"You don't want to get in the business of moving life, Liam," he said. "We aren't gods, and it's damn important you understand that."

"What's the point then?" I asked. "Why bring me here just to say that?"

"Because you need to focus."

Dad's finger glowed again, and he traced his luck charm

onto Maggie's cheek. The symbol shimmered, but then he kissed it and it sunk in.

"I won't take someone's life to make your sister better, but I can give her all my luck that she pulls through, and I can make her a lightning rod for all those who would do the same. That's what I've done." Dad motioned for me to stand closer to Maggie's head. "If you want, you can too."

"It doesn't work though," I said. The muscles around my eyes twitched as if I might cry, but I shouted instead. "My magic doesn't work!"

"Just focus," Dad said. "Feel it run up and down your spine and tingle across your skin. Feel it in your chest—like your heart is swelling. Direct it into your finger and trace the symbol."

The bags under Maggie's eyes were deep purple, and her lips were dry. Her breath was strong, though, and she had the memory of a smile at the corners of her mouth.

I couldn't feel her skin where my fingers touched her face, but I knew how it felt when she pressed her cheek against mine every time we hugged. My finger began to glow at the tip, like I'd brushed it against a star, and I wrote my luck charm on her cheek.

It was the first time I'd ever seen my magic. It was a different color than Dad's—maroon tinged with orange—and I stared before I leaned down, as Dad had, to give her a small kiss.

When I looked up, Dad was smiling. He snapped his fingers, and I blinked again.

I didn't open my eyes in the kitchen, though. Instead, I was back at Dad's bedside. I wanted to go back—to see Maggie again.

"I spent that whole week stubbing my toe, forgetting pencils for class, and spilling food on myself," I said.

Dad smiled. "Me too."

"It wasn't enough, though, was it?"

Dad's smile burrowed back under his beard, and all he could manage was a curt nod.

"I would've taken a lifetime of stubbed toes to keep Maggie alive," I said. "But that's not what it would've taken, was it? And you knew that. You just didn't think I was ready to consider what it *would* take, so you lied."

Dad's eyes were cold and hard as they shot up to meet mine, but they were wet too, and he trembled under the strain of crying.

"You were never to go in my study," he said. "You were never to look through any book I didn't give you. Those were the rules!" His voice literally thundered from all corners of the room as if we stood alone in a desert tempest.

I didn't know if the house actually shook or if it was my imagination, but I cowered for a second all the same. No boy ever becomes immune to his father's shout.

"It's my fault, though," he said, as he surrendered to the soft shake of crying. "I could have guarded the books. I could have charmed them. I could have booby-trapped them—anything. I didn't."

"You could have told me about the transference charm and let me decide for myself."

"You weren't old enough!" he said. "Ask any fool child to give up some years and some health so his dying sister will have a fraction more, and he'll say yes. Giving life is an uphill battle, Liam. Minutes are hours, and hours are years. Death doesn't make even exchanges." He looked up at me, pleading. "Even now, Liam, you're still just a boy." Dad said it as if he were disappointed—as if I should have been more. "You have more years in front of you than behind. You don't know how precious they are—how much you'll want more once you can count how many are left. You can't even fathom what I wouldn't give for more time ... lying here now—"

"Wish I could help," I said more coldly and cruelly than I'd intended.

"No," Dad said, shaking his head. "No, you don't, but that's my fault too." Tears streamed down his face.

The way he said it, he meant it every which way, and that struck somewhere deep, and I shook as the blow revealed how hollow my anger had become. I wanted to take it back, but Dad squeezed my hand harder than he ever had—so hard I was afraid he'd break it—and we were gone again.

I was in Maggie's hospital room again, but I was floating above the scene just like in my birth memory. Dad and Maggie were the only ones there, and Maggie was asleep.

"Hey, baby doll," he said, his fingers on her cheek. "I know you're tired, and the doctors say you don't have a lot of fight left." He ran his fingers through her hair, and his mouth smiled, but his eyes were angry and confused. "I told 'em they don't know you, if that's what they think." He laughed, and it was a real laugh—a full laugh. "I told 'em you're the only kid to ever get what you wanted by holding your breath. That you actually passed out." The smile and laughter fell away, and the caverns below Dad's eyes and in his cheeks ran deep. "I need you to fight a little more, baby doll. I need you to fight a little longer so we can all say goodbye. Mom, Liam, Grandma, Grandpa— everyone's on their way." There was real pleading in his voice as he said, "Everyone just loves you so much, sweetie."

It was one o'clock in the afternoon—December 14—right in the middle of fourth period. Mom would pull me from school soon. Normally, it would take about forty minutes from the school to the hospital, but with the bad snow and an accident on the highway, we wouldn't be there until almost two thirty.

At 1:12, the machine hooked up to Maggie squealed, and her vitals went flat. I watched her chest rise and fall and then not rise again. I couldn't shout her name. I couldn't interact. All I could do was watch, but Dad didn't hesitate.

The squealing cut off no more than a second after it began, and all other motion in the world stopped with it except for Dad's fingers as he completed the time charm. It was a charm so complex I'd never learned it, but he carved it into the air in a blink.

"No," Dad said. "Not yet."

His hand left the glowing charm and hovered by Maggie's cheek. He didn't touch her because if he did, time would begin to move for her again.

I didn't know how time charms worked—how they interacted with time or what exactly they did with it—but I did know they put great strain on the wizard. Dad's face was pensive, which it often was, but it was also confused and horrified. He seemed lost in a way I'd never seen, but then he nodded his curt nod and burned a symbol into his hand that I would recognize anywhere—the one that eventually made me leave home.

The transference charm.

"Don't tell your brother," he said as he pressed his marked hand to her cheek, his fingers resting just under her ear.

The veins on Dad's face leapt out just as Maggie's eyes popped open, and I could tell it was all he could do not to scream for that long moment.

"Hey, baby doll," he said as he sat back down a few moments later, winded, and took Maggie's hand.

The hospital began to move again, but the squealing monitor had stopped.

Mom and I got there about an hour later, and I got to talk to my sister one last time. I got to hear her laugh and see her smile —to feel her cheek nestled into the crook of my neck during our last hug. I would have given years for that, but I hadn't had to. Dad had taken care of that for me. I had gotten one last evening with Maggie, and that night, at 11:35 PM she passed in her sleep.

I didn't realize at first that I was back in the present moment because my eyes were closed, and I was crying. I really was still just a boy. I should have been more.

"I'm sorry," I said as I looked down at Dad as if through a rain-washed window.

He nodded, but not his curt, efficient nod. This one was more of a soft bob.

"Me too," he said, in a single, weak exhale.

It was as if it took every ounce of his energy—every bit of his breath—to form those words.

Then I watched his chest fall and fail to rise.

"Dad?" I drew in a sharp breath. *No lilac. No dogwood.* "No, Dad!"

I didn't freeze time, but I didn't have to. I carved the transference charm into my hand and placed it against his cheek like he had Maggie's.

I had more to say. I wanted to tell him everything—all the things I wished I had for years. I wanted to tell him that I loved him.

His beard brushed my palm, and I waited for the pain, but it didn't come. Instead, a symbol rose to the surface of his forehead—a blocking charm. He wasn't going to let me make the same mistake.

I moved my hand from his cheek to his palm. I'd never wished more that I was a god, but I wasn't. Dad had taught me that.

"I love you," I said.

I don't know if he heard me or not, but all the charms around the room glowed just as the ones in my birthing memory had. They surged with magical light, but it wasn't my father's. It was mine—maroon tinged with orange—and the symbols swam down to cover my father's skin. Their light flowed from all over, down his arm, and into the thick, powerful hand I still held.

I felt my father's life—his knowledge, his joy, his memories—flow into me, and I knew that when I left the room, he'd be with me, as he always had been.

Storm Humbert grew up in Ohio, got an MFA and taught for a bit at Temple University in Philadelphia, and now lives with his wife, Casey, in Michigan. His writing has appeared in *Andromeda Spaceways*, *Interzone*, and *Apex*, among others. He is also a winner of the Writers of the Future contest, and featured in the 36th edition of the Writers and Illustrators of the Future anthology.

Storm has been lucky to have had tremendous writing instructors and mentors throughout his life, including Lee K. Abbot (who first drew him to this craft), Samuel R. Delany, Don Lee, Tim Powers, and, of course, David Farland, so he tries to teach and facilitate others whenever and however he can.

Inspirational Theurgist
N.V. Haskell

William spread a clean newspaper neatly over the grimy subway floor, sat down, and leaned against the yellowed wall. He scratched his chin beneath his gray-and-white beard as one train glided to a stop, the paper's curling edges lifting in the wind. A mass of bodies careened toward the stairs as he quietly pressed himself away from their hurried shoes and analyzed each wave of energy with keen interest.

One man tossed a few coins at the elderly man, who pulled his long, tattered coat around his chin. A woman paused, and William shifted his foot, his toe peeking between the sole and the upper part of his worn shoe. She retrieved a five-dollar bill from her bag, but William didn't have a cup set out to receive such offerings, so she placed it atop his hands before rushing away.

William caught a hint of an energetic tug, but it was stale and quickly lost in the hustle of the commuters. He sighed and watched the crowd change as one train departed and another took its place.

People walked by filled with purpose and goals, their eyes locked on their phones or staring numbly ahead. Their voices struck him like blunted arrows, easily deflected with practiced defense. The years he'd spent searching for an anomalous soul had made him patient, and he no longer resented the time he waited.

His transition was looming, as evidenced by last night's shimmers that had wafted down his arms. His fingers had trembled and gone translucent; he'd lost his grip on the mug, which landed with a thud on the bar. Thankfully, his fingers quickly solidified again. It was the third time in as many months.

There.

He caught a hint of bright yellow in an otherwise black-and-gray palette and struggled to his feet as the pull called to him. His hips and knees protested, groaning under the sudden unauthorized demand. Leaning against the wall to steady himself, he spied the boy. Black curls, acne, with recently sprouted sparse hair braving his upper lip. The boy adjusted his backpack while throwing his shoulder against the crowd.

Painter.

William huffed, tucking the five dollars into his pocket before loping after him. The crowd parted thoughtlessly around the old man, neither cursing nor grumbling as they also tightened around the boy and slowed his pace. It was a subtle shift of energy that none but the truly aware could feel. And the boy was unaware of much, other than his hormones and newly complex emotions.

The energy connected William to the boy, and for a moment, the old man could sense the world as if through a new lens.

He felt the boy—*Zack*—grip his pack tighter and struggle like a salmon swimming against the current toward the train. With a collective sigh, the pack of bodies scattered from his path one second before the subway doors slid shut. The train darted away without him.

William was close enough to both feel and hear Zack curse.

The old man placed his hand on the boy's shoulder, which strengthened the energy passing between them. The energy was subtle at first, the giving of it happening at a molecular level and growing larger. William felt the magic fill Zack's arm before wriggling simultaneously into his neck and down into his torso.

Zack spun defensively, slapping the old man's arm away. The physical connection was broken, but the energy still flowed.

"A gift," William whispered, lifting his thick white brows, a smile on his thin, haggard face.

The arrival of another train kicked dirt into the air as it shuddered to a stop. Zack closed his eyes, and William slipped away into the crowd.

Still linked through the shared energy, William watched Zack claim a seat on the subway, briefly scanning the other passenger's faces. A moment later, the train jerked forward, and a surge of creativity sparked through the energy bridge like fire. Zack pulled a sketch pad from beneath five cans of spray paint in his backpack. As he began to cover the paper with new ideas, William withdrew the connection—and smiled.

Of all the comrades that e'er I had
They're sorry for my going away
And all the sweethearts that e'er I had
They'd wish me one more day to stay

The words drifted through the thick tavern air as drunken men and women sang in fractured unison. William wondered if they were still called taverns. It certainly felt like a tavern. But that could just be the alcohol and questionable decisions being made that gave it that air. He blended in with the crowd, his beard neatly trimmed, his clothing comfortably middle-class.

People saw what they expected to see, and unless he magicked otherwise, he changed accordingly. He warmed his hands in the pockets of his leather coat and reclined against the wall as he listened. The energy pull waxed stronger, like a thread tugged taut. It had potential.

Hidden behind five overly confident and mostly off-tune men, a woman sang shyly near the bar. Mary's voice lilted toward him with a rosy hue. He felt her desire to be heard contrasted with self-limiting fear.

Musician.

The inebriated people swayed apart easily as he strolled across the room. He brushed gently against Mary's arm in passing and felt her shiver. The sudden connection forced her voice to rise in volume, and when the moment ended, she did not readjust her voice.

Faces turned to her with new appreciation as she hit each note with a richness and raw emotion that overrode better tone or pitch. People lowered their voices to give space for hers. William saw a man in tears, his lip trembling as the golden energy of Mary's voice resonated inside him.

By a time to rise and a time to fall
Come, fill to me the parting glass
Good night and joy be with you all

Connected as he was to Mary, William could easily imagine her later, sitting at her table and filling old music paper with new notes and clefs. Tomorrow she would restring and tune her father's dusty old guitar, too long abandoned in a closet. With Mary's passion reignited, she would not question the new uptick in inspiration. She would not remember the well-dressed man who brushed into her at the bar.

William reclined on a park bench beneath the warming spring sun as the newly returned robins sang amorous pleas. He sipped his coffee, paid for by the generosity of a passerby in the subway. The warmth oozing from the cup eased the nagging of his arthritic fingers. He sighed, enjoying this simple pleasure his younger self would not have understood. But it had been such a long life, and it was nearing its end. Two painters, a sculptor, a poet, an actor, and a handful of musicians. It was a good haul for one night's work.

Unfortunately, none of them had been the one he sought. The artists he had touched were too full of other goals and familial obligations, things they could not put down with good conscience. Things that interfered with their ability to focus on creating.

He needed someone who had no such ties, but with the constant demands and impatience of this world, it had become like searching for a hint of ultramarine blue in a pre-1500s painting. Impossible. So, he simply gave each artist enough magic to inspire and rekindle their creative energies, to keep them going as he continued his search.

"Someday, you will have to choose wisely, too." That was what David, his mentor, had said before he transitioned. Back then, William had not understood what could happen. He thought that David's peaceful transition to an onyx-black raven that roosted in the Rockies was a lovely standard.

It hadn't been until his brother-in-service, Giotto, had failed to secure an adequate successor that William understood how dire the situation could be. Giotto's arrogant protégé had abandoned him before finalizing her commitment. She had taken most of his energy and inspiration and become famous, with no thought or intention of ever helping others.

When Giotto's last moment came, it was William who held his hand as he vanished into a long exposition of fusion jazz that filled a New York club for the better part of a night. When the music faded, several patrons had saved Giotto among four digital recordings that were never listened to again.

William shivered; it was the worst kind of ending after a life spent inspiring others. Worse, he knew how much Giotto hated jazz.

How well William chose his successor would determine his own last form. He didn't want to be a breath of wind that wafted through an orchestral pit. Nor did he want to be the worn sole of a ballerina's shoe. William wanted something more substantial, something that would linger and last. But after witnessing Giotto's end, it was hard to hope for an end like David's, and William found himself afraid to commit to anyone.

He closed his eyes and tilted his head back as the sun pierced the thin skin of his eyelids and turned his interior world shades of muted gold and amber. William thought of the boy from yesterday—Zack. He reminded William of himself when he had been a youth. But the artist was too young. He hadn't lived enough yet. And Mary, the soulful soprano, had recently taken on the role of defense attorney. She had too many distractions with a big trial coming up.

"Excuse me."

A woman's voice jerked him out of his musings. His coffee sputtered through its lid and onto his hand.

"I'm so sorry. I wasn't trying to startle you." She was a familiar, fortyish-year-old woman with strands of silver highlighting her brown hair at her temples. She was well-dressed in a simple business suit, but the designer bag on her shoulder was fraying and worn at its edges. Her brown eyes were warm with concern.

He transferred his cup to the other hand while wiping the coffee onto his tattered coat. "It's alright, miss."

She fretted, pulling a wadded napkin from her purse before shoving it at him.

William eyed her thoughtfully as a subtle, energetic tug drew his attention. There was an emptiness about her, a void that had been filled with more than she allowed herself to have now. William remembered a similar hollowness back when he was struggling to create. But that had been a long time ago.

"Did you need something?" he asked.

She thrust a five-dollar bill at him with hands he remembered glimpsing the day before. "I was going to leave it on your lap but didn't want to startle you. I suppose I did, anyway."

William glanced down; his leather jacket had transformed into a tattered woolen coat. The toes of his right foot chilled as a breeze wafted through the split sole of his shoe. She must have recognized him from the subway yesterday.

"Can I get you another cup of coffee?" she asked. She clutched her purse awkwardly, and he suspected the five had been the last of her bills.

He waved her away. "No, thank you. I appreciate the offer, though."

William glanced around, noticing the other park benches were full of couples or families. He scooted to the edge of the bench, leaving enough space for her to sit a comfortable distance away. The sun was bright; more office types would be coming out to enjoy their lunch breaks on a day like today.

"What's your name?" he asked.

"Tamara." She cleared her throat as he slurped the spilled coffee from its lid.

"William."

He waited for her to settle into a comfortable space without attempting the immediate small talk that might send her scurrying away. She wasn't timid, he thought. She was drained. Her energy was barely reaching for him. "You must work around here."

She nodded toward 47th Street.

"Lawyer?"

"Paralegal."

He grunted before taking another sip of his drink.

"And you?" Tamara asked. "You must have done some work ..." She trailed off as her cheeks flushed pink.

William gave her a small smile. "Artistic Inspirational Theurgist, wizard class," he replied. No one had asked in a long time and, whether or not she went running, he enjoyed being able to say it.

Her posture stiffened, but she didn't move to leave. "Artistic theurgist ...? Oh. That's nice. And, um, wizard class, you say?" She dug through her bag, eventually pulling out a sandwich in a zippered silicone bag. "That must have taken a lot of work."

"Four hundred years, give or take."

Her eyebrows raised as she glanced sideways at him, as if his answers were not wholly unexpected. "Well, you look awfully good for your age, William." She took a bite of her sandwich.

William watched her with increasing interest. "Any hobbies? You seem like the sort who might be good at a lot of things."

She covered her mouth, chuckling as she swallowed. "Nah. I used to be, you know, when I was younger."

"Musician?"

She shook her head, smiling. "Can't carry a tune to save my life. I'm the black sheep of my family. Everyone else plays instruments or sings."

He rubbed his beard, trying to determine how to categorize her. "Painter?"

"Only walls, and I still make a mess." Tamara sighed as she leaned back against the bench. "How about you, theologist? Any hobbies?"

"Theurgist. I used to be a writer, but that was a long time ago."

A spark lit behind her eyes. "I did a little writing back in high school."

"What made you stop?" William leaned toward her, attempting to reel in the energetic line that was spooling tentatively outward.

Her shoulders sagged slightly. "My folks died young, and I had to look after my younger brother and sister." She shrugged. Her voice held no self-pity. "You know how it goes. Life is messy and busy, and it has a way of turning out different than you thought it would." Her gaze shifted guiltily to his tattered coat and worn shoes. "I'm sorry. I should have filtered that before it left my mouth."

He smiled. "No offense taken. I'm curious though—why don't you write now?"

She half shrugged and did not reply.

"Would you if you could?" He tugged gently on an ink-black thread that spun from her chest, giving it a thimbleful of energy. With a gentle nudge, that creative line hummed to life.

"I'm too old for that now," she replied, but there was still that light in her eyes.

It was William's turn to chuckle. "It is never too late to start again, Tamara."

Tucking her empty sandwich bag into her purse, she narrowed her eyes thoughtfully. "Been nice talking with you, William. Hope to see you again."

He nodded, studying her as she hurried away.

Maybe he should revisit Zack. The boy had potential. William felt strongly that whoever his replacement would be should dive into the work with passion.

A middle-aged man scurried past while quietly reciting lines that William knew too well.

"Our doubts are traitors and make us lose the good we oft might win by fearing to attempt."

Actor.

It was easy to place a small stone in the man's way that slowed him down, and equally easy to keep the man from tripping as William imparted a bit of magic into him. A little inspiration improved every performance.

A week later, he saw Tamara sitting outside a café on a Sunday morning. She was sipping black coffee while typing one-handed on her laptop. William watched as she set the coffee down and attacked the keyboard with the full focus and fury of both hands.

"William?"

He turned to see a petite woman with black hair pulled into a neat bun behind him. "Jane, I didn't expect to see you again."

"I thought I might have missed you," she said, giving him a quick peck on the cheek. "I wondered if you had transitioned already."

"Soon, I think," he mumbled in a low voice. "Just some loose ends to take care of."

She nodded, catching the implication. "Have you finally found your successor?"

"Remains to be seen. There are several with potential." His eyes slid back to Tamara as she continued typing.

"Don't dawdle, William. You are running out of time, and I know how indecisive you can be." Jane said it with a smile, but her tone was serious. She patted his shoulder. "Just pick one, and let the cards fall where they may."

There was a yell behind them from the café, followed by a crash of dishes. A woman screamed as her companion, a short, round man, attempted to cough and could not. His face morphed into shades of maroon as he clutched his throat.

Tamara darted from three tables away. She wrapped her arms under the man's, hoisting him to his feet. Clasping her hands at the top of his abdomen, she made sharp thrusts upward. A chunk of barely chewed apple flew from his mouth.

The man leaned onto the table as Tamara released him. The man's companion embraced her, crying. They tried to repay her, offering to buy her another meal, but she declined. Gathering her computer and jacket, she hastened away with flushed cheeks.

"Huh." Jane cocked her head like a curious dog. "Writer?"

William nodded.

"Of course." She clucked her tongue. "Likes the action but not the attention. Just like someone else I know."

"I was thinking about someone else, actually. There is a young man who—"

"A young man? Are you joking?" Her look stung his pride.

"He has a lot of potential," William said.

"All young people are full of potential, William. *You* need someone who enjoys the process. Someone who wants to help others. Someone who has lived a little." Jane tapped her shoe on the concrete.

"But Zack seems like a good kid."

"A kid." She glared at him. "Should I remind you about what happened to the last good kid? Should we talk about Giotto?"

He scowled and bit his lip. His vision suddenly darkened, as if his eyelids had closed and refused to open. He swayed gently on his feet.

"William?" Jane's voice rose in concern.

Her worried face greeted him when he opened his eyes again. She shook her head slowly.

"You shimmered for a moment." She swallowed nervously. "Like sunlight moving through morning lake mist."

He sighed, wondering if that might not be such a bad ending.

They parted, and William felt the quiet pain of knowing they would not meet again in this realm.

William spent the better part of the next two days following Zack through crowded subway tunnels, down dark alleyways, and, eventually, to a small gallery in Soho. After the boy was removed by security, he graffitied a large, colorful phallus on the side of the building.

William tried to intervene, telling Zack about the life of an Artistic Inspirational Theurgist, but when the boy's eyes glazed, he switched to saying *wizard*. He bought the young man's time with food from a street vendor, but when the last of the jalapeño-and-shrimp tortillas disappeared down the boy's throat, he hurried away without a backward glance.

When William pursued, Zack threatened to hurt him.

William resigned himself begrudgingly to the thought that Jane had been right.

He spent the next week watching Mary's trial, which was almost over. But on the weekend, she met someone while singing another Irish tune. He played the fiddle and sang in a bass that complimented her soprano. William had to admit they made wonderful music together.

The shimmerings were happening more frequently, sometimes three to four times a day, and William worried that each one would be his last.

He was afraid of transitioning alone.

Sitting and leaning against the subway wall, he closed his eyes. The noise did not stifle his thoughts. He hoped he wouldn't get stuck down here as a worn-out harmonica tune, or worse, a reedy treble note of an abused accordion. Depending on the words, graffitied poetry might not be so bad. Until someone scrubbed it off.

"How are you doing, William?" Tamara wore a pleasant smile and offered him a small cup of still-steaming coffee. "Thought you might want this."

William lumbered to his feet and nodded his appreciation before taking a long swallow.

"I've been looking for you for a couple of days, actually," she said.

"You have?" He frowned at the strong energetic tug that drew him toward her. She was different. The void he had detected when they first met was gone.

Writer.

He smiled.

"I wanted to thank you," she said, standing her ground as people jostled against her.

A tingle worked its way up William's spine, and the hair on his neck bristled with an electric surge. "I'll walk with you."

They headed up the stairs and made their way out into the morning light. William shimmered for a moment but returned before Tamara noticed. He walked beside her, his knees aching at the brisk pace she set.

"Our little talk that day in the park really inspired me. I've sold a poem and written a couple of short stories," Tamara said.

"Already? That was fast." He tried not to let her see him struggling to keep up.

She glanced at him and slowed her pace. "It doesn't matter if I'm late for work today." Her smile widened. "Today is my last day."

William paused. The crowd around them thickened and stopped. "What?"

"I quit my job."

"What are you doing now?"

She laughed delightedly. "I don't really know. Take a couple of months off. Figure out what I want to do."

He examined the multicolored energy line coming from her. "What do you want to do?"

"Help people. I just don't know how, yet."

The crowd moved again, but they stood staring at each other. William swallowed.

"I think you would make an excellent Artistic Inspirational Theurgist, wizard class," he said impulsively.

She shook her head and laughed. "What kind of job is that?"

He shoved his coffee cup into her hands. "Just watch."

Pulling at the collar of his shabby coat, he tugged at the thinning line of magic within him. His clothing glistened, morphing into a tuxedo with a black overcoat. His beard sparkled and vanished, along with twenty years of wrinkles. A black oak cane materialized in his hand.

People paused and gasped at the transformation, offering a round of applause.

"See?"

She shook her head, handing his coffee back to him. "Not really. Being a street performer doesn't appeal to me."

They walked slower up the street toward her office.

"I just inspired two poets and an artist to create something today. An actor will think about my showmanship when he steps on Broadway tonight. A dancer will—"

"Uh-huh." Her tone was skeptical.

William moved in front of her and blocked her path. "This is what I do. I inspire people—people like yourself who have lost their passion. People who think they are not good enough or who just need a nudge to focus on a canvas and paint for an hour. Or pick up a musical instrument. Or sing loudly at karaoke. Or even write something buried inside them."

Her eyes narrowed, but he continued, undaunted.

"The stress of the world makes it difficult for people to find their own inspiration, so I give them some of mine. Where would societies be without its artists and visionaries?" He licked his lips, hoping she would understand. "Art gets us through the difficult times, and *everyone* is an artist, Tamara. My job is to find out what that means to them and how to coax its growth. Then hope that they feel called to pass that inspiration on to others."

He felt a shimmer ripple through him; his magical display had taken too much from him. His vision clouded as a moment of panic took hold. He had waited too long.

Tamara's warm hand rested on his arm. The energetic line

inside her reached into him, winding around his frayed thread without hesitation and making William solid again.

She sighed, studying the lines of his face. She removed her hand a minute later. "Inspirational wizard, huh? Tell me more."

He cleared his throat. "Theurgist."

But he smiled as he spoke.

"Is it time?" she asked. Sadness deepened her voice as they sat beneath the full moon on their park bench.

William nodded slowly. His hand trembled. "I'm afraid, Tamara. What if I don't ...?" His voice trailed off in a whisper.

She squeezed his hand. "I got you. You don't have to worry." She wrapped an arm around his shoulders. He had grown thin over the last months. "If you turn into a string of music, I will record it and put it on repeat forever."

William laughed, which seemed a strange thing to do in his last moments. But it felt good too.

"Even if it's jazz?"

"Yes, William. Even then." Her arms were warm around him. "I love jazz."

He leaned against her and closed his eyes. With a long, soft sigh that rustled the leaves like wind, William let go of all that he'd been.

The caw from the bird that roosted in the branches above was muffled by the late-spring snowfall, but it still pulled him from his slumber.

William stood and stretched. He sniffed the air, appreciating the scent of pine and juniper and catching the more intriguing smells of other animals.

Other animals.

He stood tall on four legs and paws. His gray-and-black fur was thick and warm. A full tail swished the snow behind him.

"Morning, William."

An onyx-black raven watched him with sharp eyes while shuffling from foot to foot and ruffling its wings.

"David, is that you?" William's words came out as a soulful howl.

The bird cocked its head as a hawk landed on another branch. The surrounding bushes rustled and parted as a black bear waddled forward. A moment later, a white-tailed deer sauntered into the circle.

The raven landed softly before him. "I'm so glad you made it, William. We've been waiting for you."

N.V. HASKELL is a Writers of the Future winner, featured in Volume 38. Her works have appeared in the *Deep Magic* ezine and *The Last Line*. She writes speculative fiction and is only slightly obsessed with non-European history and mythology.

N.V. can be found in her favorite costumes at Comic Cons or Renaissance Fairs, reading multiple books at a time, running badly, traveling, or teaching yoga. She lives in the Cincinnati area surrounded by old souls, a rescue dog with a large personality, an indignant cat, and too many squirrels. After many years in healthcare, N.V. continues to be stubbornly optimistic, believing that there is goodness in this world if we dare to look for it.

An Abundance of Wizards

Linda Maye Adams

Finding things is its own special kind of magic. People put out all types of junk to the curb, labeled with a crude sign, hoping *free* will get someone to it take away so they don't have to.

Most of it is junk.

But sometimes there's a good object we can use. My husband, Alex, and I fix those up and sell them online. Can be pretty profitable.

But not this morning.

We'd passed on three free piles. Old books, stained and stinking of mildew. A child's toy car, the red-and-yellow plastic faded from the sun. That dresser of fractured wood, covered with stickers of a *Star Trek* fan.

"We'll do better at the next place, Jennie," Alex said.

Disappointed, I yanked open the passenger door to our aging minivan. A cloud of heat enveloped me. I stayed on the curb, scooping my carrot-red hair into a ponytail while I waited for it to dissipate.

"We weren't even gone for fifteen minutes." Alex glowered at the pollen-crusted roof. "Look at it!"

It needed washing. After two weeks of rain, the oaks and maples were putting out their all. A crow cackled from the tree-tops, as if mocking us.

"Says you," Alex called up to it.

"Humidity's going to be bad today," I said. "Do you want to go back?"

His gold wedding band glinted in the pounding sun. "Bills are coming due. We can't go home empty-handed."

My shoulders slumped.

We both felt the pressure of the almighty budget. Ever since we inherited my family's historical Queen Anne house, everything needed fixing. We went through money so fast that I'd resorted to painting river stones to sell as garden decorations.

The cloth seat scraped at my sweaty legs. Guess I shouldn't have worn shorts and flip-flops.

Paper crackled as Alex passed me a bag. From the smell, the double-chocolate chip cookies I'd made yesterday.

"It's too early for cookies," I said.

"It's never too early for cookies," he said solemnly. "Besides, I need cookie fortification after all our bad luck."

Truth be told, so I did I. So I nibbled on one with a bit broken off the end. Damaged cookies didn't have calories.

"Where do we try next?" Alex uncapped a bottle of water, knocking it down.

"How about we try over on 15th? The houses are being demolished. Might be something there."

The row of five houses had been bought by a construc-tion company looking to build monster-sized houses without any yards. Same company offered us a lot of money for our house. Didn't care that it was historical. Just that it was on a big lot they could turn into as many houses as they could jam on it.

The stucco houses might have been generously called bungalows by a real-estate agent. More like shacks. Tiny, empty-eyed windows. Weeds battled for dominance in patchy yards.

My flip-flops slapping at the pavement, I trudged across the street to the first house.

"I'm leaving the window down this time," Alex said.

He ran after me. I turned, walking backward to admire his legs. He'd dressed in neon rainbow board shorts and a T-shirt that didn't match. I ignored that, glad I could sightsee.

"All right, but if someone steals the van, it's your fault."

"Who'd steal that? It's fifteen years old. Hardly a getaway car. What are the thieves going to do, turn it into a clown car of robbers?"

I smiled, picturing black-clad robbers wearing masks spilling from a clown car.

As I reached the sidewalk, I said, "I've been thinking. Is there another area we should branch out in? Additional cushion when the pickings are slim?"

The problem was that we had to spruce up the free junk. Paint, woodworking supplies, sometimes repairs. I'd used the last of my coral paint on a music stand.

"How about we take photos?" he said. "Put them up on one of those online photo sites."

"No one wants blurry pictures of my thumb or your crooked ones."

"My pictures are not crooked. You just have to hold them at an angle."

We passed the first house, a pale gray that hadn't aged well. Alex stooped to inspect the lumber dumped at the end of the yard, likely part of an old fence.

The boards clattered as he dropped them, spewing pollen. "Dry rotted."

A rusted garden rake lay in the next yard. Alex tested the metal tines. Tossed it back.

My nose itched. "Stop doing that. The pollen doesn't need any help."

"Sorry. This looks like the junk no one thought worth hauling away."

"Someone will take it."

There was always that person who would pick up the broken junk, telling themselves they could fix it. Then it became their junk, a project forever waiting but never finished.

The third house was painted an ugly coffee-stain brown with a flat roof and squinty windows. Stank like someone had peed in the yard. But we hit the gold standard.

Two—*two!*—steamer trunks!

Not the kind you buy for your winter blankets. These were old, possibly antiques.

Jackpot.

Alex shoved his hands in his pockets. "We aren't this lucky, Jennie. Why hasn't anyone else picked these up?"

"Maybe they stopped after the first two houses."

I ran my hands over the pine and oak wood, finding small dings and other damage from use. The flattop trunks must have been beautiful in their day. They'd need restoration work by someone who knew what they were doing.

More money. Living in a historical house, I knew how that added up.

"Looks like all original hardware," Alex said. "Still has all the end caps."

He unlocked the iron latches. Hinges, long unused, squealed. The smell of mothballs joined the pollen.

"Looks like Halloween costumes," Alex said.

He pulled out a wizard's hat—a pointed cone in a deep amethyst, stars and moons embroidered in yellow. A matching cloak lay underneath, the material amazingly soft. They looked like costumes from an old movie.

I shook my head. "Too good for cheap costumes. Maybe a theater production?"

"Or vaudeville." He grinned, his cheeks dimpling. "Let's get these home and see what else is inside."

We really should have opened the second one.

Our Queen Anne house was marked by the brilliant purple flowers of a magnolia blooming happily at the end of the football field-sized yard. Okay, the yard wasn't that big, but it took two hours to mow with a riding mower.

First time I saw the house, when I was ten, I believed it was haunted. It looked like something from *Scooby-Doo, Where Are You?* You know—tower, gables, old stone. Just needed the lighting flashing over it.

Now I saw the house as a stately gentleman, dressed up to attend a black-tie party. I still couldn't quite get over that this piece of artwork was mine. My great-great-grandfather had designed it in the 1880s, and in its day, many parties had been held here. I could picture women peeking through lace curtains in the three-story brick tower, waiting for guests to arrive. A husband escorting his wife, dressed in a lavish gown with a bustle, up the five steps to the oak door under timber arches.

Alex pulled the minivan up the serpentine driveway that had once served horses and carriages. Now it was paved with smooth asphalt. Still, I sometimes fancied smelling horses and hay when the day was hot.

We unloaded the two trunks in the backyard. Startled, a brown cottontail bunny hopped into the bushes.

The green grass tickled my ankles. "Grass needs mowing again."

"Grass always needs mowing," Alex grumbled. "When we get more money, we could pay a gardener."

Yeah, it was an old discussion. We'd never had enough money for anything that we hated doing.

Alex had gotten laid off a year ago. The job hadn't paid well anyway. My boss was so bad I'd left to keep sane.

The saddest part? We made more money selling junk than both our jobs combined, and we were still broke.

Yup.

I opened the first trunk, shaking out the amethyst robe. Baby soft. I wanted to pet the fabric. Instead, I clipped it to the laundry line to air out the mothball odor.

The rest of the trunk was packed tight with five more robes, all in deep, jewel tones, rubies and emeralds.

"Everything's hand-stitched, hand-embroidered," I said, hanging all the robes on the line.

Alex shrugged into a peacock-blue robe that almost fit his lanky form but left his ankles exposed.

"What do you think?" He waved a wand made of blond wood.

"What are you planning to zap?"

"How about Mr. Oberman? He's always spying on us with those big binoculars."

"Pain in the ass," I muttered, laying the rest of the wands on an old sheet.

Mr. Oberman called the cops on us regularly. The first time because he was convinced we were burglars. After that, he blamed us for vandalism to his mailbox (kids) and stealing his paper (probably the carrier just didn't want to deliver the paper).

I turned to the second box, flipped open the latches. They were stiff and needed some oil. The hinges groaned. Preparing for the mothball assault, I pushed open the lid.

Cold washed out from the trunk, a gray fog swirling up.

"Jennie!"

Alex surged at me, robe flapping around his shins. He hooked his huge hands under my armpits and dragged me to the driveway. He was amazingly strong.

And so frightened, he didn't realize I had bare skin on scratchy grass. One of my flip-flops had come off. I barely had time to get my feet under me when we reached the concrete.

An eerie moan rose from the fog, the chill reaching into my bones.

The fog swirled, then whisked away, disappearing into the sunlight. The old wood of the trunk creaked and groaned.

An ancient man rose from inside the trunk, stretching his long legs. Wrinkles nested in his face. Cloud-white hair touched his shoulders. He wore a simple shirt of silk, buttons running down the front, and wide-legged trousers. Practical boots in a soft, well-used leather. The toes were scuffed. All of it was the same color as the first robe I'd hung on the line: amethyst.

He shook out his shoulders one at a time, then rubbed at a thick white beard.

I stared at him, afraid to move. Alex's chest heaved against my back. Visions of every horror movie flashed through my mind. Had we unleashed a paranormal serial killer?

"Out of the way! Out of the way!" squawked a second voice.

The white-bearded man stared down his nose at the interior of the trunk. "Patience, Bartley, patience."

"You try being patient after being imprisoned in this trunk forever!"

With a put-upon sigh, the first man stepped from the trunk. He gazed around our backyard, cocking his head.

"Tobias, help me out of this coffin already!"

"Very well." Tobias reached down to help a fireplug-shaped man out of the trunk.

Bartley was no more than four feet tall, his hair rumpled. He applied a squinty eye to survey our yard. "There it is!"

With short, quick steps, he cut across to the laundry line. Glared up at the ruby red robe.

"Who put that up there?" he demanded.

"I'll get it." Tobias gave us a sympathetic smile. "My apologies, dear lady, gentleman. We're not going to hurt you."

Alex jumped to his feet, fists balled at his sides. The peacock-blue robe slipped halfway off his shoulders. "Who are you? How—"

"A moment, please. Bartley won't calm down until he has his wizard's robe." Tobias passed down the red robe to his companion, then pulled on the amethyst one. "That's better."

"Says you." Bartley seemed to be the bad-tempered sort. He marched back to the steamer trunk to retrieve the crooked wand.

Tobias leaned over the open trunk. "It's safe to come out. We're ... somewhere." His pale eyes met mine. "Where are we? Where is your other shoe?"

Oh, right. My legs jangling with tension, I bounced to the errant flip-flop. Alex squawked in protest.

I ignored him. He was supposed to be the brave one. "Who are you?" I asked as I slipped on the flip-flop. Better. Even the grass was too warm for bare feet.

"We're wizards, of course," Tobias answered.

"Wizards?" Alex blinked and joined me. "You mean, like magic, love spells, and all that?"

Tobias helped a woman with stone-gray hair step out of the trunk. Her Victorian-style dress was peacock-blue. Alex hastily shed the robe he was wearing and held it out to her.

"Oh, no," Tobias said with all seriousness. "We don't cast love spells. Possible, of course, but immoral."

"There are some things no one should interfere with," the peacock-blue wizard said, taking the robe from Alex.

Three more wizards, one man and two women, climbed out of the steamer trunk. The very air seemed to shift. My stomach took a hard lurch, nausea swelling up. Alex gripped my hand tightly.

Then: *Snap!*

The sensation was gone, and the trunk looked normal again. But now we had six wizards in our backyard. What were we supposed to do with them?

Not sure what else to do, I invited the six wizards onto the screened service porch on the back end of the house for lemonade and cookies. There wasn't quite enough seating for so many people, so Alex moved the painted river stones I'd left drying on the two-foot-wide sill framing the screens.

I left Tobias and the Green Wizard inspecting the river stones. I hoped they didn't comment on my painting job.

"What are these for?" Tobias asked.

"We sell them to pretty up people's gardens," I said.

Yellow Wizard tried to follow Alex and me into the kitchen. I shooed her out. She bowed three times, nervously, then retreated through the back screen door, not saying a word.

"This is too weird," Alex said as he dumped double-choco-late chip cookies on a bamboo tray.

"You think you could arrange the cookies so they look nice?" I asked, feeling waspish.

"Why? They're going to get eaten." But he sighed and lined them up.

Ice clinked as I dumped a scoop into the pitcher. Did a quick headcount of the glasses. "We can't even explain them. And they all stand out. What's Oberman going to do when he sees them?"

"Call the cops."

We both laughed, too hard, at the absurdity of the whole thing. I pictured myself trying to explain the colorful wizards. Pity it was spring and not almost Halloween.

I wiped tears from my eyes, then hefted the tray with the lemonade pitcher and glasses. "One thing at a time."

Alex picked up the cookies. "Onward!"

The wizards pounced on the cookies.

"It's like we threw food to piranhas," Alex said.

"Maybe they haven't eaten in a long time," I said.

"Manners, please, manners," Tobias called over the crunching and munching. "We apologize, my lady. We haven't tasted anything so delectable before. Even the king's cook could not create anything like this."

"It's the chocolate," Alex said.

I handed Tobias one of the cookies I'd held back, kept the other for myself. There were priorities, and chocolate was always a priority.

We sat on the wicker sofa, squeezing in beside Green Wizard. He eyed my cookie.

Alex smacked his hand. "She can make more."

"How did you get into the trunk?" I asked around big bites of my cookie.

"The palace was attacked," Tobias said. "The black wizard cast a spell that imprisoned us in the trunk. He said only a woman with fire hair would free us."

I touched my hair. No wonder he thought I was the one he was looking for.

"You don't have anyone with red hair in your world?" Alex asked.

"No." Bartley drained his tumbler of lemonade. "Brown and black, some straw."

Straw? It took me a minute to translate that into blond.

"You must be the fated one," Tobias insisted, looking at me.

"Can you go back to your world?" I asked.

Tobias shook his head. The other wizards glanced away, shifting uncomfortably. Green Wizard plucked at a thread on his robe.

"You don't want to go home?" Alex asked.

"Even if it were possible, I fear we would be killed," Tobias said. "Please, my lady, you would honor us by letting us stay here."

Here? In the house? With us?

I blinked, exhaled. The house was big enough, certainly, with six bedrooms. But why was I even considering it? They'd just shown up on our doorstep.

But where else would they go?

Alex's warm hand closed over mine. I squeezed it, swallowing. Hated the heat in my eyes.

He leaned in close. "What would we do with six wizards?"

"Beats me. We can't afford to feed everyone."

Tobias frowned. "Afford?"

"Money, uh, coin," Alex said.

Tobias's blue eyes brightened. He picked up one of the river stones I'd painted as a lavender ladybug. "We can enchant these. You can sell them. Right, Bartley?"

The red wizard gave the rock the squinty eye. "Yes. A charm to make the garden grow."

"Could we sell that?" Alex asked.

My mind worked through the possibilities. I'd heard of people putting their souls up for sale—and someone else buying it. Why not enchanted rocks? "We'd have to put a disclaimer on it, you know, 'Just for entertainment.'"

It might be possible to set up a table at the farmers' market and sell them there. It was scary how fast we agreed to keep the wizards. But what would we do about Oberman?

Two weeks later, and we aren't hunting for free junk anymore. It only took one enchanted rock sold at the farmers' market and a raving comment from a gardener about our ladybug rocks making his azaleas shoot up, and suddenly I couldn't paint them fast enough.

Of course, we were adding to the pollen, but still ...

It was surprisingly easy to get used to wizards walking through the house, their robes sweeping the hardwood floors, bright against the oak paneling. Somehow, I could see them fitting in at those past parties my great-great-grandfather hosted.

Mr. Oberman was beside himself. He called the cops on us again to complain about the "strange people." I told the officers we had tenants to help pay the bills.

After that, though, Bartley cast a spell over the front of the house to hide the wizards. He'll need to renew it about once a week and after it rains. I've also been trying to convince the wizards to dress in modern-day clothing.

Yeah, a work in progress.

Alex and I sat out on the service porch and watched as

Green Wizard chased the cottontail. As I leaned into the curve of Alex's body, I realized how glad I was to not have to hunt for junk anymore.

Free junk felt like desperation. Wizards walking through my house felt like home.

Linda Maye Adams is the author of "Alien Pizza," published in Kevin J. Anderson's anthology *Monsters, Movies, & Mayhem. Publishers Weekly* reviewed her story as "especially delightful." She is a two-time silver Honorable Mention winner in the prestigious Writers of the Future contest and also has received five honorable mentions. Her novel *Crying Planet* was selected for the Military Science Fiction Storybundle. She is currently writing two series, GALCOM Universe and Dice Ford, Superhero.

A Sprig of Wolfsbane

Mary Pletsch

We were given a wizard as well as an inn.

My in-laws had said nothing about a tenant on the property, and, having never seen a wizard before, I thought he was just another customer. A strange one, mind, but there were plenty of folks in Dobovor who seemed strange to my provincial eyes.

My husband had been a soldier, the kind who died young. I had also been a soldier, the kind who had to pick up the pieces after the war. Our attempt to defend our home against the vastly superior elven army had been both brave and futile. With nowhere else to go, my son and I fled to my husband's kin for refuge, to this nation under the shadow of the mountain citadel. My in-laws asked me to take over the day-to-day operation of Dobovor's inn, replacing the leadership of their recently deceased matriarch.

Yes, I'd heard the stories about this country, and the dark tales of what slept in the castle high on the mountain. Yes, I'll confess I was relieved to find that the nation had a functional government, a regent chosen by the elected mayors of its towns.

But was I afraid to live in this place? I could not manage fear. After facing the elves in combat, I would never again be frightened of rumors and fireside stories. If those terrifying tales were keeping the elves at bay, then I would happily spread them.

Our fireside's regular occupant was not interested in scary stories. The wizard spent most of his time with a big book open on his lap and a potted plant on the small table at his side, where an ordinary person would place a drink. He wore black leather gloves, black boots, and a simple green cloak with black underlayers. There was no way to tell how old he was: he wore a cowl low over his eyes and a black veil that completely obscured his face. This manner of dress, among his other eccentricities, explained why the rest of my customers generally preferred to ignore him.

In the beginning, learning the day-to-day operations of the inn kept me too busy to pay much attention to the wizard. It also kept me too busy to pay enough attention to my son, which is why I failed to notice that he'd developed a certain attachment to the tenant who lived in the little cottage at the back of our property. We'd been in Dobovor for several weeks before the day my son called me over to the hearth to see the wizard at work. Before my eyes, the wizard's plant produced a single additional leaf.

It wasn't appropriate for my boy to be disturbing him. "Couras!" I chided. "Leave the customers to their business."

The verdant cowl lifted and turned in my direction. "He's no trouble," the wizard said in a low murmur. "Honestly, I find it refreshing to have young company." A pause. "Which reminds me. I owe my monthly rent." The wizard produced a small bag from beneath his robes and handed it to me.

I paled when I saw how many gold coins were inside it. "Is ... this ...?"

"The customary amount, yes."

"Mama!" Couras's eyes shone with excitement. "Could I do magic like that someday?"

In our old life, there would have been next to no opportunity for Couras to seek an advanced education. Now? With the money the wizard paid in rent, it might be possible.

My throat choked up at the thought of my son's future wide open before him, so the wizard beat me to an answer. "It requires talent," he said quietly, "and study, and much, much practice. But if your mother gives her permission, I could help you discover whether you have such talent."

Couras looked at me pleadingly.

"Perhaps when we're established," I said. "Right now we don't have the money to spare."

"I would seek no payment. It is I who owe you for your generous hospitality," the wizard replied. "It would have been entirely within your rights to evict me." Again, a pause. "You would not be the first."

"You mustn't teach him anything dangerous," I said firmly.

"Just hedge magic. The enhancement of living things. Practical little spells," the wizard agreed and rose to his feet. "May I introduce myself properly. I am called Wolfsbane."

"Ratsbane, more like," muttered a customer sitting behind me.

I didn't understand the comment. The wizard explained, "Gregor here wants you to know that I am responsible for keeping the town free of pests."

Gregor startled at the mention of his name, but his sneer returned as he leaned toward the wizard. "Never see you doin' anything about them."

The sound from under the wizard's hood might have been a chuckle. "Then I must be good at it."

"He's got you there," one of my servers said as she passed

by with a tray laden with glasses. "Can't remember the last time I saw so much as a mouse."

Gregor snorted. "It's not as impressive as it sounds. We've had no vermin problem in my lifetime. Most of the wee beasties fled these lands a thousand years ago." He leaned forward, resting his elbows on the bar, and gave me a nasty smile. "Ever since this land fell under the shadow of the King of Darkness."

"*In*," the wizard said, and I could hear the disapproval in his voice.

"Excuse me?" Gregor snapped.

Wolfsbane sighed. "King *in* Darkness. Not *of*."

"What's the difference?"

"I would think rather a lot." Wolfsbane gathered his things and stood up, as though he'd had enough of Gregor's attitude.

Meanwhile, I had forgotten that although I had heard the rumors and stories before, Couras had not. The second my back was turned, my boy asked Gregor about the King in Darkness.

"They say the King in Darkness sleeps undying in the citadel on the mountain. If he awakens, he'll reduce us all to bones and dust, like the doom he loosed upon the land a thousand years ago. He is the one thing worse than those bloody elves. The one thing they fear."

My lip curled with anger. I wasn't worried about ghost stories, but I didn't want Couras reminded of the things he'd seen as we fled our former home.

Wolfsbane must have sensed something, because he paused at the door and said, "Couras, would you like to come for a walk with me?"

Couras looked back and forth between Gregor and Wolfsbane, clearly struggling to choose.

"Where are you going?" Gregor taunted. "To fight the King in Darkness with hedge magic?"

"To do what I do every day when I'm not hunting rats."

Wolfsbane's voice reflected an austere dignity. "To repair the Blight."

Couras tugged on the wizard's sleeve. "What's the Blight?"

Gregor belched. "It's the doing of the King in Darkness. You can see it at the border of the realm, just over the hills to the south. Wiped out all living things in a one-mile radius."

"Two," Wolfsbane said softly.

"Huh?"

"The original radius of the Blight was two miles. It's shrunk over the centuries." He lifted his finger, and his plant unfurled another leaf. "Nature is always a work in progress."

"It'll take a few more centuries at that rate," Gregor sneered.

The wizard stretched out his hand, and his plant began to flower. What he said next took me back to the war, back to the elven war pack and the bloody banners they carried.

"Longer, if there are wolves."

Five years later, another wizard came to town, campaigning to become our nation's next regent. She was middle-aged, fit, and looked like a proper wizard, with a floppy hat and a crystal ball on a staff and blue silk robes embroidered with arcane sigils. She gave her name as Kessem and rented a room in my inn, where she became quite popular among the townsfolk, as though they'd never seen a wizard before.

Couras, now ten, knew a number of practical spells that he had learned from Wolfsbane. He was thrilled to show Kessem how he could light a candle with a snap of his fingers or sprout a plant from a seed within hours. When she asked who had taught him, he pointed to the chair by the hearth.

Kessem took one look at our resident wizard, and her expression changed.

In five years I'd rather forgotten how uncanny Wolfsbane looked at first glance. I'd grown so familiar with him—he'd always been so kind and so generous with my son and me—and I'd become so accustomed to the fact that, save for Gregor, the townsfolk preferred to avoid him.

Kessem rose to her feet and leveled her staff, pointing the crystal ball directly at him in a surprisingly aggressive gesture. "I am Kessem of the School of Artigas. Declare yourself."

He rose slowly to his feet, looking like an old man instead of the youthful adult I'd always assumed him to be. "I am Wolfsbane. I have no school."

She snorted. "Self-taught?"

"Something like that."

Gregor, as usual, graced us all with his opinion. "He's the town ratcatcher."

Wolfsbane drew himself up. "I hardly think Kessem is here to challenge me for my job."

Kessem blinked. Laughed. Leaned her staff against the table and left it there. "If I win the election, you might challenge me for mine someday," she teased.

Wolfsbane softly demurred.

Gregor laughed. "You should have a contest. A wizard's duel."

"A friendly one? Certainly," Kessem replied. "It's always a pleasure to see another's mastery."

Wolfsbane turned his cowl away. "I have no interest in competitions."

Couras tugged on his teacher's sleeve. "Please?"

Our wizard looked down at my son, sighed, and agreed.

The match was painful to watch. Initially, Couras was excited by Kessem's flashy magic, but with every spell she cast, his smile slipped further away.

Kessem opened with a bolt of light that sprang from the crystal ball on her staff. Wolfsbane cast a shield that slowed the bolt barely long enough for him to step aside. I could see the surprise on Kessem's face. She had clearly expected him to deflect it. It was then that I began to suspect that, by wizard standards, our local garden-grower and rat-killer might not be a particularly *skilled* wizard.

Wolfsbane caused vines to grow around Kessem's feet. Kessem simply stepped free.

Wolfsbane charmed a nearby oak tree to pelt her with acorns. Kessem raised a ward, and they pattered harmlessly against the barrier.

Wolfsbane summoned a swarm of biting flies. Kessem summoned a wind to blow them away.

I saw Wolfsbane step back, his arms trembling, as he raised his hands to cast one more spell. Clouds gathered in the skies overhead, and Kessem cast a magical canopy, but the only thing to fall from the clouds was a gentle rain.

Kessem recalled her canopy and whispered, "Enough."

I felt terrible for Wolfsbane, who leaned against a tree, as though too tired to stand on his own.

"Don't be downhearted," Kessem said gently. "Mastering magic without formal training is an impressive achievement."

"Well." Wolfsbane's voice was weak. "Perhaps I shouldn't take hedge magic into my next battle."

Kessem looked at him oddly. "What other kind would you take? Magic is a river. It's not so easy to change its flow."

Later that evening, Kessem drew me aside and inquired about Wolfsbane. Her initial questions were all public knowledge, so I answered them as best I could.

"Do you trust him?" she asked abruptly.

I blinked, startled. "If anything were to happen to me, I would entrust my son to no one else."

That was the moment when I understood what Wolfsbane had come to mean to me, to us, in the time we'd lived here. It wasn't what I'd had with my husband. It was something different, but it was also something precious: his quiet steadiness, his generosity, his endless patience with my curious son. It took Kessem's question for me to realize that Wolfsbane was more family than tenant to us.

I became suspicious of her interrogation. "Why do you ask?"

Kessem glanced at the fireside, where Wolfsbane and Couras sat in front of a tray of soil, nudging plants to rise from the earth. "His magic is something I don't understand."

A chill ran down my spine. "My son?"

"Oh, your son is a hedge wizard, make no mistake, and someday he'll be a fine one. Wolfsbane has taught him well. Taught him *correctly*. But Wolfsbane's own techniques are highly eccentric, incomprehensible really, and they're not particularly effective. I don't understand why he doesn't use proper form when he's taught it so well to your son."

"He's a strange one," I said noncommittally, and changed the subject.

Where I'm from, we defend our own.

Five years later, Kessem returned to Dobovor, this time as the leader of our nation—and the commander of an army. Rumors began to fly around my inn the moment the soldiers rode into town, and Kessem called an emergency assembly in the town square.

Couras and I joined the throng of townsfolk gathered before the steps of the mayor's offices. The mood was somber—curious people who came to see the goings-on quickly became subdued. For me, I felt a chill the moment I heard the whispered word "Wolfpack" passing through the crowd.

Memories and nightmares roared to life in my mind. I cursed myself for ever thinking for a moment that we were secure, for daring to believe that rumors and stories would be enough to keep us safe.

Wolfsbane came up behind me and murmured, "Where is the Wolfpack?"

From behind my other shoulder, I heard Gregor's sneering voice. "And what do you expect to do against wolves, Ratsbane?"

I'd had about enough of him and turned to him sharply. "Not wolves. A Wolfpack. A battalion of the Lupine Army."

Gregor's face went white. "The elves."

Couras clambered up on a hitching post and yelled above the noise of the crowd, "What about the King in Darkness?"

Sudden silence fell.

Kessem climbed the stone steps to the porch of the mayor's offices, where she addressed the crowd. "I have traveled to the mountain citadel and found it empty. The King in Darkness, if he ever really existed, is long gone from his crypt, leaving no magic, no treasure, nothing of value behind." She shifted her weight, failing to hide her unease. "The elves know that too. There is a Wolfpack, an elite combat unit, headed our way. They ride with an army at least a thousand strong, and they use magic to cloak their passing. We have had next to no warning of their approach. I have assembled an army and brought what soldiers I can, but make no mistake: we are here to buy you all time to flee."

"Should we prepare defenses?" Gregor shouted.

Defenses. I felt my blood run cold. I remembered exactly what good my husband's defenses had done, a kingdom and a lifetime ago.

"Your defenses are useless. You must *run*, and pray they do not chase you." Kessem's eyes shimmered with tears, but her words were firm. "Leave here, gather your belongings as quickly as you can, and flee. You must understand how severely we are outmatched. I'm sorry. I truly am. *Go.*"

I guided Couras back to the inn, feeling caught in two times and places: Dobovor, now; Kerascc, ten years ago. I barely noticed Gregor stumbling after us. In my mind I was thinking over everything I was about to do.

But when I opened the door of the inn, I met Wolfsbane coming out. He wore a black cloak that I'd never seen before, and he held a long object wrapped in cloth. I thought it was a sword until I saw the wooden tip protruding from the end.

"I didn't know you had a staff," Couras said.

"It's useless for hedge magic," the wizard said. "But I *did* say I wouldn't take hedge magic into my next battle."

"Battle?" Gregor shouted. "We need to run!"

Wolfsbane's voice turned to a low hiss. "I have *work*. My kingdom's *infested*." He turned his back on me and Gregor with a sweep of his black robe and stalked away through the crowd, which parted like water for his passing. He brushed past Kessem, and she stumbled into me.

"Where is he headed?" she demanded. "We could use some small magics to repair carts and ward crossroads."

"I think he's going to war," I said, as ten years' worth of little suspicions suddenly bloomed in my head, a dark flower.

"He's going to get himself killed. For *nothing*."

I had to be wrong. If Kessem didn't suspect …

She suspects only that his magic is strange.

I couldn't possibly be right. I knew next to nothing of wizards.

Kessem startled me when she suddenly pulled away. "Hurry! Go!"

My first obligation was to my son. I had to get us both to safety. Yet as I looked at Couras, I saw not a boy but a young man on the verge of adulthood. I saw that boy gripping his sword and vowing to rescue his mentor.

I fulfilled my obligation. "Couras, I need you to help Kessem with those minor magics. When the townspeople leave, you leave with them."

His face brightened with pride at the responsibility, then fell when I spoke again.

"I need you to promise me you'll do that."

Couras bit his lip, the little boy peeking through the ripening man. "Where will you be?"

"With Wolfsbane." I put my hands on his shoulders. "We'll come after you as soon as we can."

He looked at me with a weight in his eyes that told me he understood we might never come at all.

"I love you," he said. "I love you both."

Then I entered the inn, took the old, rusted sword from underneath my bed, and set out once again in pursuit of a loved one gone out to face the Wolfpack. This time I did not have a horse—I'd left it for my son. I wondered if, once again, I would be too late.

I crested the rise of the hill and looked down upon impending disaster.

The border between the realm of the King in Darkness and the neighboring territory was marked by a simple wooden fence cutting across a wide plain that I can only describe as a desert. This was the epicenter of the original Blight, a place where life had never returned.

A dirt road led across the plain, but only the vanguard of the elven army used it. The rest of the Wolfpack were spread out in formation across the plain. Kessem had warned of a thousand, but there were more—many more—the sunlight glinting off their war helms. Our town's garrison could not fight off a hundred men, let alone a thousand elves.

Kessem had been right. We stood no chance.

Wolfsbane stood alone in the road on our side of the border, his staff lying at his feet, an utter madman staring down a cavalcade. He raised his arms, and a tall thicket of thorns sprang up along and above the fence. With another gesture, a swarm of flies descended on the plain.

The lead elven riders slowed their horses. From the center of the group rode forth an elf dressed in golden armor, mounted on a powerful steed. He waved his hands, and a strong wind blew the flies away. The elf walked his mount down the center of the road to the very edge of the border rather than attempting to jump the thorns. He looked down on Wolfsbane with a cold and condescending smile.

"You can't stop us with your agrarian charms, hedge wizard." He raised his head and stared directly into my eyes. "You. Would you be the representative of the border town of Dobovor? Is this your pathetic wizard?"

From the corner of my eye, I saw the elven archers raise their bows. I raised my hands to indicate peace—there was no point in doing otherwise. Their arrows would have struck me down before my sword could harm them.

Wolfsbane looked at me over his shoulder and then

gestured for me to come join him. As I reached his side, I admitted, "I am merely an innkeeper."

Wolfsbane's reply shocked me with its audacity, even as his voice strained with exhaustion. "I am the representative of this kingdom."

I watched as the rest of the elven war band reined in their horses. They moved toward us until they surrounded us in a half-circle.

I wondered how difficult it was for a hedge wizard to raise plants from the nutritional void of the Blight.

I wondered if I saw Wolfsbane's hands shaking.

And I wondered if I was mad to ever suspect that the patient mentor who'd taught my son hedge spells to grow plants and call animals and summon rain might, in fact, be able to do so himself because all life exists in a slow progression toward death. To take that river Kessem spoke of and force it to flow backward. To work necromancy in reverse.

"This is my only offer," the elven prince said haughtily. "Surrender and live. Resist and die."

"This is my only counteroffer." Wolfsbane dropped to one knee, but his words were firm and steady. "Depart and live. Advance and die."

The prince laughed. "I am Lobau, grandson of Queen Silvia, and this land is mine by birthright."

Wolfsbane hung his head. "Please don't make me do this."

"Little wizard, who do you think you are?"

I reached out my hand and closed my fingers over Wolfsbane's thin and bony shoulder, knobby under my touch. "I forgive you," I whispered.

Wolfsbane's hand closed around the shaft of his staff. "Lobau. Your final chance. Your grandmother named me Wolfsbane."

"What?" Lobau's smile slipped, just a little. "A hedge wizard?"

The cloth wrapping fell away from the staff as Wolfsbane rose to his feet and leveled it like a weapon at the elven prince.

"What is life but the passage toward death?"

Lobau's expression changed from malicious glee to abject terror.

Abruptly, Wolfsbane threw his cloak around my shoulders and pulled me hard against him. His arm was like a metal rod, thin and cold and unyielding. His body—and I'd never been so close to him—felt much the same.

"Perhaps in another thousand years, my hedge magic will be strong enough to stop your granddaughter's army. In the meantime, to protect the people I love, I will stop you *how I can.*"

A vicious wind rose from out of nowhere, blasting past my face, and my eyes closed reflexively. I struggled to force them open and saw nothing but Wolfsbane's cloak fluttering madly in the wind. Blinded, I clung to Wolfsbane's side until the wind receded and the cloth fell away from me.

Before me, a pair of skeletons crumbled to the ground. Their skulls rolled until they settled side by side: the elongated head of a horse, and the fine-featured skull of an elf.

I raised my head, and the elven army was gone. The plain was a battlefield after the battle was won. Swords, spears, and packs of provisions littered the ground, scattered among the thousands of bones and the dried husks of the plants underfoot.

Something fell from the sky like a shower of hail and pattered in the dust at my feet. I'd cooked enough pheasants in my time to recognize the bones of a bird.

The wizard who'd struggled so hard to coax blooms out of buds had let his magic follow its natural course, like water down a river, and sucked the life from an elven army in the blink of an eye.

I was still frozen in terror when the King in Darkness released me, turned away, and walked off in the direction of town.

I don't know how long I stood there staring at the devastation around me, trying to comprehend how it felt to be the only living thing for a mile around. At some point, I drew a deep breath, turned around, and fixed my gaze on the green trees over the crest of the hill. Dead grass crunched beneath my feet as I started walking.

The bushes were shriveled, the flowers desiccated, the landscape turned to the brown and gray of rot. Still, up ahead, a few shoots poked bravely through the ash. A lush carpet of greenery still existed between the edge of the blasted earth and the trees that marked the perimeter of the original Blight. At the end of that carpet was Wolfsbane, sitting in the grass, gesturing to the ground. A single sprig of wolfsbane pushed its way up from the devastated earth.

"That's going to take an eternity," I said as I sat down beside him.

He didn't look at me. "I've got one."

"A wise wizard once told me that nature is always a work in progress."

The hood lifted. I knew what was behind that black veil now. I didn't need to see. I could no more easily read an expression on a skull than on a piece of cloth. I would measure Wolfsbane as I had always measured him, by the tones in his voice and the shape of his actions.

I raised an eyebrow. "Dead things are part of nature, aren't they?"

"I suppose they are." The hood tilted. "Yes, I suppose they are." A low, musical chuckle rolled out from beneath the veil.

I took his leather-gloved hand, gripped the bones gently. Another wolfsbane shoot rose. It unfurled. Budded. Flowered.

MARY PLETSCH attended the first Superstars Writing Seminars in 2010 and learned from the best. In the years since, she has published short stories and novellas in a variety of genres including science fiction, fantasy, and horror. Superstars holds a special place in her heart; it made the difference between writing as a hobby and writing to be published.

To Mend or Rend

Morgan J. Muir

45:00 / 0-0

Her skates squeaked with every step along the rubber mats lining the path to the ice rink. Annoyingly, it was not something fixable by any of the magic Mels possessed, even had she been whole. The soft cloth of her shoulder pads rubbed rough against her back and shoulders as she walked, and she tugged the front of her jersey away from her neck. It wouldn't be long now.

Sounds of anticipation bounced around the hockey rink, echoing the feelings in her gut. She swallowed back the tightness in her throat, stopping a few steps from the mass of teenage testosterone that was her male teammates. This time would be different. There were rules on the ice, limits to what force could be used, and how, and when. But the ice also provided freedom.

Mels touched her long, dark braid, double-checking that it remained tucked fully into the back of her jersey.

The boys cracked their usual crass jokes with each other, a

couple sparking their magic in small flashes. A few heckled the team waiting down the boards as the Zamboni finished resurfacing the ice. Kerr, the team captain, smoothed the fresh tape on his stick with a puck. A trio of tiny wolf illusions he created paced alongside each stroke of his hand.

Mels forced herself to breathe, ignoring the familiar stink of the boys' hockey gear, and ran her eyes over the other team. They gathered at the other end of the rink, blue-and-silver mirrors to her own team's red and black. Her stomach tightened. The Wizards team was all about the same height, with a couple shorter guys. He wasn't there.

Relief flooded through her as she looked away, followed quickly by irritation. She wanted this to be over already. Confront him, take back what was hers. Be whole. If he wasn't here—

"You finally gonna knock someone down this time, Rouk?" Kerr asked her with a friendly shove.

Mels shrugged, shifting her weight on her squeaking skates. No one else's skates squeaked. Kerr turned away with a chuckle.

The sharp thud of the gate closing behind the Zamboni echoed through the rink. She grinned as Munro lifted the latch, opening the Wolves' door, and her team flowed onto the ice.

As Mels neared the door, her world pared away to the frozen boundaries of the rink that waited a single step away. No matter her problems outside the rink, they would all fall away the moment her skates touched the ice. Despite her terrified hopes, this would be just another game.

Something tugged at her magic, drawing on it, gently, subtly. Mels froze, her head whipping back toward the other team.

He strode toward the ice, a head taller than anyone on his team. Mels's breath came in gasps.

Joel.

She could still hear him laughing at her. He stopped and looked at her.

Mels immediately dropped her gaze, her hands tightening on her stick. She could *feel* his amusement through her magic. It sickened her.

"Move it, Rouk," someone behind her said, hitting her calves lightly with their stick. "Game's on the ice."

Scowling, Mels stepped forward, shifting from a world of stillness and friction to one of smooth, effortless freedom. The ice crunched beneath her blades as she pushed forward, the chill air cooling the heat in her face. She could feel him still.

Mels slammed her stick onto the ice, deftly maneuvering past the red-and-black uniforms of her teammates as they warmed up. This time they would be in public, and Joel wouldn't be able to fight back. Mels's stick, nearly as tall as she was, shot out and picked up a puck, sliding it along the ice.

His magic had sliced into hers. Mels's blades sliced the ice with each stride, driving toward the net. Sliced away bits of her soul.

Stealing her magic.

This time, she would do whatever it took to get her magic back.

Even if it meant Rending.

Mels pulled back her arm then slammed her stick into the puck. A slight twist of her wrist as it connected lifted the puck from the ice, the slap shot echoing with a crack in her ears. Her goalie snagged it out of the air with his glove and threw it at her as she sped past. The puck hit her shoulder pads and dropped to the ice behind her as she queued up in the corner.

"We're trying to warm up the goalie, not kill him," Kerr said, his voice tense. "Save it for the game."

"Right," Mels muttered as he passed his puck and skated

out into the warm-up. Translucent images of wolves flowed beside him, obscuring his movements.

She couldn't feel her fingers in her heavy gloves. She was here, with Joel, on the ice. The last missing piece of her soul not a hundred feet away, a connection unseen, unknown to any but her and him. Suddenly, all her plans for taking it from him fled her mind. She could still leave. She didn't have to face him.

Munro slapped her shin pads with his stick, jerking her from her thoughts. "Good to see you worked up. You finally going to check someone tonight?"

"You guys keep asking me that." She could check Joel and rip her magic from his grip. She was tall and strong. She could out-check everyone on her team. She could do that.

But he's bigger. Stronger. The quiet voice twisted in her mind. *He destroys, and you only bind. You won't be able to Rend it from him.*

"Well, you know, there's a bet on if you'll finally do it this season. We all know you can, we just don't get why you don't."

Mels shrugged. Munro laughed and took his turn in the warm-up.

You can't beat him at his game. You're not aggressive enough. Mels shook her head. It's why she played defense. But if she wanted her magic back, she needed to be something she was not. She had to.

Or you can leave. He'll just hurt you again if you stay.

Her senses pulled at her, and Mels glared at the other team. At Joel.

He would just keep hurting her if she didn't do something.

32:07 / 0-1 Wizards

At the shrill tone of the referee's whistle, Mels swung her legs over the boards, pulling her ethereal shields tighter around her.

She dropped lightly to the ice as the previous line returned to the bench. So far, her line had not been out against Joel's.

Every time she made it through a line change without facing him was a relief. And a frustration. She needed to face him somehow, and while they were on the ice. She couldn't get past his defenses out in the real world, where there were no rules to hold him back. There she was like a child beating against a wall while he laughed. But tonight they were both playing defense.

Had he chosen defense deliberately? He'd played forward when he'd been with the Wolves.

Mels flowed across the ice, taking position in front of her goalie for the face-off. She set her stick into position as the Wizards' wing lined up against her, the click of his blade against ice echoing hollowly across the rink. Minding the movements of the ref in her periphery, she watched the blue-and-silver mass before her.

But the part of her Joel carried called to her from where he sat on the Wizards' bench. Did the connection go both ways? Did he feel her too? Her chest tightened with anger at the thought. If she made it through his defenses, was she really capable of doing what she needed to get it back? To tear it from him as he'd done to her?

A chill stole across her at the thought of Rending a soul.

Even his.

"Stupid girl," the boy across from her hissed as the ref held out the puck. Almost as one, all ten players moved into place, sticks on the ice. "No wonder your team sucks."

Anger flared through Mels as the puck dropped. Instinctively, she dropped her shoulder as the wingman surged toward her, the centers to her right fighting for control of the puck. The chorus of stick hits, blades, and crackling shields hitting together rose above the dampened silence of the rink.

Several pucks rushed away from the fighting centers. Mels ignored the projections while others flinched. The real puck burst toward Mels, and the wingman shoved her out of the way.

For an instant, options flashed through her mind as the players moved around her.

She could send a quick light flare over the puck and deflect it to her forward.

She could knock the wingman's stick aside when he reached for the puck.

Or she could power forward and check him.

Attack.

Instead, Mels hesitated. She was a defender. The dark puck landed safely on the wingman's stick. Bursting forward, Mels slid her stick beneath his and lifted. There was no resistance in his shock; he'd thought she'd try to check him. Mels kicked the puck onto her own stick as she passed.

Mels glanced up, and a flash of light tried to blind her. She knocked it away with her shield. Before her the ice lay clear. Ahead and to her left skated a black-and-red Wolves jersey. To the right charged the wingman she'd just beat.

Mels passed the puck and braced. She dug her skates into the ice and dropped a hand from her stick as two hundred pounds of solid teenage boy slammed into her shoulder like a tank. She pushed back at the moment of impact, feeling the power in her legs and back, and *lifted*. The crash of their shoulder pads swallowed the small *pop* of their shields. A moment later, the Wizards' wingman sat on his butt on the ice, and Mels was halfway down the rink.

Behind her, she felt her own thrill at the game echo. Joel had come onto the ice. Mels wanted to scream at the intrusion. This world, this emotion was *hers*, and he had no place sharing it with her. Sound faded as she watched the play, moving her position in tandem with the puck, her heartbeat filling her ears. He was on the ice.

Her chance was now.

She could try. She would try.

You will fail.

The puck shot past her, and Mels started, her breathing rapid. She hadn't been paying attention.

The whistle blew, and Joel skated past, smirking at her. She tugged at her shoulder pads that rode up against her neck, choking her. Someone hit her shoulder and gestured to the bench. Nodding, Mels retreated to safety. Off the ice. Away from Joel.

Sound returned to her as Mels dropped into place beside her fellow defensemen, shoving them down the bench with her hips. Everyone shuffled to make room for the players fresh from the ice, and she reached for a water bottle. Kerr reached behind the guy next to him and gave her helmet a friendly pat. She knew exactly what he was going to say.

"Next time, check him first and don't throw the puck away."

Be aggressive.

17:56 / 2-4 Wizards

Mels watched from her point at the blue line as her forwards shot at the Wizards' net. Her job was simple. Don't let the puck pass the blue line. Catch any loose puck and dump it back toward the net for her forwards. She was a defenseman. Not a forward.

Mels was not aggressive.

But she could be.

This time she would be.

She crouched, her stick on the ice, watching the puck dart

from player to player, shifting along the ice with the play. She tried to ignore Joel. Right now was not the right time. Right now he was just another player. A force unto himself. Using *her* stolen magic for something as stupid as a high school sport.

There are worse things.

Mels shivered despite the heat of the game.

A Wizard broke free, angling toward center ice.

Joel.

She should check him.

Mels spun toward her net and powered forward, skating parallel with Joel. They passed the center line, and she lengthened her stride, gaining speed and pulling ahead of him. He was stronger, more powerful. But she was faster. He angled toward the boards. She would herd him into the corner behind the net.

Deftly, she flipped around, skating backward and gaining speed. The second blue line passed beneath their blades as they entered the Wolves' defensive zone.

In one stride she pulled in front of him, meeting his eyes.

He looked back, pulling harder on her magic to shield himself. It twisted inside her.

She should check him.

Instead, she swung her stick at his, trying to knock the puck free.

Another stride. Joel leaned his weight on his stick, refusing to be moved.

They were only a heartbeat or two from the net.

Joel allowed himself to be herded to the boards. The other eight players, rushing toward them, had not yet made it across center ice.

Mels stood between him and the goal. She could lean into her blades, gather her power into her knees, and drop a hand from her stick. She could reach for the slice of her magic he held. Tear it from him.

She could be the attacker for once. Not just the defender.

A heartbeat passed.

He feinted left toward the boards, and she followed, obscuring his chance at a clean shot. Suddenly, the puck bounced off the boards to her left as Joel cut hard to the right, sweeping around her.

He had outmaneuvered her. Again. She resisted the impulse to charge at him, her stick swinging. Anything to stop the laugh echoing through her magic and into her mind. She turned, keeping her face toward him. Joel picked up the puck, but was too deep to get a good shot on net. Snow sprayed into the air from her blades as she stopped, taking her place to reinforce the goalie.

The second Wolves' defenseman crossed into their zone, but not quickly enough.

Mels could *feel* Joel gloat as he wrapped around the net and slipped the puck past the Wolves' goalie. Her hands formed fists around her stick.

Next time, she *would* check him.

Next time, she would win.

6:02 / 2-6 Wizards

Exhaustion pushed at Mels. She fought back. Weakness had no place here. Bodies of blue and silver contended with black and red, fighting for possession. Fighting for the goal. Fighting back the invaders and protecting the all-important bit of black rubber.

Mels stood her ground as her opponent shoved her. She would not be moved. She reached out with her stick, knocking his away as the puck neared him.

Suddenly, the puck lay cradled on her stick. She glanced around for someone she could send it to. All her teammates were covered.

For a moment, panic froze the world around her. She was a defenseman. She had no business with the puck. But she could not pass it without risking an interception and goal. They would score again.

Not they. Him.

Joel.

No. He would not have this. Gritting her teeth, Mels surged forward, the puck firmly on her stick. The others were occupied, but the ice beyond Joel was clear.

She needed only to get through Joel.

And he would come to her.

Mels twisted past the other players; few of them could match her speed.

This time she would do it.

This time she was the aggressor.

She could feel Joel grinning, challenging her. Rage built in her chest as he drew on her magic, on the scrap of her soul he had stolen—the part he had kept. He pushed forward at her, squaring his shoulders to hers.

She braced herself, hands gripping her stick as she slammed straight into him.

She shoved her rage into him, pushing against his thick chest. Light exploded around them, and she grasped for that which was hers, ready to Rend it from him. Ready to tear it free.

She brushed against it, touching her own soul. As familiar as her own reflection.

It slid away from her like silk.

A deep, deafening boom ripped through her, throwing her back.

A whistle blew, and she found herself laying on the ice, Joel already up on his knees a few feet away. The force of their impact ached through her bones as she stood, a sharp pain flaring in her hip. The scrap of her soul called to her, still held firmly in the prison of his grip. Still behind a shield he'd used her own power to create.

He met her eyes and pulled on her magic again, her stomach twisting.

Mels charged toward him, but arms in red-and-black jerseys held her back, bodies in the same colors came between them. Mels raised her fist at Joel, ready to scream her rage, but her hand disappeared under a glamour as her voice went silent in her throat. She glared at Kerr.

"Light, Rouk, I didn't mean like that." Kerr scowled, forcing her to turn away from Joel.

She snapped her teeth shut and dropped her hand, and Kerr released his magic.

"But that was pretty damn impressive." Munro slapped her on the back.

The ref called out a penalty, and Mels recognized her number. Cross-checking. So stupid. She'd let herself get angry enough that she'd forgotten to drop her hand off the stick. Too angry to grasp her own soul. She'd been so close.

The referee called a second penalty, this one against Kerr for using his magic out-of-bounds. He'd saved her from a second penalty that might have removed her from the game entirely. She might have lost her chance. And Joel knew it. He'd manipulated her. He'd won. Again.

The referee escorted them to the penalty box as she glared at Joel.

4:43 / 2-6 Wizards

Mels dropped onto her seat in the box, Kerr beside her. Leaning her stick against her shoulder, she rested her elbows on her knees. She was an idiot. She would never get it back. She slipped her hands from her oversized gloves, rubbing her wrists. No one could help her; it was her word against his. Even her friends had disappeared, off with their own troubles. And she could not stand against Joel on her own. He always won.

"Hey, Mels," Kerr said hesitantly.

Mels looked up. No one on the team ever used her first name.

"Look, I don't know what it is you have against Joel." He raised a gloved hand. "And don't tell me you don't. I've never seen you so ... well, so not like yourself.

"Here's the thing. Everyone keeps telling you to play more like us. Be forceful and whatever. But you're no good at it. I mean, well, you are good at it. But you're not.

"The thing is, you're good at *you*. Like, you do the tricky stuff. Moving sticks and whatever. No one expects that. They all think you're gonna be like them. Checking. Forcing your way through. That sort of thing. But you don't, and it surprises them. And that's what you gotta do. You know. Be you. Play your way, not theirs."

Mels rolled her head toward him. "That's the longest speech I've ever heard you give."

"Yeah, well." Kerr looked up at the blade of his stick, twirling it around. "I never liked Joel anyway. Even when he was on the team."

Kerr's time in the box wasn't long. The Wizards quickly scored on the shorthanded Wolves, and he dashed back to the ice.

4:10 / 2-7 Wizards

What did they want from her, anyway? Mels rested her head against her stick and closed her eyes, ignoring the game in the solitude of the penalty box. Munro and the others wanted her to play more like them. Kerr said to play like herself. Why did it even matter?

Her teammates kept playing even though they'd already lost. Winning was impossible.

So why keep playing?

And none of it even mattered when her only chance of something far more important than a high school sports game—even one she loved to play—was slipping away. She was never going to get it back. He would always have it, siphoning away threads of herself until nothing that was her remained.

And it was her own fault. She'd been so stupid. Getting angry, letting herself lose focus. And now she was helpless to change anything. The story of her life. Alone, and unable to even help herself.

For three years her teammates had teased her about checking in a game. Now she could take down anyone on the team. But not in-game, apparently. Not when it mattered.

Just like how she'd spent the last year working to improve her skills, strengthen her magic, hold her shields without thinking. And she was good. Very good. She'd even, reluctantly, carefully taught herself to Rend. But not like Joel did.

Never like Joel.

Bitterness colored her small smile. She was a defenseman. Defender. D. That was what she did. It was what she was. But defensiveness never scored points. Passivity never won.

Aggression had never done her any favors before, either.

It certainly didn't now.

Yes, she'd worked hard and could compete with the boys.

She played as well as any of them. But she couldn't beat Joel at his own game. She never had. She never would.

She had clearly lost.

But can you really stop trying?

A tapping on the glass made her look up. Her teammate gestured to the clock and then to the bench, indicating she should return rather than play out. She glanced up, and only a few seconds remained of her penalty.

Familiar anticipation filled her at the thought of getting back onto the ice. Why keep playing, even though they'd clearly lost? She couldn't help but grin.

Because the game was not over yet.

Taking a deep breath, Mels stood and reached for the door.

2:17 / 2-7 Wizards

Findley charged toward the bench. "D! D!" he shouted, throwing himself over the boards.

Mels swung her legs over the boards to replace him, her skates on the ice before she had time to think. Play had shifted to the offensive zone as Findley had made for the line change, but now it moved quickly back toward the Wolves' goalie.

And Mels had the advantage. Their bench was in their defensive zone. Mels was already in place.

She moved to intercept the lone forward.

Be you.

She grinned, feeling the chill air slide over her hot neck. The thrill of life surged through her as she moved effortlessly across the ice.

The forward bounced the puck off the boards to her left while moving to the right, the same move Joel had used earlier.

Play your way, not theirs.

Feeling almost casual, Mels twisted around, grabbing the puck with her long reach.

This time no one stood in her way.

She pushed forward, redirecting her momentum away from the opponent behind her. He could do nothing to her now.

Why keep playing?

Her Wolves harried the remaining Wizards as they all moved down the ice.

Mels played because she loved it.

She swung to the left, around a pair of Wizards, dancing out of their reach.

Mels played because she could.

She wasn't one of the guys. Aggression wasn't her game. It never had been. But sometimes a defender still needed to be a forward. For a moment.

Mels was past all the others. A single, familiar form remained between her and the net.

Joel.

Sometimes the best way through an obstacle ...

Mels grinned as he squared up to check her, dropping his hand from his stick. He pulled at her magic, drawing strength into his shield as she mirrored his movements.

... is to not go through it at all.

At the last moment, Mels abandoned the puck to its momentum and danced to the left, pivoting around Joel's hulking form to face his back. She picked up the puck he'd unwittingly skated past and twisted around to shoot.

Caught off guard, the Wizards' goalie missed entirely.

0:00 / 3-7 Wizards Final

Mels stood in line with her fellow Wolves, each with their right hands ungloved to bump fists with the other team. Good sportsmanship and all.

She took a spot near the end, pleased to see Joel do the same. She pulled her braid from her jersey and draped it over her shoulder. With her stick tucked casually under one arm, Mels passed through the slow gauntlet, muttering "good game" with each fist bump. One kid pulled his hand away, muttering about girls and hockey. Mels rolled her eyes, resisting the urge to "fist bump" his shoulder instead.

As Joel approached, Mels's heart sped up, but she kept her breathing slow. Relaxed. Only two players away now. One.

Instead of a bump, she grabbed Joel's fist in her hand and met his eyes.

"You have something of mine," she said quietly. She reached through the touch and found it. The piece of her self that he'd stolen.

And she would not need to Rend it from him.

This was her game. Calm, now, it did not recoil from her. Keeping his eyes, she sent a thread of her magic out, touching her own orphaned soul shard, and *Bound*.

The ties dissolved from Joel as she let go of his hand, her missing magic flowing home.

He spluttered as she turned away, shoving her hand back into her glove. Mels didn't look back.

She was once again complete.

Morgan J. Muir has always loved telling stories, especially stories with magic, hardships, and—eventually—happy endings. She is working hard on becoming a crazy cat lady and on curating her collection of hobbies. Morgan lives with her family in Utah. You can find more of her work at morganjmuir.com.

Last Call

Nic Lishko

ealer!" Crystobal shouted as he kicked open the door of his brewery. "I need a healer now!"

Holding the body of his best friend in his arms, Crystobal scanned the bar. No one was there. He knew that. Wolfman had flipped the *open* sign to *closed* earlier that night to deal with that loser arms dealer, Fats McMud. The mobster was still pissed at Crystobal and Wolfman for helping heal a rival gang's henchman. How were the friends supposed to know the brute knocking on death's door was actually the brother of the biggest wand and staff dealer in the West?

"Annabelle," Crystobal called out. "Annabelle, where the devil are you? I need a Reviver's Fire or ... or something."

He fell to his knees. Despite Wolfman's six-foot frame, thick torso, and solid build, the man felt as light as a tray of empty mugs. Could it be possible his soul's spirit might still be in there?

"Stay with me, bud," Crystobal begged, laying Wolfman on the peanut-shell-covered floor. "Come on, you're not supposed to go this way, remember? 'Gotta grow old to die young' and all that? That's what we say, right? Wolfman?"

Crystobal moved his face to his friend's nostrils and wide-open mouth. The slightest shallow breath escaped his nose.

There's still time, he thought.

He slapped his pockets, searching for his phone. Yanking it from his vest, his fingers swiped until they dialed Annabelle.

"Grandpapa?" came the teen's sleepy voice. "It's five in the morn—"

"Belle, Wolfman's hurt. Like 'end of the line, down the old dirt trail' hurt. Do we have any Reviver's Fire left?"

"Wolfman? Uh, did you check the cellar? I thought we sold —Wait, where are you?"

"Get to the brewery," he said. "We've gotta act fast."

"Should I bring my staff?"

"Girl," Crystobal growled.

"I can help, Grandpa."

"This isn't the time. I gotta go; I'm losing him."

"Losing him? Isn't he immort—"

Crystobal tapped the red x and dropped the phone. He leapt behind the counter and fumbled at the cellar door.

It was locked. It was always locked.

"Gotta say the enchantment." He heard Wolfman's tired voice in his mind. *"How do you always forget?"*

"Click it, click it, lock free now. Open this damn door and don't have a cow."

The latches unclicked, and the door popped open.

Racing down the stairs, Crystobal cast a wicked-quick illumination spell and scanned his fingers against the bottles. Reviver's Fire was at the top of the rebrew list, but if there were any bottles left, they'd be down here.

Countless products now filled the once-bare shelves. Labels covered in dust boasted drinks strong enough to knock out the toughest of men, but they also warned of the many possible side effects, from rapid healing to regrowing blown-off limbs to changing the drinker's face when camouflage was needed.

Every recipe was another adventure Crystobal and Wolfman had enjoyed. Sometimes years of testing was required before the mixture was just right. The fun hadn't solely come from creating elixirs and having them blow up in their faces; they also loved crafting funny names with double meanings like "Reviver's Fire Stout" and "Chameleon's Cream Ale."

When they established their potion shop nearly a hundred years earlier, the duo never imagined it would one day be a top-ten brewery in the state. WolfCrystal Potions & Elixirs had been every front imaginable from apothecary to saloon to speakeasy and now microbrewery. In a city that thrived on attracting all types of magical beings, Crystobal and Wolfman never took a side despite all the squabbles, battles, and mini-wars the magical folks deemed necessary.

"That's just not our style," Wolfman would say. "We're a hospital for sinners and a house for saints alike. We don't slam our doors to those in need."

Things had been so good for so long. Every year, in their "State of the Friendship" address, the two would weigh the pros and cons of staying where they were, and despite Crystobal's best logic-based arguments for wanting to move, Wolfman always won out. He believed they had found their peace.

Crystobal gasped at the row of bottles of Reviver's Fire. Grabbing one, he flipped it over. Nothing from the spout. He grabbed another and another. No caps. No wax seals. No liquid. Simply recycled bottles needing to be refilled.

Thus the sign on the shelf—To be Filled.

He barked a curse and swept his arm across the shelf. Once the bottles stopped tinkling on the floor, he caught his breath. He slammed his back into the wall and sunk to the floor. Was this truly the end? He wouldn't know how to go on without his best friend at his side. The benefit of them both being wizards meant they never said goodbye. Crystobal wouldn't even know how to do such a thing.

A tone similar to the clinking bottles came from upstairs.

"Grandpapa?"

Belle.

Rising and taking one last look at the shelf, a bottle caught his eye. The glass was a dark shade with a small square of tape slapped on the side and a name crudely written in marker. The concoction had been created on a rainy night after seven years of cauldron aging. Crystobal remembered the bottling all too well.

"Why would anyone buy that?" he'd asked. "Seven years of aging for a seven-minute use."

Wolfman grinned. "It's a pretty clever name, though, eh?"

"People want permanence."

"People want problem-solving. It's kind of the bread and butter of what we do."

"It literally has 'temporary' in the name, not to mention it's a short-term solution for a permanent problem."

"Then we'll put it back here," Wolfman said, sliding it to the very back of the shelf. "Save it for a rainy day, eh? Might sell for a pretty price."

Now Crystobal held the bottle in his hands. Would it be enough? He already knew the answer, but the contents might at least promise a little more time.

Thunder boomed from upstairs as Belle shouted louder.

"Grandpapa? Can you hear me?"

"Coming," he shouted. Pocketing the bottle, he snapped his fingers, killing the light.

As he closed the cellar door, a hefty snort nearby made his blood grow cold.

"Let's, uh, let's not do anything too funny."

Crystobal raised his hands. Slowly lifting his gaze, he found his great-granddaughter's neck held steady by a large man in a purple-and-yellow zoot suit. Three goons wore similar uniforms, poised for a fight. Stepping in front of the line was Fats McMud.

"Keep on, uh, keep on a-keepin' them hands up," Fats said.

"Bar's closed 'til noon," Crystobal said. "Why don't you give me the girl, and you can come back for lunch. I'll make sure the police will be here with a full plate of appetizers. We'll make it a whole thing."

"Fu-fu-funny guy," Fats said. "Always with a joke."

The goon holding Annabelle flexed his arm, causing the girl to squeal from the choke.

"Enough!" Crystobal barked, slamming his hands onto the bar. "Look at your feet. See what you did? My best friend's life has ended thanks to you. Can't this be enough bloodshed for one night?"

"Mayb-b-b-be," Fats said. "Or maybe I got a t-taste for more."

Crystobal sighed, slowly sliding his arms off the bar and lowering his head. "You don't understand what you've done, have you? Wolfman and I ... We've been through so much together. Two hundred years of fun really wasn't enough."

"You knew the rules," Fats shrugged. "He knew 'em good. You can't claim neutrality then pick a side."

Crystobal slipped one hand into his pocket and carefully retrieved the bottle. "Just when you think you've finally figured out life—boom. It's over. I thought we had hundreds of more years of good times and adventures ahead. But I guess that's how life goes, you know? It's over before you know it."

"Especially when you've got a f-f-friend like me to help speed up the pr-process. Eh, boys?"

The goons chuckled.

Fats squinted and looked at his men. "I said, 'Eh, boys?'"

To that, the men's meager chuckles morphed into full-on laughter.

Just my chance.

Pressing the edge of the bottle against the sink under the bar, he pulled down until the cap popped up.

Fats blinked and shifted his head. "Hey, wait a sec," he said. "You'd b-b-better put those hands up now, or the girl—"

"Alright," Crystobal said and slid the opened bottle back into his pocket. "I'm coming out. Just don't hurt her."

Moving around to the front of the bar, Crystobal stopped a few feet from Wolfman's body. He'd have one chance to slip the drink in, so he better make it count.

"Well?" he asked.

Fats snorted and spat. "Well, what?"

"Did you have a plan when you walked in here, or did you really just want food for that pig trough you call a mouth?"

At that, the goons busted up laughing. Fear fell across Fats's face, followed by red-hot anger.

"Shadup, you freaking lo-lo-loons," Fats said.

But the men couldn't help themselves.

With a shaking fist, Fats unsheathed a wand, pointed it at the goon laughing the hardest and barked a command. Red energy blasted from the stick, slamming the goon into a brick wall and unconscious onto the floor.

One down, Crystobal thought.

The other two men immediately closed their mouths as Fats waved the wand in their direction.

"You laugh at my jokes," he spat. "Not his. Got it? Now we're makin' an exchange, wi-wi-wizard. You come with us, and we let the girlie go."

Crystobal's eyes narrowed. "You'll let her go? Like how you let Wolfman go?"

"That was different."

"How?"

Fats sputtered for a moment before shaking his doughy face. "We could kill her and take you anyway. What's it gonna be?"

Crystobal sighed and took a few steps forward. "Fine."

"Fine? Really? Nothin' funny?"

"I'm not laughing."

Crystobal scanned the floor, searching for the table with the most amount of peanut shells beneath it.

Have to make it believable. Have to make him think it was an accident.

He spied a pile near the table closest to Wolfman's head.

"Then let's g-g-g-get it on already," Fats said.

Crystobal sighed and walked toward Fats. Stepping onto the peanut shells, he flung his foot back and slammed onto the floor.

"Dammit," he cried. "Stupid peanuts!"

Fats let out a gasping laugh and lowered his head to slap at his knee.

Crystobal crawled over to Wolfman and slid the bottle into his dead friend's open mouth. He dragged himself in front of Wolfman so Fats wouldn't see.

"Ya gotta get a cleaner," Fats said. "Place is a disaster. Lucky for you, you won't be-be-be coming back."

Crystobal rose and grabbed at his own knee. He needed to buy more time to give the elixir a chance to work. If it would work at all. They'd never tested it. Never could.

"Alright, dat's enough of that," Fats said. "Let's go, old man."

"Think I twisted my ankle," Crystobal said, putting on his best limp.

"Don't care. Grab h-him."

The other goon moved to Crystobal and yanked him by the shirt.

"Alright, fine. I'm here now, so let my granddaughter go."

"We still haven't left with you yet," Fats said. "When you're in our keep, we'll let her be."

"That's not what you said, porky."

Fats pushed his wand into Crystobal's forehead. The tip was still red-hot and burned Crystobal's skin. "Well, I changed my mind!"

"Just kill him now, boss," one goon said. "He dies, his potions and recipes go with him."

"Then we've got this town," the other one said. "Just do him in."

A smile crept across Fats's face. "Sure, boys. Why not? Let's let the wizard join his old friend in death."

"Or life."

All heads spun to Wolfman, who chucked the old bottle directly at Fats's face.

As the portly gangster yelped, Crystobal elbowed the goon holding him and broke free from his grasp. Dodging past Fats, he grabbed an empty chair, darted up another onto a table, and leapt at the goon holding Annabelle. He brought the chair down on the goon's shocked face, causing it to splinter into dozens of pieces.

The goon fell into a heap on the floor, freeing Annabelle.

"Nice hit," she said.

"Get behind the counter," Crystobal said. "Don't let them see you."

"What in da hell is this?" Fats said, holding up the bottle. "Temporary Necromancy?"

"Good to know that worked," Wolfman said. "But the flavor profile—"

"We can discuss later," Crystobal said.

"Don't think there'll be time later, so just know it's too bitter for a stout."

Fats roared in annoyance and shot a blast from his wand at Wolfman, who, having died by a similar blast an hour earlier, had learned his lesson and ducked.

Fats spun on Crystobal and fired at the old wizard.

Crystobal held up a hand and absorbed the blast in its entirety.

Fats eyes widened "Without a wand? How is that possible? I destroyed yours!"

"Yeah, but you blew it up in my hand," Crystobal said. "The splinters in my hand are painful, but I don't think I'll tweeze 'em out. Seems to be a nice kind of side effect."

Focusing all of the energy in his body into his hand, Crystobal's eyes turned white. Despite Fats flicking his wand time and time again, Crystobal absorbed all of the energy shot his way.

With a quick swing of his finger, the wand flew from Fat's hand into Wolfman's. The two wizards cornered the gangster.

"Hey, Crystobal," Wolfman said. "Smell that?"

"Yeah," Crystobal smiled. "Smells like fear."

"Really? I was gonna say piss, as in Spam here just pissed himself."

"Hold on," Fats cried. "I'm so-so-sorry I-I-I-"

Wolfman tilted his head. "You're sorry you what? Killed me?" He flicked the wand, sending Fats upward until he slammed against the ceiling.

"Help me, you morons," Fats squealed to his goons.

Crystobal spun, expecting the two remaining goons to attack him, but was pleased instead to find them against the wall with Annabelle holding a staff on both of them. The tip glowed yellow, shining a sunny glint on his granddaughter's face.

"I know you said I'm not old enough for my license," Annabelle said, "but maybe we can count this toward my learner's test."

"I'll get you a permit as soon as break's over," Crystobal said.

"Hey, Annabelle," Wolfman called. "When this is all over, I'm giving you my stake in the brewery, ya hear?"

The girl squealed with delight as the two friends faced the fat gangster.

"I swear on all that's ho-ho-holy I'll get you," Fats shouted. "I swear on heaven and hell that I'll—"

"Heaven?" Wolfman pursed his lips. "Let's see if you can get past the pearly gates."

Together, the men raised their hands and their voices and shot a mighty blast at the gangster, shattering a hole in the roof and sending the pig squealing until he disappeared in the sky.

"What goes up must come down," Wolfman said.

"I angled him slightly," Crystobal said as his eyes returned from white to blue. "Should end up in the drink. I'll fish him out later."

Wolfman nodded and looked to the clock on the back wall of the brewery.

"How long has it been?"

"Five minutes. Two full minutes left at best."

Wolfman's face lowered. "Hey, Belle, can you take those two men outside? We'll call the police."

Belles eyes widened with pride. "Really?"

Crystobal pushed his tongue into his cheek and nodded. "You can do it, hon. We'll be out in a minute."

The girl grinned and pushed her staff on the two goons, forcing them out the front door.

Wolfman hurried to the back of the bar. Stepping onto the counter, his fingers raced across the top shelf until he found a small bottle.

"What's that?" Crystobal asked.

"A little something I cooked up just in case this would ever happen. Cheers to you."

Wolfman hopped off the counter, took a long sip, swished the contents in his mouth, then spit it back into the bottle. "Drink up, buttercup."

Crystobal raised an eyebrow. "You serious?"

"I just deposited a bit of me back in this bottle," he said. "You've gotta drink it while I'm still alive or I'll never be able to help you when I'm gone."

"Help me?"

"I call it Manmade Memory. Tastes like a spontaneous sour, but it's laced with a bit of me. Things like the way I thought and the way I approached a challenge. That way, when you're making the new stuff—and you better damn well keep making the new stuff with that youngin' out there—you'll wonder, 'Gee, how would Wolfie approach this,' and then you'll feel an itch in the back of your brain and that'll be me." A tear rolled down Wolfman's face as he sniffled. "That'll be me."

Crystobal frowned. Then he tilted his head back and chugged the bottle. The sour made his eyes pucker and the white hair on his neck stand up.

But dammit if it wasn't the best thing Wolfman ever made.

"I'll carry your memory," Crystobal said. "I mean it, the lessons you taught me, I'll pay it forward. I'll teach others your lessons. You'll live on in me and in every apprentice I take on."

Wolfman smiled and moved to Crystobal with outstretched arms. The two friends embraced as hard as they possibly could. Having mentally begun the countdown from the moment the

Temporary Necromancy had touched Wolfman's lips, Crystobal knew that only seconds remained.

"Not ready," Wolfman said.

"Never are," Crystobal said.

"Love you, man. See you on the other side."

"Love you. Rest easy, Wolfman."

NIC LISHKO has been typing ever since he mastered the underground world in *Mario Teaches Typing*. From half-finished books to short stories that his family has called "Iffy at best," Nic has trudged through years of writer's block and come out the other end smelling like an In-N-Out Burger. After a year of living in LA full of ramen and clearance rack produce, Nic's spec "Evilish" went wide in 2014. He made it onto the Tracking Board's Hit List that same year, got married, and moved to Colorado. His award-winning web series "Long Walks on the Beach" can be binged in its entirety on Vimeo and his podcast, *Cinema Gush*, can be found wherever podcasts are listened to.

He lives in Monument, Colorado, with his amazing bride, Monica, and precocious Old English sheepdog, Oliver.

The Punstoppable Catfish Stanley
Becca Lee Gardner

y name is Catfish Stanley, and I save the world with puns.

Really, the cringier the joke, the more potent the magic is. Eye rolls give additional stamina bonuses to defensive spells. And the best knock-knock jokes can throw a troll right through an office window.

I'm telling you this because the world isn't as safe as you think it is. I've seen ogres crawl out of manholes. I've watched goblins terrorize a playground. I've met more than one Baba Yaga in Human Resources. Threats from the Rune Realm are everywhere. I need you to belie—

"Catfish?"

I startle in my chair and rip my headphones out of my ears. Lisbet stands at the entrance of my cubicle, clutching a red file folder to her cardigan, with a polite stiffness to her face. She's the only one in the office who talks to me in the lunchroom. The rest of the marketing team schedule their lunches at odd hours just to avoid me.

"Lisbet. Hi!"

I pause the audio track on my phone. It's the first draft of my own podcast. I'm still working through some technical revisions on it, but that can wait.

"I like your shirt," she says.

I glance down at the wolves howling on my chest against a tie-dye blue background. She could be making fun of me. Most of the time when people pay me compliments, that's what they're going for, but this is Lisbet. I smile back. "Thanks!"

Her kindness is a strength. I can see it in her eyes. I wonder if she knows that about herself.

"Barker just asked me to present at the client meeting today," Lisbet says. "Would you mind helping me get ready? I need a few copies of this report."

I want to say yes immediately, but I pause. This office building has an inherent closeness with the Rune Realm, and the proximity affects any technology plugged in for too long. It's why I unplug everything in my cubicle every few hours.

For the rest of my coworkers, the threat is small. I constantly cast protective jokes on them, and, in full daylight, the biggest menaces of the Rune Realm aren't tempted by regular humans. Only the chance to feast on a Word Wizard could tease the most dangerous creatures of the Rune Realm out into the light.

"If you're busy, I can ask someone—"

"No!" I say, too loud and too fast. "I'm happy to help." I smile again. I keep thinking if I smile around her, maybe she'll do it, too. "When is the meeting again?"

Lisbet looks at her phone. "It's in ten minutes," she says. "In the other annex."

I hold out my hand for the file folder. "Do you know what you call a factory that makes okay products?"

Lisbet hands me the folder and stiffens.

"A satis-factory."

She groans, but a shimmery turquoise energy flashes around her. It will offer her temporary, low-level protection. I'll need to land at least a dozen more jokes in the next couple of days to give her proper protection for a weekend of unknowns.

"Thanks, Catfish." Lisbet hurries back into the maze of cubicles.

With the folder in hand, I make my own way through the cubicle city to the copy machine. I smile and greet everyone I pass, but few are willing to exchange more than a head nod with me. And fewer still have the turquoise sheen around them that signals their magical protection. It might be time to tell another joke over the intercom.

The copy machine is tucked in a cubicle of its own, surrounded by several fake trees and a table crowded with rubber bands, paper clips, and highlighters. As I approach the machine, it crackles with a purple light.

I pause, and my pulse amps up inside me.

As a Word Wizard, I can see magic. I see my own spells on other people. I could—in theory—see other Word Wizards' magic. And I can see the work of my enemies in the Rune Realm.

And this isn't the color of my own magic.

I approach the copy machine stiff with caution. Sometimes the closeness of the Rune Realm can betray my eyes. There could be nothing wrong with the copy machine at all.

Or it could be an active portal to the shadowland.

My heart thumps fast as I work through the options. If I don't get Lisbet the file soon, the meeting won't go well for her. Barker doesn't give junior team members second chances.

But if the copy machine is connected to the Rune Realm? Whatever comes of it—well, Word Wizards are supposed to work in pairs, but even in the realm of magic, I am alone.

I suck in a long breath. I can't let Lisbet down. There hasn't been a big event in months. I am probably just paranoid.

I pull the documents out of the red file folder, slide them into the feed tray, press two-sided, collate, and staple. Letting the air out of my lungs, long and slow, I push the wide green copy button.

Purple energy zaps out of the copy machine in wild arcs. One of them slaps me in the chest and sends me staggering backward and breathless.

The machine shudders on its wheels, shaking and spewing more tendrils of purple light as the document feeds into the copy machine. Three papers in, and the machine groans, a jam alarm growling out from the possessed office equipment.

I yank the knock-knock joke book out of my back pocket. They are my only offensive magical spells, but they rely on a second person to answer.

Black ink spews out of the copy machine like a mortal wound, pooling in a wide puddle on the gray carpet. As the puddle grows larger, a black hand reaches out of it. The hand grasps at the carpet, and an arm and a shoulder emerge, and then a wet, sticky black head lifts out of the ink puddle.

In another breathless moment, the black, wet figure rises into the hulking form of a golem born not of stone or clay but ink. It looms high, its head missing the ceiling by centimeters. It stares down at me with black, hollow sockets where its eyes should be and opens its dripping mouth to reveal a white maw deep within the black. It pulls at its legs; its feet not quite free from the Rune Realm from which it was born.

For a chilling moment, the golem looks down at me and I up at it. It must be a level fifteen creature, at least. A dire enemy, even if I'd prepared for it. Even more so when it schleps its way into my work schedule.

I lurch to the left, duck out of the cubicle, and dash along the wall to the nearest fire alarm. I pull it, and a chirping sound erupts throughout the office, followed by a silent, flashing light. People slowly emerge from their cubicles, pausing to chat with each other.

I wave them toward the exit. "The copy machine is on fire! Hurry!"

They look at me with glazed eyes. Fire alarms mean administrative drills and unscheduled breaks, not danger.

I shift tactics, spreading a fractured smile across my face. "Did you know smoking will kill you? And bacon will kill you. But smoking bacon will cure it!"

Turquoise energy flashes around the half dozen people around me, and no one seems willing to wait out the alarm anymore. They evacuate with an eagerness to flee only my jokes can inspire.

I don't see Lisbet among them.

The ground shudders. The golem has mastered its ink legs into a single, trembling step.

We don't have much time now.

I tuck my joke book under my arm and cup my hands over my mouth. I shout, "Someone threw all my 70s records in the fire! It was a disco inferno!"

More turquoise magic sparks up around the last stragglers as they hurry to the back exit and down the stairs. Hopefully Lisbet is with them.

Another heavy footstep shakes the floor. I am alone. I cannot lead the golem out of the office and into the crowd of my coworkers.

It's time to get creative.

I hold tight to the knock-knock joke book in my hand and sprint around the edge of the cubicle maze. There might be a way to fight alone. I've been thinking about it a long time now, and I guess today is the day to test it.

Most of the office is a wide-open space with carpeted

cubicle walls delineating the borders between workspaces like countries on a map. Each cubical kingdom lacks the very thing I need to fight back against this monster: doors.

A knock-knock joke requires two participants. Ordinarily that means two Word Wizards. But if I can find an actual door, then maybe the golem can play a physical comedy approach to the spell.

And I might just live through the next few minutes.

This annex has four solid doors: one to the back stairs, one to the front lobby, one to Barker's office, and one to the bathroom. I will not lead the golem toward my retreating coworkers. Barker's office is on the other side of the annex. So I head to the bathroom.

Boom!

I glance behind me to see the ink golem kicking down cubicles like dominoes. The cubicle city has fallen.

Arriving at the bathroom, I grab the doorknob, but it turns on its own in my hands. I startle back as Lisbet exits. She pauses to scrutinize me. Then her eyes widen as she sees what's behind.

I don't have time to explain anything, so I push her back into the bathroom and lock the door.

"Catfish! What was that?"

I rip open my joke book and begin turning to a few dog-eared pages near the back. "Do you know what the pirate said on his eightieth birthday? Aye matey!"

She looks incredulous. I can feel her confusion like heat radiating from her. But I also catch the flash of turquoise enveloping her. Two jokes directed right at her in the last ten minutes would be decent defense stats if there wasn't an ink golem about to bust through the door and consume us both.

"You're really joking right now?" she asks. "What the heck is out there?"

"A level fifteen ink golem," I reply, still flipping through pages.

"A golem—"

"Ink golem," I correct. "And the jokes are spells. They will keep you safe."

"Jokes will keep us safe?"

"No," I correct again. "They will keep *you* safe. I deal the protection, but I don't get it."

Lisbet shakes her head. "Nope. I must be dreaming. That's what this is. A bad, very bad, terrible dream."

The next thundering footsteps shiver through the tile and rattle the faucet.

I raise my hand to the door and knock. For a moment, all the sound outside the door stills.

"Icing!" I shout through the door. Another pause. "Icing so loud my neighbors complain!"

The spell works. Kind of.

The door bursts backward, but the ink golem catches the piece of metal in his sopping, black hands. It squeezes the metal, and the door screams and groans and compacts into something that could pass for abstract museum art.

If the golem takes one more step, we'll be cornered in the bathroom with no hope of escape.

"Run!" I yell, just as the golem half-steps into the bathroom, crouching below the low ceiling and aiming a swipe right at Lisbet. I dive between Lisbet and the blow, catching an inky fist to the head and cracking against the wall.

Lisbet screams.

My vision blurs. The black blob of the ink golem swirls as I stagger back to my feet. I have to find Lisbet. I have to protect her.

"I was wondering why the Frisbee kept getting bigger and bigger," I say as my legs buckle. "And then it hit me!"

I spot the flash of turquoise energy a few feet away from me. There she is! I blink and stumble closer. When my vision clears, I see her cowering in the corner, holding her knees tight to her chest. Her eyes meet mine, and they're wide and full of terror.

The golem rips a bigger entrance into the bathroom, pieces of the ceiling thumping down around us. I turn to the golem again, standing between it and Lisbet. It senses my power and screams a challenge at me, its face so close I can see the mangle of white within is jaw.

But the white isn't teeth. It's paper. A crumpled-up piece of the file I tried to copy for Lisbet is jammed in the ink golem's mouth.

And golems have a thing about paper.

I stand tall between Lisbet and the golem, blood leaking from my head and into my eyes. "Lisbet, knock-knock!"

The golem lunges forward and snags me in its grip before I can even flinch.

"Catfish!"

The golem pulls me closer, its mouth opening wide. "Lisbet! Knock-knock!"

"Who's there?" she says with a choking sob.

"Cereal!"

"Cereal who?"

I wriggle my hand free of the golem's grip just as it shoves me headfirst into its mouth. I grab the jammed paper lodged there with all my strength. It's the only other solid object in the warm, dark, oozy black around me. Holding onto it keeps me from going further into the golem.

The golem squeezes my waist and tries to force me down its throat. I hold fast to the paper in my fingers.

"Cereal pleasure to meet you!" I bellow as loud as I can.

The ink gurgles, and for a moment I wonder if the joke

won't work when I'm halfway down the golem's throat. The thick ink is everywhere, and whatever pocket of air the golem gulped down with me is shrinking fast.

Maybe I didn't enunciate clearly. That seems to be a thing with spells, even ones as ridiculous as knock-knock jokes.

I yell the words again with all the clarity I can muster: "Cereal pleasure to meet you!"

This time the punchline does its job.

The golem shrieks and explodes. I free-fall through black muck and slap against the wet ground. My skull aches, and I gulp in the bitter-tasting air. I try to wipe ink from my face and eyes, but my hands are coated in the stuff.

Lisbet uses her cardigan to wipe my face. "Catfish! Are you okay?"

She helps me to my feet; I manage to stay upright for a moment and then wobble as my vision spins. I tend to under–estimate a good head thwacking. And I had two in a row.

She moves to my side, steadying me. "Are you alright?"

Lisbet's brown hair sticks out at odd angles. Splatters of ink cover her from head to toe. Her eyes search mine. "How can this be real?"

"What do you call a fake noodle? An impasta!"

"Gosh. Does it ever stop?"

Her lips don't even twitch into a whisper of a smile. But the sheen of turquoise encircles her, and I decide I'd take a few more head thwackings to see her real smile.

"The ink is still moving," she says.

I really should have noticed that. This isn't my first brush-up against a level fifteen-er. Although, it is my first time doing it with someone else. And the last time involved an abandoned construction site, a port-a-potty, and a fortuitous amount of concrete.

Turning from Lisbet, I watch ink slide about the floor.

Searching. Droplets join with other droplets, globules with other globules. Ink slides off my skin to meld with its fellows.

Lisbet cringes as the ink leaves her skin, too.

It's fast. A few blinks and I have no sign of ink on me at all. Instead, the ink pools in a dozen splotches across the ground. Each of the pools shiver as new forms push up and out of the ink. The two-foot-tall creatures have long, hooked noses and protruding brows.

Goblins.

Or, in this case, Globlins.

"When will this stop?" Lisbet breathes.

"We have to get to the copy machine," I say. "It must be powering the connection to the Rune Realm."

The Globlins charge. I dodge to the left, and a jagged dagger stabs into the air I had just occupied. Lisbet yelps, but a turquoise light flashes, and a Globlin staggers back. They're too low-level to get through Lisbet's defenses. For now.

My own jokes don't protect me, so I duck and weave around the slashing weapons, trying to draw the majority of the Globlins away from Lisbet.

"Get to the copier!"

"Catfish—"

A scimitar lodges in the desk chair inches from my hand. "Unplug it and get out of here!"

"But—"

"I'll come when I can," I say, twisting away from several more slashes. "Hurry!"

She darts across the debris toward the other side of the annex, and I hold back the truth of her mission. Yes, unplugging the copier will keep the Globlins from morphing again, should I defeat them.

But alone, I have no chance of doing that at all.

I can't outrun the horde like I did the golem. And Globlins

don't have a paper jammed inside them keeping them animated. They are pure hatred and sharp things.

I had to get Lisbet away from them.

The Globlins attack again, this time with a wild ferocity that makes the first ambush feel like a warm-up. I dance around the office chair, rolling and swiveling it to keep it between me and the strikes and stabs of the tiny Globlin horde.

They quickly adapt, forming a circle around me so that anywhere I turn, a blade awaits me.

For a moment, I imagine Lisbet running for the exit, down the stairs, and out of the building. I think about her escaping and living a safe life where she smiles a wide, full smile all the time.

A dagger catches me deep in the shoulder, and the breath rushes out of me. In the next moment, three more Globlins rip the chair from my hands. They're on top of me in an instant.

I fight the tiny hands and bat their sharp weapons away as best I can, but they take me to the ground. My head hits the floor, and purple flashes across my vision.

One Globlin leaps atop my chest. Black ink drips from the small figure like ichor, and its dark eyes shine with a purple hue. The rest of the Globlins clutch tightly to my limbs, pinning me to the ground. The Globlin standing on me wags his scimitar in my face. It's not every day that a goblin of any sort gets to end a Word Wizard.

The Globlin presses the wet, warm ink blade to my throat. Its face is so close to mine our noses nearly touch. It smiles a cruel, impish smile.

"What do you call a pony with a sore throat!" someone shouts from behind the Globlin. "A little hoarse!"

Yellow light flashes around me, throwing all the Globlins six feet back.

In a blur, I see Lisbet running toward me. She's carrying an office chair, and the next second she hurls it at the Globlins.

The Globlins scatter, and the chair crashes against the wall.

I push myself up, and more blood weeps from my wound. My head spins, but I lean forward and force my feet under me. When my vision steadies, I find Lisbet kicking debris and throwing keyboards and monitors at the Globlins with a ferocity that surprises even the creatures of the Rune Realm.

My legs wobble, but I stagger closer to Lisbet.

The Globlin horde eyes us, uncertain of their odds.

"That was a good joke."

"I heard it from my dad," she says as she tosses an instruction manual in the Globlins' direction. "He would have liked you."

"Would have?"

Lisbet's intensity wanes, and her lips twitch up into a sad smile that holds a thousand different happy memories turned cold with grief.

I feel her hurt inside me. My own buried grief and loss thumps like an old battle wound. "I'm so sorry, Lisbet."

Her smile shifts, like sunlight beaming through a stagger of gray clouds. She turns to the Globlin hoard. "Catfish?"

"Yes?"

"Knock-knock?"

A wild smile spreads across my face. "Who's there?"

Becca Lee Gardner is an award-winning short story writer, novelist, and 24/7 geek. If she could live anywhere, it would either be New Zealand (near the Shire) or Batuu (Galaxy's Edge in Disneyland). She loves being a mom of three young kids who challenge, inspire, and often deprive her of sleep. Becca writes epic fantasy and sci-fi.

Silver Sentinels
Jen Bair

I know better than to do magic in school.

Most of my freshman year had been spent trying to bury my junior high reputation, but never in a million years was I going to turn down Vivian Everly. I would run around the sun for her if she asked.

Not that she'd asked for anything so impossible. It was just a magic trick. Make her book disappear. That wasn't so hard. I'd made things disappear a million times. Petty magic was part of my heritage.

I, Edger Lee, come from a not-so-proud line of sleight-of-hand hacks working dead-end jobs filling space between acts with true stage talent. Never mind that my family's magic is real; it isn't impressive, which is what sells tickets.

I was no exception. My magic was as petty as my ancestors', but if it got me an actual conversation with Vivian Everly, I'd take it.

We should have gone to the library, or at least outside where it was less populated, but I was afraid she'd think I was being creepy if I asked her to go somewhere secluded with me.

The school cafeteria was the number one most dangerous place to do any kind of magic. There were too many people shambling about. I knew it, but I ignored it because I'm a teenage boy and we're not all that smart when pretty girls are around.

It wasn't hard to convince myself it would be fine. All my common sense evaporated with Vivian standing in front of me, her raven-black hair spiraling down around those big, dark eyes, mouth parted in a half-smile.

I'd been hugging one wall of the cafeteria to steer clear of the lurch of humanity that shifted and flowed through the room, pockmarked by gaggles of kids blocking aisles as they talked, oblivious to the poor saps that had to go around them, when I heard Vivian's voice next to me.

"You're Edger, right?"

I had frozen, unable to believe she was talking to *me*. The smell of her, smooth and floral with a hint of vanilla, momentarily drowned out the prevailing scent of instant mashed potatoes and bean burritos.

"I hear you can do a trick where you make things disappear. That's really cool. Can I see it? Will you make my book disappear?"

The next thing I knew, I was holding her book. *Her* book. One she had touched with her own hands. I was now *associated* with the coolest girl in school. Even if it was only for the two minutes it took to do a single magic trick.

Suddenly, I was grateful for my reputation as the lamest kid in school. Vivian didn't seem to think magic tricks were lame.

I know, I should have been more careful, but what was I going to do, say no? Of course not. Not when she looked so intrigued, and that intrigue was directed at me. It was my wildest fantasy come true.

Besides, the trick wasn't hard to do.

I stared at the book, the words *To Kill a Mockingbird* scrawled across arching tree branches. I ran my fingers over the silky-smooth cover, which told me either her book was new or she took very good care of it.

I concentrated, blocking out the cafeteria and the kids laughing with their friends, the clatter of trays and the bustle of bodies. Last of all, I blocked out Vivian. Nothing else existed but the book.

Then I opened my mind to the empty dimension, which was a pocket of space that was ... well ... empty, which made it a great place to hide things.

I did my little trick where I "fumbled" the book, the sudden movement startling my audience of one, and the book disappeared, tucked away in the empty dimension.

At least, that's what was supposed to happen.

Greg Sluff shoved into me at the worst possible instant. Greg was a Silver Sentinel, captain of the school basketball team. He was one of the cool kids.

I was on the team, too, but I wasn't a star player, and I definitely did *not* count as one of the cool kids. My basketball skills were mediocre at best. Honestly, I didn't even like basketball, but I was tired of getting picked on for being the dorky magic kid, and the sports kids always seemed cool, so joining the team felt like the obvious solution.

Except the only popularity I gained was the attention of all the sports kids who had their perfect target show up to practice so they didn't have to hunt anyone down. You'd think I'd get off easy for making it so convenient for them. No such luck.

I knew I was in trouble the second Greg shoved me because his phone smacked into Vivian's book just as it disappeared, and they both ended up in the empty dimension together.

"Watch it, dork," Greg said, as if he hadn't been the one to shove me. I was against the wall, so it's not like I was in his way.

He "accidentally" ran into me multiple times a day. For a guy with all the moves on the court, I didn't believe for a second he was that clumsy.

Still, if I survived high school with only a few bruises, I'd count myself lucky.

Unfortunately, I didn't think Greg would be limiting himself to bruises once he realized—

"Hey, where's my phone?" he said after a cursory glance at the empty floor.

Vivian let out a squeal of delight. "That was amazing! You really did it. You made my book disappear!" She did a little dance, bouncing on her toes.

As much as I loved the sound of Vivian's voice, I really wanted her to stop talking.

Greg looked at me, and I could feel tension radiating up my spine and settling at the back of my skull. His look was stormy, and the furrows of his lowered brow were much deeper than when he was fake-mad at me for being in his way.

"Disappear? Did she just say you made it *disappear?*" Greg's tone of disbelief warred with disgust. "What, like with one of your stupid magic tricks?" He turned in a circle, staring at the floor like he didn't believe for a second that I could possibly have made anything disappear.

"That was *so* good," Vivian continued to gush, oblivious to my impending doom. "And you did his phone, too, at the last second. You're, like, a total genius."

She waited for me to respond, but my eyes were locked on Greg's face, waiting for the moment he realized his phone was not, in fact, on the floor. It didn't take long.

"You hid it in your pocket, didn't you, you little twerp," he said, lunging for me like I was going to sprint for the exit.

I probably should have.

He grabbed my arms and started wrestling me to the ground.

I didn't even fight him. He had far more experience slamming into people, on *and* off the court, than anyone else on the team. Aggressive was the only way he played.

I was used to getting knocked down, but the basketball court wasn't full of cafeteria tables. My head caught the corner of one of the benches, and lightning shot down my spine.

I slammed onto the floor with Greg on top of me. I couldn't think with the world tilting crazily and starbursts sparking in my vision, but I could feel Greg patting down my pockets. I was wearing a short-sleeved shirt and blue jeans, so there weren't many places to hide a phone.

I didn't have a phone of my own because my parents wanted me to save up for one. I wasn't in a hurry to do that because I knew my teammates would find all sorts of new ways to make my life a living hell if I had one.

Greg was in the process of pulling off my shoes, presumably thinking I had somehow managed to hide his phone in one, when a stern voice spoke up.

"What is going on here, young man?" It was a woman's voice, no doubt one of the faculty members.

Greg grunted as he gave my second shoe one last yank. "He stole my phone."

"Mr. Sluff, don't think being captain of the basketball team lets you get away with manhandling your fellow students. As you well know, our school has a no-bullying policy."

"Yeah, yeah," Greg muttered.

My vision cleared enough for me to focus on him, leaning over me and shaking the shoe out before peering into it.

"Respect yourself by respecting others." He repeated the team motto in a mocking voice under his breath. "Your team is your family."

I was an only child, but I was pretty sure most of my teammates treated their family like week-old trash. The coach was always trying to motivate us to work together and form connections so we'd work harder not to let our friends down, but the message seemed to be selectively absorbed.

Silver Sentinels were supposed to be all about diligence in our pursuit of what mattered and standing up for what's right. Fighting the good fight and all that. It sounded nice, but the reality always seemed to end up with me on the floor with a concussion.

Vivian was also standing over me, but she had her hands over her mouth, worried, which was something, at least.

"Ms. Everly, will you escort this student to the nurse's office?" the faculty member asked with a sigh. "Mr. Sluff and I need to have a chat with the coach."

Greg glared down at me. "You better get my phone back by practice," he said, pointing ominously at me. He turned and stalked off, leaving the faculty lady to scurry after him.

Vivian tried to help me up, but she was built pretty, not strong. I managed to get myself up and insisted I was fine, though I wobbled and had to grab the wall for support. She insisted I go to the nurse's office, so I followed her, feeling weak and dorky and miserable.

The nurse gave me a cold pack to put on the lump growing on the back of my head and made me lay down for a few minutes. I ended up falling asleep and didn't wake up until the school bell rang.

The clock in her back room told me that was the final bell. School was out, and basketball practice would start in fifteen minutes. I debated skipping it, but I knew Greg would find a way to track me down. It was Friday, and there was no way he was going phoneless for the entire weekend. I just needed someplace out of the way to concentrate long enough to retrieve it.

Luckily, I was in just such a place. All I needed was a couple minutes of peace.

I closed my eyes only to be distracted by Coach Nelson's voice in the next room.

"I hear one of my players was here at lunchtime. Edger Lee?"

Before the nurse could tell him I'd been asleep all day, I hopped off the bed and made my way to the door. "I'm here, Coach."

He gave me a cursory look. "You good? I heard you took a tumble."

Of course Greg hadn't told him the whole story. "Uh, yeah. I'm fine."

Coach Nelson had this weird way of buoying up the team's spirits by assuming we were the best, even when we weren't. He lived in a fantasy world where all the motivational sports movies held true for his team. Missed a three-pointer? Just a fluke; we'll get the next one. Twisted ankle? It'll heal stronger than ever. This time was no different.

"Attaboy. We're tougher than most, right? Sentinel strong!" He pumped his fist before glancing at his watch. "See you on the court in a few." He flashed me a grin and was gone.

I signed out of the nurse's office after she checked my pupils and took my temperature and asked me four times if I was feeling okay. I thanked her for letting me sleep through class, though I knew it meant I'd have to catch up over the weekend. Greg was in my sixth-period biology class, so I was happy to dodge that bullet.

My plan was to head toward the gym, but pass it and head out the back door of the school where I might find a minute of solitude to concentrate long enough to retrieve the phone, but I heard dark laughter behind me in the corridor after leaving the nurse's office.

Greg must have realized where I was when I hadn't shown up to biology. He and Tony, another teammate, had been headed for the nurse's office when they spotted me. The ball of nerves in my stomach plunged to my feet.

Abandoning my last chance at getting Greg's phone before confronting him, I resigned myself to a brutal practice session. Luckily, Coach was in the locker room, so the most Greg could do was glare at me as if fantasizing about artful ways to decorate the walls in my blood.

I changed quickly and stayed close to Coach when he headed out to the gym. The lacquer-sneaker-sweat smell always made me think of stale almonds.

My luck didn't last long.

At the start of practice, Coach told Greg a new transfer was trying out for the team. Coach was going to run him through some drills on the court outside, so Greg was in charge of the team. I volunteered to go scrimmage with the new guy, but being a mediocre player, I wasn't surprised when Coach chose more qualified players for his three-on-three.

That's when I knew I was toast.

I watched the group of handpicked players head for the door, the sunlight shining through the opening like a passageway to heaven. And I was stuck inside with Greg, a place that currently felt like the opposite of heaven.

Greg's dark chuckle sounded behind me, and I let my chin drop to my chest, already knowing what was coming.

"Where's my phone, dork?"

"I can get it for you as soon as practice is over." I left the sidelines, heading to where the rest of the team was doing full-court drills. It took effort not to glance behind me, but I strained my ears, listening for Greg's footfalls past the squeaking of shoes on waxed flooring.

He waited several seconds before shoving me, no doubt so I would think he was going to let it go for now, but I'm not that dumb.

Greg never let anything go.

His shove was hard enough to make me stumble. I would have fallen if I hadn't been expecting it.

"I want my phone now, dweeb. Not after practice. Not in ten minutes."

I turned to face him. He was angry. Like, *really* angry. I'd never seen him look so murderous.

I took another step back from him.

"Okay, okay." I tried to temper the note of panic in my voice. "Let me run to the locker room, and I'll get it for you."

"Bull. If it was in the locker room, you could have gotten it while you were changing. You're just looking for a chance to escape." He shoved me again, harder.

I landed on my backside and bit my tongue, the tang of blood coating my molars.

"Too bad you can't make *yourself* disappear."

I rolled over, getting to my knees but staying low. The Silver Sentinels logo, a silver wolf outlined in magenta, gleamed waxy fresh beneath me. I was at center court, and the interruption to the team's drills meant they were gathering around us.

"Hey, Greg, what's going on?" Isaac asked.

Tony answered for him. "Magic kid stole his phone at lunch."

I heard a few low whistles.

"If you're so good at magic tricks," Greg said, "make my phone reappear." He stepped up next to me, shoving me off my knees and onto my side with his foot. Since I was already so close to the ground, it didn't hurt much for once.

"I can't," I protested. "I need to concentrate. I need some privacy."

"Performance anxiety?" Greg scoffed as some of the team snickered. "You stole my phone in the middle of the cafeteria. I'm not buying it, dork. Cough it up."

"*Copperfield* it up," someone joked.

Greg kicked me, though not hard. "Get started, Houdini. I'm going to keep kicking you until I get my phone back."

The way I saw it, I had two options. I could try to focus long enough to get his phone back or I could sit there and get kicked for the next hour. Greg kicked me again. Harder.

"Okay, okay. Give me a minute," I grumbled. I sat up, keeping my legs spread in a *V* so I wouldn't fall over every time he kicked at me. I stared down at the magenta lines outlining the wolf, tasting the coppery blood on my teeth, and tried to concentrate.

Every time Greg kicked me, it pulled me out of my trance. I think I growled at him around the fifth kick. Accessing the empty dimension wasn't difficult, usually, but doing it while being assaulted made concentrating ridiculously hard.

I was able to feel the empty dimension's presence, but it was shaky. Finding the empty dimension was like staring at one of those 3-D posters, where blinking at the wrong time would make you lose the image, only I wasn't using my eyes. I didn't want to reach into it while Greg was kicking me. I wasn't sure what would happen if I lost track of the dimension, but there were some crazy stories in my family's history that made me not want to try it.

Somewhere around the tenth kick, I heard murmurs from the rest of the team.

"Quit kicking him, man."

"Yeah. I want to see what he can do."

Greg snorted in reply and kicked me again. "If he knows what's good for him, he'll either bring my phone back or make himself disappear."

As soon as he kicked me, I put extra effort into my concentration, hoping to open the dimension in the uninterrupted time between kicks.

It worked.

I opened the dimension, but I was terrified of reaching inside. I knew every second I waited meant I was closer to the next interruption, but I didn't want my hand to disappear. The lingering taste of copper in my mouth had me picturing fountains of blood spraying from my severed hand.

The kicks would be better than that.

Unless I *could* make myself disappear. Wouldn't that be a neat trick? Only I had no idea if the real dimension could be accessed from inside the empty dimension. Nobody I knew had ever tried it.

I waited too long. Or maybe Greg didn't wait as long as normal. He kicked me just as I'd mustered up the courage to reach into the emptiness. The borders of it wavered, coming close to my hand. I froze, focusing my concentration, and the wobbling settled, solidifying once more.

My frustration spiked. Greg's impatience was going to get me killed. Stupid nonbeliever that he was, he didn't even realize what he was messing with. My frustration flowed through me, a tingling sensation that grew until the energy of it seemed to solidify into an almost-glow, invisible to the eye, a sort of astral force that was hard to describe.

It flowed into the empty space, and something echoed back.

Something cosmic and ancient and powerful.

Hearing it, *feeling* it, was like standing on a beach watching a hundred-foot wave come at me. I wanted to run, but I was too mesmerized by the sheer awesomeness of its power. Its energy pinged me, and it felt like a giant, spirit-question-mark hovered before me.

What do you want?

Greg kicked me again. The void didn't waver. The connection between my frustration and whatever lurked in the emptiness was too strong.

I answered, though it seemed infinitesimally inconsequential compared to such a force. Like asking someone to use a jackhammer to snap a toothpick. I felt silly, but the force had asked, and I felt compelled to answer.

I want Greg to stop kicking me. I want to stop being picked on. I want to go through my day without being harassed all the time. I want justice.

The being shifted. There was no other way to describe it. It was as uncompromising as a cyclone, as indisputable as planetary rotation. It moved on the spectral plane, and there was no stopping it.

I heard gasps and the scuff of feet on the waxed floor. Something was happening in the real dimension.

I opened my eyes to see the floor glowing.

Bright lines of magenta shone up from the floor, so bright I had to shield my eyes, though I didn't dare look away from it. Like when the tingling of my frustration grew into something solid, the light grew in intensity, resolving into solid matter. Light made flesh. Well, not flesh, but ... *something*.

My mouth dropped open as the emblem of the silver wolf, lined in glowing magenta, rose up from the waxed wooden floor beneath me, solid and semi-real. The magenta glow surrounding it shone through me like a light cutting through shadow. The shaggy fur was as insubstantial as air, yet it held me up.

The wolf grew beneath me, lifting me off the ground. I sat

astride its back, clutching at its fur, though my balance atop it was perfect. Just as my hand was part of my body, I knew the wolf was a part of me, my will made manifest, mixed with something far beyond my comprehension.

The wolf—*the* Silver Sentinel—stood with its head just below Greg's chin. The basketball team, true to form, had plenty of tall kids on it. I wasn't sure how big natural wolves were supposed to get, but this thing was almost the size of a horse.

It growled at Greg. At least, I thought it growled.

It emanated a deep vibration that rattled my bones until I thought my cells might shimmy apart. I'd never heard anything like it in my life. Like reality itself was tearing.

Greg let out a high-pitched squeal and went white as a sheet.

I wasn't sure my heart was still beating. My body was one giant tingle after the growl faded.

The wolf was part of me, but it was also part of the empty. Instead of reaching into the empty the way I always had, I had somehow manifested the essence of the empty dimension in the material plane.

And that manifestation was protecting me.

I had always been more lanky than muscular. I'd never fit in with the cool crowd, but looking around at the team, their mouths open in shock, I finally felt powerful, like I held all the cards. Only I didn't know what to do with them.

The wolf pinged me again. *What do you want?*

I had wanted Greg to stop picking on me. He was literally shaking in terror, so I didn't think he would be a problem for me anymore. I kind of felt sorry for him.

All I really wanted was to give him back his phone and continue on with my life in peace.

Since the wolf was the emptiness and that's where the

phone was, I used my senses to feel inside it. The phone was easy to locate.

"You wanted your phone?" I asked Greg. I waited for him to nod, but he was too far gone. I wasn't even sure he'd heard me.

The wolf sensed what I wanted. It let out a hacking cough, like a cat with a hair ball, only much, much louder. With a retch, it hocked up the phone, which landed with a clatter and a splat on the gym floor, covered in a silvery slime. It looked super gross.

I hoped it still worked.

"Welp," I said, trying to sound nonchalant, as if I summoned giant ectoplasmic wolves from the empty dimension on the regular. "There's your phone."

Greg didn't move. He stared at the wolf like it might drag him into the void.

I patted the wolf, trying to convey my thanks to it. I concentrated on the connection between us and loosened my hold on it. Slowly, the wolf sank back into the floor, its stare never leaving Greg until its head turned to gelatinous goo and disappeared into the familiar emblem of the silver wolf outlined in magenta. I was left straddling the image, trying to gauge the reaction of my teammates.

There was an awkward silence until the slam of a door drew us to our senses. Coach was returning with the rest of the team, all of them patting the new kid on the back. It looked like we had a new member.

Greg swallowed hard, then scurried forward to snatch up his phone, grimacing at the silvery goo coating it. I heard Isaac squeal in an imitation of Greg's reaction to the wolf. I couldn't blame Greg. If he had summoned a giant wolf that glowed magenta and growled at me like that, I'd have peed my pants.

Someone near Isaac let out a nervous chuckle, and Greg,

realizing he was the butt of their joke, straightened his shoulders. Glaring at me, he said, "I should make you lick this phone clean."

The words were tough, but he had lost his credibility and it felt like false bluster. The team must have noticed, too, because Isaac spoke up.

"Back off, Greg. He's part of the team. Treat him with respect."

"Him?" he said, gathering his indignation. "What about me? Look what he did to my phone! You're gonna take his side? It's not right."

"Your phone getting goobered is the least of what's right," the guy next to Isaac said. I thought his name was Ronnie or Robby; I couldn't remember which. "You've had it out for him all year."

There was a murmur of agreement from several of the team members, and Tony, usually Greg's right-hand man, kept his mouth shut.

"Fine," Greg said, glowering at the group. "You want to choose the dork over the captain? Be my guest."

Isaac let out a heavy sigh. "The captain is supposed to keep the team together, not tear it apart." There were more murmurs of agreement. "Edger represents what this team should be. You've been picking on him since middle school, but he still shows up to practice every day."

John joined the discussion. "And he's funny. He always cracks jokes after we lose a game, keeps the mood light."

I hadn't realized he thought I was funny, but cracking jokes was part of being a magician. Part of directing the audience's attention away from what you didn't want them to notice.

"He's cool with me," another kid pitched in.

Greg turned in a huff and stomped off to the locker room.

"Wow. Thanks, guys," I said, at a loss for anything more eloquent to say.

Isaac slapped me on the back and held up a basketball. "You're good people." He handed me the ball. "I'll admit, though, I thought the magic schtick was lame."

"We were wrong about that," John said.

Isaac laughed. "Yeah, we were. That wolf was ... something else."

I felt a smile stretch across my face. "Want to see me make the ball disappear?"

The team let out a cheer, and Coach hollered at us to get moving.

"Later. After practice," Isaac said, his eyes alight with excitement.

I nodded and tossed him the ball.

I knew better than to do magic in school, but really, what could go wrong? I needed to get Vivian's book back, anyway.

I couldn't wait to talk to her again, and now I had an excuse. I didn't even have to run around the sun for it. News of the magic wolf would make the rounds by tomorrow. We'd have plenty to talk about.

JEN BAIR is an Air Force brat, Army veteran, and military wife. She loves traveling with her family to foreign places, real or imaginary, whenever she can. Her family is her life. Her writing is her passion. You can find her published works at jenbair.com.

The Immortal Dez'itny

Jesse Sprague

On her return from the Well of the Gods, Dez'itny approached the fallen body of her father. She clutched her newly created mask to her chest. Dried blood flaked from her fingers. Part of her wanted to sink to the white tiles of the colonnade's interior walkway and weep. Her father's sword hung at her side; his blood stained its blade as well as her hands and her soul. The rhythmic bang of enemies pounding at the walls of Bouraster's capital city—*her* city—reminded her why her deed was necessary.

The dead king's eyes stared up at her. After her lover's death and learning the child she carried would be born without breath, her father had been all she had left. Yet it had been the king's life or the survival of her people.

That was no choice at all.

Her father's advisers stood beneath the white arches separating the walkway from the balcony that overlooked the city. Out there, all the way to the huge stone walls, her people cowered inside their homes, tents, and canopied public gardens. If the city walls fell, those people would die. The advisers had been the first to whisper that patricide was her answer.

How quickly would her people tear her to pieces if she couldn't save them?

The king lay just outside the doorway into her private chamber. His war mask, carved to resemble a boar, was askew on his face, showing the man beneath the king. A man, whose last word had been his daughter's name—Dez'itny. His cold corpse did not concern her anymore; it could not if she wished to keep her countrymen alive.

Her father had been weak.

She would not be.

Stepping into her private room, Dez'itny shoved down her terror and ignored the desperate hammering of her heart. Her father had failed to protect the city—he'd suggested treaties, offered payoffs, even allowed their enemies to claim hunks of Bouraster for themselves. All to avoid fighting. He'd given in to his fear.

Dez'itny touched her mouth, which had spoken words of love so often in times past, spoken promises of a life with her lover, words of comfort to her father even as his fear ate him from inside out. Silk swathed her black hair and bare shoulders. Dez'itny was a woman stranded with no oasis in sight—a woman who had lost her lover to raiders, her child to fate, and if she did not act soon, would lose her people to war.

Dez'itny looked down at her mask for the first time since she had entered the Well of the Gods and lifted the mask from the waters. The totem of station had been created for her, a sign from the gods of her right to rule, but also possessing a piece of herself in its wafer-thin white stone.

It resembled nothing more than a twisted death mask of her own features.

She traced one finger over the too-wide red lips and the

skull-like pit of the cheek. Its single eye was a red jewel. Like half a freshly cleaned skull, the mask would cover only the right side of her face. The mask was a promise between her and the gods of what she would do for her people.

With shaking hands, she set the mask into place. The hooks reached behind her ear and pressed against the back of her skull like bony fingers. The stone felt light, as if she were wearing nothing, as if all that covered her face was the kiss of her gods.

She looked out her window at the city walls manned by guardsmen who had never known battle before. The red jewel eye painted the world in blood.

"It's beautiful," she whispered. She allowed herself to gaze a moment longer. The mask stared out at the reddened walls. The other side of her countenance, though not hidden, was forgotten. That was not her face.

The plain features of a human girl would never inspire warriors to repel the hordes beating at the city's gates.

The walls of Bouraster's capital city were stone, pressed from eon upon eon of sand and sun. Carved of the same stone, the gates were too heavy to move by hand. That was the only reason the city wasn't already overrun. Bouronians were peaceful people, many of them nomads who stopped in the cities only to trade. The city was built to welcome, not to repel.

The gates would not hold the night.

Her father had known this. He'd intended to submit to the Ram Lords—to let them win. He'd told her, as if it were a comfort, that she would survive such a surrender. What was the purpose of surviving if your people were either dead or enslaved?

But he'd been right about the rest. The Bouronian warriors were outnumbered, outmaneuvered, and soon to be outplayed. The small Bouronian army trained mostly with drunken brawls. They fought like their country's totem animal, like boars.

They had always been the people of the boar, but the old ways would not be enough. Charging out the gates to meet the army of the ram in battle would mean death for the Bouronians.

Turning, Dez'itny left the room. This time, she didn't spare her father a glance. Her mask had never known him; it did not mourn.

Her father's advisers bowed their heads, hands over hearts. They had lacked the bravery to do as she had done, but they would follow her.

Out in the stone courtyard, her warriors waited, bloody and tired. At the sight of Dez'itny, the warriors froze. Most of the hundred-odd men wore their fur cloaks with the hoods up, boar tusks jabbing out from beneath their chins. Their chests were bare except for the deadly tools of war and the scars of battle they wore proudly. These few, and those on the wall, were all that was left of the Bouronian army.

Warriors of the ram roared on the other side of the gate. Above, a statue that had once been a boar was now weathered down into an undefined snarling beast.

Staring at that statue, she knew it would become a wolf. But how could she tell these men that the boar was dead and a new age had risen?

She'd walked into her private rooms as their princess, a creature of silk and perfume. Wearing the same perfume, the same silk, she had exited those rooms transformed into their queen.

She would become anything, sacrifice *anything*, for the survival of her people.

Dez'itny rested one hand over her belly. The child was still; it had not moved in days. Its name was unchosen. The dead could not carry a name—they were nameless and forgotten. Her country would not share that fate. When she spoke, it was as much to the unborn child as to the warriors.

"Don new masks, men," she said.

The artisans would be busy, carving in wood and stone, dying leather. These warriors wore the hoods of the boar; they fought in the boar's army. Under her rule, they would be something new.

"The rams have come searching for pigs to slaughter. We will teach them we're not pigs, not even boars; from this day forward, we're wolves. We attack at dusk from the tunnels. They'll learn to fear our snarls in the night."

The warriors were silent, and the mask's grip pressed into the back of her skull.

"Let them call me Destiny—for I will be theirs. And it will be a dark destiny!"

The warriors raised their weapons and roared in salute.

She raised her father's blade to the sky. It was her blade now, but Dez'itny knew it was not her true weapon. The mask gave her people something stronger than flesh to follow.

The mask would give her enemies something immortal to fear.

For generations, the mask served Bouraster.

Only the mask knew how many Dez'itny's there had been since the first had declared Bouraster the land of wolves. People altered. The mask did not. The ancient mask whispered to its new queen. It whispered words of siege, turmoil, and pride; it knew nothing else.

In the mask, Jezryn was Dez'itny; she was Bouraster's queen.

Jezryn had worn the mask as she rode into the swampy grounds of Cassadon, the land of the owl. The mask's drive remained the same—it would find Bouronians safe harbor in a hostile country by slaughtering their enemies.

Watching through Dez'itny's jewel eye, Jezryn walked the ranks of sleeping warriors, sword thumping against her thigh. The corpses of the men who had originally inhabited the camp no longer tainted the soil. Dez'itny's warriors had descended on them under the ripe moon. Several riders were transporting the bodies to hang near the gates of the enemy's city—a warning that the wolves were coming for the owl.

When she finally came to conquer, the Cassadonians would be too afraid to fight.

The remainder of her warriors rested in their new camp, wearing their cloaks over their heads, so it was the silhouette of the wolf that anyone passing would see.

Dez'itny loved her people. Everything she did was for her people—this was the first truth of the mask.

Among her warriors, Jezryn indulged herself in forgetting the greater world and enjoying the scent of a simple rabbit stew over cook fires and the conversational tones of frogs in a nearby bog.

The mask whispered to her how dangerous it was to cling to any of her life before. Anyone but Dez'itny might fail, might allow their people to fail. They might not understand the mask's second truth, that the only way to be strong was to be feared, to cut and slash through enemies until no one dared stand against Bouraster.

She stepped into her sleeping tent and saw her former life-partner sitting on the finest fur rug with their daughter. Dez'itny would have called for warriors to arrest the fugitive. Jezryn pressed her lips shut—she had not let go of the fondness they'd once shared.

She let the tent's door flap fall shut behind her. Before the mask, she had loved Calustus for his carefree spirit and desire to live peacefully off the land. But those ideas were only daydreams, and the world was not forgiving of dreamers. Calustus needed to be contained so his vile words did not contaminate her warriors. If only he could understand that as long as their enemies walked the world, Bouraster would never be safe. She saw the good intentions he had. The mask saw him through a blood-red lens.

Calustus stood to face her, placing his back to the child. He did not stand alone. Tall for her age, at almost eleven, Machite positioned herself just behind her father. She was their daughter, conceived and born in peace before Jezryn ever wore the mask. Before she had taken the mask from her mother's cooling face and assumed the immortal name passed in secrecy from mother to child.

Machite would one day don the mask and take the name Dez'itny. To the view of the world, the mask had only ever belonged to one woman, and Dez'itny's strength came in part from her deathless youth. Jezryn could not be Machite's mother with the mask on; she could be no one but the same immortal queen who had worn the mask before her, worn it since the day the boar became the wolf.

Not even she knew how many years had come and gone since the creation of the mask.

Machite watched both her parents, calm and still.

A slit in the back of the tent showed where Calustus had entered. And where he'd leave if he valued his life.

Jezryn looked at him. So did Dez'itny through the mask's red jewel. No part of her viewed him as an immediate threat.

"I have declared you a traitor," Jezryn said. No, Dez'itny spoke; as long as she wore the mask that was all she was. There were other words that Jezryn might have uttered, words of sorrow and regret. Those remained unvoiced, discarded as weak, useless things.

"You don't need to go on with this war," Calustus said, walking toward her.

Machite remained where she'd been standing, young but already with a warrior's stance. She watched. Some part of the queen wished the child would look away, but she didn't know which part that was.

Calustus spoke softly. "Bouraster's borders are clear. This is not your battle—not your place. We are not invaders."

Jezryn had once thought his gentleness was his strength, but now, the mask knew it for the weakness it was. Surrender meant death. The mask had always known any path except the sword was doomed to fail.

Dez'itny said, "For generations, they have come for us. It is the wolves' turn to stalk. If you don't believe in me anymore, then go."

Calustus reached across the space and touched the mask on Dez'itny's face. "I support you. I always will, but Dez'itny has gone too far."

"Stop," Machite said, though whom she spoke to was unclear.

"Take it off, Jez," Calustus said, his fingers hooking around the edge of the mask.

The mask's bony fingers gripped the back of Dez'itny's skull. "Never."

"Take it off and walk away. Violence isn't noble in its own right—this mask, and its legacy, was forged in blood, but we can change."

Dez'itny drew her blade—the same curved sword her riders wore. In one fluid movement, she pressed it to his neck.

Machite let out a brief cry and started to move, then stopped, frozen in fear.

"You're lucky I don't kill you here and now," Dez'itny said. "I loved you once—but peace is not the way of the wolf."

"Do it then," Calustus said, his voice too weary for fear.

But Dez'itny could not kill him any more than Jezryn could. Even at that moment, he was one of her own, and she would not let him fall, not even to his own weakness. He was one that she must protect. "There are fools out there who stand against us. I will be their Destiny—and it will be a bloody destiny."

Blood marked the edge of the blade, and yet Calustus stood still. Running would not save him from the wolf.

Machite screamed and threw herself against her mother. Though small, her weight was adequate to push Dez'itny aside. Her fists smashed into her mother's chest.

Dez'itny grabbed the child's hand and turned to her, holding her blade away from them. This child mattered. She was the next queen. "You're old enough to understand. We cannot let our softer emotions rule us. We must always be strong."

When Dez'itny turned back, her partner was gone, only a few red drops on the floor of the tent remained in his place. Good.

Bouraster would be safe no matter what it took.

Weak people had no place here. The mask called for blood, and it would be answered in kind.

A new Dez'itny traversed the Bouronian sands.

The mask now wore Machite.

Her riders howled as they rode toward the gates of one of Bouraster's border cities. The sand howled around them, cool with the evening air. And Machite howled with them, tilting her face to the sky until she saw the moon bathed in the red of her jeweled eye. The patrol had been successful, and they were excited to be home.

No enemy braved Bouraster's borders.

Fear was the masked queen's best weapon—fear was immortal, transferred from generation to generation in stories of blood. That was Bouraster's protection.

Even though sand and sweat from the journey covered her riding breeches, Machite did not enter the city with her warriors. Instead, she walked around the side of the gate toward a familiar oasis. She knew she'd find her family there; Dez'itny sensed many things, and among those things was the blood of her own.

When she arrived in the clearing, she saw her son splashing in the water of a small pond. Trees, twisted by the wind and harsh climate of their homeland, hovered protectively around the child. He was safe here, in the arms of Bouraster, but Dez'itny knew he was not alone.

Carefully, she reached up and touched the mask, her fingers caressing the bone-sharp cheek and the wicked curve of the red lips. The mask whispered its truths, gripping the back of her head. Yet this was not the time for the truth of Dez'itny.

For a moment, she could be just Machite. She unhooked the mask and slid it reverently into a bag at her hip. The right side of her face felt cold and naked. She felt naked.

"You look beautiful," said a man from the shadows of the trees.

"Come out, Father," she said. Her hand went to the firm shape of Dez'itny's mask in her bag. The sensation comforted her. It made her feel safe. "I notice you waited for me to remove the mask to call me beautiful."

Calustus stepped out. "Intentionally," he said. His hair had gone white, though he was not old enough for the look.

The mask whispered that he must be captured, that he must be stopped. But it was easier not to listen with it off her face. Calustus stood between her and her son, Va'ashlan, blocking her view of the boy as he played at the edge of the water.

"You know you're banished," Machite said. "You shouldn't be here; it's dangerous."

"You could lift the banishment."

Machite shook her head. This was an old dance between them, and she doubted Calustus even wished to return home. "Dez'itny would never reverse her word. She's constant and infallible."

The mask never changed. Machite understood that for the flaw it was. The world changed, yet the mask did not allow them to follow suit. Even now, it whispered that any deviation was weakness.

Calustus spoke softly, as if afraid of spooking her, "You're not *only* Dez'itny."

This was an even older fight between them. "What am I without her? What would Bouraster be?" This was the first time she'd meant those words.

The mask admonished her from the bag. She ignored it.

"Wouldn't it be lovely to find out?" Calustus leaned close, eyes plaintive.

Behind Calustus, Va'ashlan dove under the water and returned to the surface with a handful of mud, which seemed to delight him.

Machite said nothing. The mask was not so easily set aside. Even standing there without it, she felt the wrongness. Deprived of the immortal grin, she was nothing. This face, the one of flesh and blood, was the mask for her.

If there was another path, she could not walk it. She'd danced to the mask's tune too long.

"The woman you see now," Machite said softly, "she's just a mirage. I am the mask—the longer I wear it, the more I become her. And yet I always was her. Ever since I was a child, there was no other path."

Calustus looked at the boy in the pond, still splashing and laughing. He had not yet seen his mother, or he would have come running. Va'ashlan was a lovely child, but he could never be Dez'itny; his very gender barred him from that. Machite liked that she could raise him, not for the mask, but to be himself and find his own path.

"You're not Dez'itny," her father said. "You're Va'ashlan's mother. It's hard to love a mirage; don't you want to be more for him?"

Machite set her jaw. She'd seen war, knew it in her bones. "Bouraster would fall without Dez'itny. Outsiders fear her; they tell stories of her mask and her riders. When I wear the mask, I *am* Destiny." She rested on the mask in the bag at her side. It goaded her on, reassuring her that her words were right. "I'm their nightmare, and as long as that destiny is feared, we're safe."

"What if you're wrong? Change doesn't happen on its own. We make change ... and we do it for them." Her father motioned toward the boy.

"I appreciate you trying." Machite didn't look at her father but at Va'ashlan. As if feeling her gaze, the boy looked up and grinned.

No one looked at her like that anymore—without fear, only love. The mask cast its shadow on everything else. But Va'ashlan didn't belong to the nation yet, only to his mother. Malleable with youth, there was nothing out of reach for him, yet.

An idea hit her—her son was not yet tainted by Dez'itny. Change was in his nature. Not in the mask's nature.

If Dez'itny were to continue, the mask needed to pass to a woman—someone who could bear the name along with the mask. Machite could have another child, a daughter to feed Dez'itny's immortality. But she wouldn't. Machite couldn't see another path; she couldn't change. But that didn't mean she had to set another along the same course.

"How would we protect ourselves? How would we make them fear without Dez'itny?"

"Those are words of fear," he said. "You seem to believe, as your mother did, that fear is immortal, that it's stronger than all else. Fear isn't the only path. Fear is born of love. There are other ways to protect the ones who matter to us."

"None that I see. It's my duty to keep Va'ashlan safe. If I am a nightmare to others, then he need have no nightmares of his own."

And for that reason, she plucked the mask from the bag and settled it back on her face. Her father looked different through the red jewel; the gentleness in his eyes seemed like weakness. Va'ashlan had that same weakness, and the idea of what it would mean to stamp that out chilled her.

She would not sacrifice another generation to the mask's lusts. She'd raise her boy—not to be afraid, but to be a man who understood the power of peace as well as war. Maybe Dez'itny need not be immortal. Maybe there could someday be a world that didn't need the mask.

She couldn't see a new path. Maybe he could.

Yet, she could not imagine a force more timeless, more immortal than fear, than Destiny.

But Calustus was correct about one thing: it would be lovely to find out.

Va'ashlan approached the body of his mother, which was being prepped for funeral rites in the center of the royal pavilion. She wore furs and riding leathers. Her wolf's cloak had been wrapped snuggly over her body, and its muzzle shaded her brow. A tan line bisected her face where her mask had lived.

The time had come for the mask to sleep.

They could continue as they had been—but why? There was a place for Dez'itny, for blood and war and strength. Bouraster would never lose that, never deny her legacy, but there was more to life.

He held tight to his daughter's hand. Liliano glanced back and forth between her grandmother's body and a white sandstone building just off the royal pavilion. At five, she wasn't old enough to understand the price the mask would demand. Her mother had been yet another sacrifice in a long line in this quest for safety earned by the sword. Many things could be earned with a sword, many things would be. But the wolves needed a new tool in their arsenal. It was his duty to see that his Liliano lived to see a better world.

In his other hand, he gripped the mask. Dez'itny's mask. Its smirk stared up at him, comforting in its way. The jewel eye promised days and nights of blood, of howling at the moon, of terror. He knew the mask's hunger well.

His mother had fallen to its bloodlust, hanged by her own countrymen. Many of their people had demanded a new Dez'itny rise to the throne. When his mother had refused to name an heir, that sect had taken it into their own hands to secure Dez'itny's name. One woman had ruled Bouraster for so long that it knew no other way. Blood was blood, and the fury of Dez'itny knew no bounds.

Yet Va'ashlan had prevailed. He was the chosen of the gods, and soon he'd have a new mask from the Well of the Gods to prove it.

He only hoped Bouraster could walk a fresh path—not for him, but for his Liliano.

They left the royal pavilion and passed into the white stone building, walking through an arched hall to an old chamber. Artifacts rested on display, wolf pelts hung on bone rods, and masks of proud warriors lined the walls. A new stone pedestal stood in the center of the chamber, carved to resemble a wolf— Dez'itny had been the mother of wolves.

Va'ashlan set Dez'itny's mask, created in the Well of the Gods centuries before, onto the stand. Its red leer stared out at him. His mother was dead. Yet, his mother was there on the stand watching him. His mother would never die.

That was comforting. But it was the past.

He would not wear this mask. Nor would he let another put it on and continue the cycle. The Well of the Gods would create something new.

"Will I wear it someday?" Liliano asked in a hushed voice. "Will I be her?"

Va'ashlan turned to his small daughter. Her mouth was streaked with berry juice from an earlier meal, hair falling in an uncombed mass over her shoulders; he had never seen anything so beautiful. "No. The time of destiny is done. You will forge your own path."

Maybe, just maybe, she would grow to be a new kind of wolf.

Looking into her eyes, Va'ashlan knew the one truly immortal thing in the universe. The mask looking down knew it too—it had always known.

Fear was the tool, not the power. His ancestors had forgotten that.

Fear had always been no more than the armor of love.

Coming from a long line of storytellers, and as a busy mom herself, JESSE SPRAGUE writes for others looking for an evocative escape. Her debut novel, *Spider's Kiss*, took the shapeshifter trope in a new direction with sexy spiders in space. Her sci-fi series, Beneath 5th City, explores what happens if there are no heroes to step up in an alien invasion. Her previous stories have appeared in anthologies alongside award-winning and *New York Times* bestselling authors.

To Jesse, words are magic—they might be the only real magic left in this world. Visit her at JesseSprague.com.

Red

Lehua Parker

With each bump, the puppy's head lolls in the wagon bed, one ear limp and the other bloody. Jammed between a carpenter's box and coils of pulleys and ropes, Elise studies it in the fading afternoon light.

Dead, she thinks, remembering how Highway Man casually twisted the dog's neck before tossing it in the back next to her. She dry swallows around the gag, the taste of axle grease and lye soap tickling the back of her throat. With the calico scrap riding like a bit in her mouth, it's hard to breathe through her swollen nose.

Don't upchuck, she prays. *Highway Man says if I upchuck, I'm dead.*

It's hot in the back of the horse-drawn wagon, but the puppy doesn't smell like death, just like iron nails in a blacksmith's pocket. Elise takes shallow breaths and shifts her weight off the sore spot on her hip. The wagon slows and takes a hard right.

We're headed toward the old sheep camps above Deer Creek, she thinks.

Her guts grip.

No one will hear the screams.

The puppy was a nice touch.

Walking alone along River Road in the waning afternoon light and carrying a satchel, twelve-year-old Elise's thoughts flittered like a mountain chickadee, bright with excitement and expectation. Tonight was her first Harvest Moon, and her eyes scanned the meadow for deer. She didn't think anything of the weathered buckboard and horses standing in the shade until a flash of yellow caught her eye. A Labrador puppy with a bright green bow around his neck scampered over the side rails and down beneath the wheels.

From behind a tree, a man called, "Chester! Chester! Come back, you naughty dog. Hey! Sweetheart! Yes, you! Thank goodness, you're here. Help me, please! Don't let him get away."

Elise sprinted, her feet slapping against the ruts in the dirt road, knees pumping high and hard, her lucky red cloak billowing out like a sail.

"Here, Chester," she said, dropping her satchel and bending down.

The puppy crawled out, pushing his eager nose against her, tail wagging.

"You're not naughty, just playful." Elise laughed. "Hey, mister, I got your dog," she said to the black boots rounding the wagon.

She tipped her head back, her eyes sweeping from the worn boots up the canvas pants and no-nonsense workman's belt to the homespun shirt, all the way to the bandanna covering his face.

But it's not dusty, she thought just before his fist landed in her face.

Stunned, she rocked back between wagon wheel ruts, deep grooves in the hard-packed dirt that cradled her pain while the puppy licked her cheek, her bleeding nose, her swelling lips.

All the better to kiss you with, my dear, purred a new voice in her head.

Don't, Elise! shouted her mother's voice from deep within. *He's just a common Highway Man. A kidnapper and a thief. It's not what you think. Scream. Fight. Yell. Don't let him take you.*

But when Elise opened her mouth to scream, fight, yell, Highway Man kicked her in the gut.

Lying in the dirt, all Elise's mouth could do was open and close like a fish on the dock. Air flowed weakly into her lungs as through a crack in a winter-tight door. While she struggled to breathe, the Highway Man moved.

Forcing her wrists together at her stomach, he looped them with a piece of rawhide and cinched tight. "Those earbobs are perfect, Honeybun. I love how them gold hoops shimmer along your throat. Very grown-up." He reached up and chucked her chin, ignoring the teakettle protests that wheezed past her lips. "But what I really wonder about is the color of your bloomers." She stilled. He held her eyes. "Cornflower blue, I'm guessing," he mused. "But don't tell me. I'll find out soon enough."

With a magician's flourish, he pulled a scrap of bright yellow calico from his pocket. "Ladies and gentlemen! Nothing up my sleeve! For my first trick, I'm going to make a child disappear." He shook the rag in her face. "Now you, young lady, have the look of a sensible child. I can just gag you if you're sensible. Far less bruising if we do it that way, but I have plenty of rope if'n I need it."

This can't be how I die.

"Well, Cherry Pie, I'm waiting. Are you sensible?" Highway Man stood and drew back his foot for another kick.

Still no air to speak, to yell, to scream. Elise clamped her lips and nodded.

Highway Man's foot stopped mid-swing. "Good girl. That's what I figured. Gag and hands only. But keep your guts in order, hear me? If you yak, you'll choke and die. It's happened before. And that's a sad thing for both of us."

Highway Man twirled the calico scrap between his hands like a cowboy's kerchief, then tucked it between her lips, knotting it tightly behind her head. "Bruises are bad," he said. "You're makin' the right choice, Johnnycake."

With his gunslinger's hands, he picked her up and half-threw, half-dumped her into the wagon like a sack of potatoes. The handle of a shovel bit cruelly into her hip, but she ignored it and scooched like a worm, moving as far from him as possible.

He snickered, shaking his head. "They always do that."

Highway Man scooped up Chester and her satchel, flinging her bag next to her. "Can't leave that lying around, now can we?"

Cradled like a baby in the Highway Man's arms, Chester wiggled, frantic to reach anything a puppy's tongue could love.

"Good boy. But I won't need you any longer now that I've got Angel Cakes to play with."

Ruffling the puppy's ears, Highway Man snapped Chester's neck and dropped him boneless to the wagon bed. "That's better, Plum Puddin'. You won't be lonely with Chester to keep you company."

Highway Man swung up to the front and raised the reins. "Hup," he called to the horses. She felt him crack the reins, once, twice. Moving at a ground-eating trot, the horses stepped out from the trees, aligned the wagon's wheels in the ruts, and vanished down the road.

Chester.

Elise screws her eyes tight.

I won't cry, he can't make me cry, not over a silly puppy, but tears spilled anyway. *With his hands on the reins, he can't hurt me. I'm okay. I'm getting through this.*

Elise tips her chin, sucking bloody snot back up her nose, swallowing the lump down her throat.

All the better to smell you with, my dear.

Cautiously, she wipes her nose along her sleeve.

Swollen and hot, but not broken. Teeth still tight in their sockets. Bottom lip thick, but not split. Blood on my new cloak, red on red—forget it. Forget about the dog, too. Don't get distracted. Stall. He doesn't know.

An hour passes like kidney stones until the wagon rocks a hard left, turning off the main country road. Her satchel tips.

Oh, no. Please, don't let it roll onto Chester. I'll never use that satchel again.

More twists and turns, and by the sharp scent of the pines, Elise knows they've passed all the low-lying meadows and fields.

Into the woods.

Trapped in her winter cloak, sweat beads on her forehead and runs dust and dirt into her eyes. Using the sides of her thumbs, she smears black streaks across her cheeks.

War paint.

Squirreled away in Elise's hope chest, the gold hoops were her grandmère's legacy. She'd never worn them before.

"Earbobs, Elise? Really?" Maman frowned, turning from

the stove to serve dinner. "Do you see what your granddaughter's wearing?"

Grandpère caught Elise's eye and smiled. "She looks fine. Sophisticated. Like her grandmère."

"*Merci, Papi!*" said Elise, taking her place at the table.

"It's the truth," he said, kissing her cheek. "I'm so proud of you. It's your Harvest Moon!"

Maman clenched her jaw as she set the meat platter next to the butter. Shaking her head, she said, "She'll lose one in the woods and then what? Some things you can't undo."

"Maman. I'll be careful. Promise."

"Uh-huh. Heard that before."

Elise picked up the serving fork and snatched the biggest steak.

"What big eyes you have," Maman tsked, guiding Elise's hand to Grandpère's plate.

As the steak dropped, Grandpère said, "She's a growing girl."

"Who needs to keep light on her feet."

Grandpère shrugged. "You're right, of course. It's better that way."

"She needs to stay sharp. Earbobs are a distraction."

"My Harvest Moon's tonight," Elise said. "I'm old enough."

Maman snorted and flipped the smallest steak onto Elise's plate. "That's not what I'm worried about."

Elise picked up her fork and prodded the meat. "It's not like I haven't eaten deer my entire life."

"It's different when you hunt it yourself."

Grandpère raised his grizzled head. "She'll be fine."

"Of course I will."

Grandpère slipped a forkful of steak past his lips. "Mmm. I remember your maman's Harvest Moon." He waved his fork. "Big buck, too."

Elise set down her fork and drank from her cup. "I don't want big; I want tender."

Maman rolled her eyes. "Doesn't matter what you want. You won't choose your Harvest Moon."

"Of course I will. The hunter always chooses."

Maman slipped her serviette onto her lap. "Not your first."

Elise paused, a bite halfway to her mouth. "What?"

"During a Harvest Moon, the prey offers itself. That's why it's called a blessing."

"That's crazy."

"It's tradition."

"You'll see," Grandpère said. "Young, old, big, small—it won't matter. You'll know your blessing when you receive it." He smacked his lips. "You may have eaten deer your entire life, Elise, but this one will be special. Nothing tastes as good as something you brought down yourself."

"I just don't see why I have to do this alone. Why can't you and Maman be there?"

"Tradition," Maman said. "Now eat. Your food is getting cold."

"Ugh. I can't eat now."

Grandpère nodded. "Nerves."

Elise set down her fork and pushed away her plate. "I'm heading out."

Maman glanced out the window. "Now? It's so early!"

Elise stood. "I'll eat later."

"The confidence of youth," Grandpère chuckled.

Maman sighed. "Be mindful of the time."

"Oh, Maman. As if I could forget!" Elise turned from the table and lifted her new cloak from a peg near the door.

Maman rounded the table, reaching for her. "Don't wear that, Elise. The deer will see you from miles away."

"But it's cold in the woods at night," she said, twirling it over her shoulders and fastening the clasp.

Maman clucked her tongue and shook her head, her eyes lingering on the twinkling golden hoops. Sighing, she smoothed Elise's hood flat against her shoulders. "Your first Harvest Moon. My baby's all grown up. Wear your red cloak if you must, but stow it in your satchel. Don't leave it too late. You don't want to ruin it."

"I know, Maman. You've told me a million times."

"And I'll tell you a million more. It's what mothers do." Maman smiled and pressed her hand to Elise's cheek. "Good hunting!"

"*Bonne chance!*" Grandpère called.

"*Merci, Papi!* I'll get a nice, tender yearling for you." Elise paused at the door to check her satchel one last time, making sure she had everything she needed.

Maman sat next to Grandpère and leaned close. "She's really doing this alone?"

"Didn't you?" He smiled and slid Elise's steak onto his plate. "Tradition!"

Elise stepped out the door but didn't look back as she strolled down the path to River Road, her red cloak swirling like blood down a drain.

The long screech of a scrub oak branch trails down the side of the wagon as it sways to a stop. Highway Man hops down and starts unhitching the horses. Elise's heart beats faster as she tries to suck in more air around the gag. Her nose is throbbing and too crusty to be much use.

She glimpses the blue of his shirt as he disappears around the side, leading the horses to a nearby stream. The cool evening air seeps in, taking some of Chester's iron-and-leather smell into the aspens. She hears tuneless humming, then the sound of leaves crackling and wood popping, then the smell of smoke.

Highway Man is building a campfire.

It doesn't take long for the first fly to come.

She flinches, thinking a bee has come to sting her. She's deathly afraid of bees—any insect that buzzes, really—and this more than anything makes her want to scream. The gag is soggy now; ribbons of blood-salt and lye coat her tongue.

She feels her gorge rise and her stomach heave. *Don't upchuck, don't upchuck, don't upchuck.*

Don't.

Highway Man's head pops over the side of the wagon. He pulls the bandanna off his face. "Don't need that anymore," he says. Without the mask, his face goes from outlaw tough to saggy and middle-aged, the face of a guy who dry-farms forty acres and prays for rain Sundays at church.

The mask is better. Ordinary is harder to swallow.

He grabs the shovel. "Going to need that next." Wrinkling his nose, he hooks a finger under Chester's ribbon and slings the dog's body to the ground. Catching her eye, he smiles. "Don't worry about Chester. He's a good dog. He'll keep you company long after I've gone." He jerks his thumb toward the trees. "There's hot chocolate and marshmallows waiting for good girls at the fire. If you come out, I'll take off your gag. You'd like that, right?"

Highway Man waits a beat, then hefts the shovel and turns. "Suit yourself." He strolls back to the campfire, whistling. Soon Elise hears sounds of digging in the trees.

The night deepens. In the underbrush, crickets sing love songs in the darkness. More flies come, but preferring Chester near the wagon wheel, they don't settle long next to Elise. The glow from the fire is rosy and homey against the trees. Leaves drift slowly from the aspens, raining yellow and red and pooling in her lap. The mountain air is apple crisp. Elise strains her ears.

Nothing.

I'm leaving.

Elise rolls to her knees. Ignoring the pins and needles shooting through her legs and the dull ache in her hip, she creeps toward the front of the wagon. She inches quietly, thinking of mice and cats and cheese. At the bench where the driver sits, she pauses, stretching her neck and spine tall like a prairie dog. Peering through the gap between the backrest and the wagon seat, she looks toward the firelight.

Facing the wagon are two stumps with rough backs notched by a hatchet. There are sticks with marshmallows leaning against them. A coffee pot warms near the fire.

"Boo!" shouts the Highway Man from behind.

Elise shrieks and hits her head on the backrest. Stars spiral behind her eyes. She barely keeps from pissing herself when she feels him grab her arm.

"Gotcha!" he chortles. "Bet ya didn't see that one coming." He wraps his arms around her and lifts her over the side and to the ground.

She doesn't want to, but she leans against him. When she finds her toes and balance, he releases her and steps back.

"What nice hair you have," he says. "So shiny." He sniffs. "Mmm. Smells like lavender, too."

Head down, Elise blinks rapidly. Moving hurts, but she can't let him know that.

"You can't run," he says. "Well, you can, you just won't get far. We're way up in the woods, and there are monsters in the dark. If you run from the fire, they'll get you." He gives her shoulder a nudge toward the fire. "Come. There's chocolate waiting for good girls."

It's better than the wagon, she rationalizes, trying desperately to ignore Chester's new friends buzz-buzz-buzzing near her feet. After the second step, the vertigo eases, and she shakes her head to bring her hair forward to hide her face, one earbob swaying gently, the other lost in the darkness. Her eyes scan the campsite and catch a glimpse of the shovel among the aspen trees. She follows the handle down to the ground and discovers it's sticking out of a big pile of dirt.

He's right. He doesn't need the mask anymore.

At the campfire, he plops down on a stump and picks up a marshmallow stick. "The coals have to be just right," he says. "Most things in life work that way. With marshmallows, it just takes a little patience and planning. If you rush, you roast them alive." He jams the end of his stick into the heart of the fire; the marshmallows blaze and blacken. He pulls them out, the end of his stick burning blue and bubbling. He sighs. "Charcoal. Patience was never one of my virtues." He blows them out, then tests with his fingers. "Take off the gag."

Elise waits for the punch line, but it doesn't come.

"Go on now," he encourages, licking white melted crème from his lips, "give 'er a try. Your wrists are tied, not broken. Tug on the end of the knot behind your head. I know you can reach it." He rummages in a sack hidden in the dark and fishes out fresh marshmallows to spear.

Elise slides her hands along the back of her neck and pulls. Like magic, the knot disappears. She peels the gag out of her mouth and takes her first full breath in hours.

I could've done that at any time. What else am I missing?

He motions to the log next to him. "Sit. Let's get acquainted." Elise gingerly sits. "Here." He hands her the other marshmallow stick. "Give 'er a whirl. Patience, remember? You look like a patient girl to me."

Elise thrusts the marshmallows into the fire, and a savage joy rises within her as she watches them burn.

"Patience, Cream Puff," he says. "You don't want to flame out too soon."

Elise ignores him as the white end of her stick collapses into molten black tar.

Good. No one will ever eat these.

"You can call me Kid," he says. "My own private joke. What's your name, Muffin?"

I have a weapon. I can take my stick and poke Kid in the eye—

"No, you can't," Kid says.

Startled, her eyes dart to his.

"You're thinking you can use your stick, but you can't. It's too flimsy, and I'm much bigger than you. I'm your only hope. I'm the only one who can keep the demons away."

"Demons?" It's her first spoken word since she found Chester.

Kid nods. "Didn't your mother tell you not to go into the woods alone?"

She looks to her lap, hiding again behind her hair.

"Thought so. You're much safer here with me by the fire." He pokes at the coffee pot with his foot. "Chocolate?"

"No," she says. *Chocolate is for good girls.* "Just water."

He snatches the marshmallow stick from her hands, lifts a canteen from behind a log, and sets it in her lap. He tilts his head, then reaches over and twists off the cap, dropping the chain to the side. "What do you say?"

Elise sits dumbfounded. There are too many words in her head to choose.

"What do you say?" he prods. "What's the magic word?"

Abracadabra? Open Sesame?

He leans forward in his seat. She feels energy coil around him, a snake about to strike.

Untie me, you madman? Please? Oh.

"Thank you," she mumbles.

His shoulders slump as he sits back. "That's right. For a minute there, I thought you were one of those rude ones who didn't have any manners. But you're not. I can tell your momma taught you proper. What's your name, Gumdrop?"

She stalls by taking a long swig, feeling the blessed coolness coat her tongue, fall down her throat, and land in the pit of her stomach. She means only to sip, but the water washes away the horror of axle grease and snot, and she guzzles most of the canteen.

Kid grunts and wrinkles his nose.

Elise comes up for air and gasps. *I can do this.*

Kid's lips thin in disapproval.

Ladylike. He likes soft, polite, and ladylike.

"Thanks for the water, mister."

He pushes his feet to the fire and relaxes. "Now I told you to call me Kid. Say it."

"Kid."

"What's your name, Gingersnap?"

"Elise."

"Elise what?"

"Rougarou." She clears her throat and takes a dainty sip. "Elise Rougarou."

"Roooo-gah-rooooh." He rolls the word around his tongue and kisses the last bit with his lips. "Sounds foreign. You one of them emigrants? Russian, maybe?"

She shakes her head. "American."

Kid narrows his eyes. "Don't sound American. Where your people from, Cupcake?"

"Grandpère says France. Before the war." She pulls against the rawhide binding her wrists, hiding the movement with the canteen.

Too tight. Patience.

"Grandpère, huh? Your grandfather, you mean. French." His eyebrow quirks. "I heard me a lot of stories about Frenchies in the war." Kid picks up the coffee pot and fills a mug with rich hot chocolate. "'Course, nothing fit for young girls' ears." He stirs his drink absentmindedly with a finger then licks it clean. "Still, apples don't fall far from trees. I'm gonna have to consider other options. Might not be a cornflower-blue girl after all."

He paws through the sack and plops a marshmallow into his drink. "Hot chocolate and marshmallows. Best thing ever." He fills his mouth, swallowing the marshmallow whole. "Well, second-best thing."

The horses snort and stamp near the trees. Through the flames, Elise spots Grandpère leaning against an aspen. Elise shifts her eyes to Kid, but he's busy with another marshmallow.

Grandpère points to the glow on the mountain ridge, bright against the diamond-scattered sky. He holds her eyes until she nods. It's still her Harvest Moon.

With her bound hands, Elise tugs on her lucky red cloak and sighs. *No way to take it off. Maman was right. I should've left it home.*

Kid picks up the sack and dumps out chocolate bars, jerky, and hardtack. When the horses whinny again, Grandpère disappears like smoke.

"French," Kid mutters. "That explains it. The scarlet cloak. Them bright earbobs. Can't help tarting yourself up now, can ya?"

Moonlight rolls down the mountainsides and puddles in the valleys like fog. Energy coalesces. She feels it humming under her skin, swarming around their camp like a hive of angry bees.

"You're too young for earbobs."

No longer afraid, she breathes the bees in. "But I wore them just for you, Kid," she says.

He stills, caught in the moment of unwrapping chocolate. Slowly he drops his hands to his lap, his eyes never leaving her.

"I thought you'd like them, Kid. See how they shine? Don't you like them?"

He breaks off a piece of chocolate and slips it between his teeth. "What, Sugarplum? What are you trying to say?"

"Chocolate's my favorite. Can—I mean, *may* I have a piece?"

Kid tosses the broken bar from his lap and she catches it, bringing it to her lips to nibble. "Thank you, Kid," she says.

"You're welcome, Elise." He polishes off the last of his drink and slides a finger across another candy wrapper, splitting it seam to seam. "You're different from the other girls."

"What girls?"

"You're not crying or begging."

"I can if you want me to."

Kid stands and walks to the woodpile. He lifts a hatchet and chips a few pieces off a log and tosses them into the fire.

"Red," Elise says.

"What?"

"My bloomers. Red. Not blue. Blue is for babies."

He hefts the hatchet in his hands. Elise sees how he likes it when the blade tips forward, eager to bite. With a flick of his wrist, he pulls the head back and buries it in a log. Returning to his chair, he contemplates the fire.

"You're a baby," Kid says.

"Not really. I'm small for my age."

"How small?"

Elise shrugs and drops the canteen to her side.

"I picked you, you know."

"I know," she says.

"I watched you walking all by your lonesome. Not home, safe eating stew meat and corn bread by firelight, but wandering the River Road in a scarlet cloak, your earbobs shining like fishing lures. Like the others."

"What others?"

"The seven. My special seven. You're eight." He crosses his arms and regards her in the firelight. "But number eight should be special, too, just like the first. I like to be first. First and only is best." He squints. "I think I've misjudged you, Lollipop. I'm not your first."

"I don't know what you're saying."

He nods. "Of course you do. The hunter always knows its prey, Apple Dumplin'. You like games."

She draws a lungful of autumn air as the tingle spreads from the pit of her stomach. In her mind, she hears Maman's voice. *There's nothing to be afraid of. One quick flash of red in the woods, and it's over. No reason to think twice. All creatures have a purpose and a place. You're just fulfilling yours.*

"Who?" He chucks a woodchip into the fire and watches it flare.

"Who?"

"Are we pretending to be owls, now? Who was your first, Peppermint Stick? Uncle?"

"What?"

"Brother?"

"I don't—" The first pain, sharp and biting, knots her hands and spine. She gasps and looks to the ridgeline. The light of the full moon hits her like a locomotive.

Another chip. "I know," he says to the fire. "You're a daddy's girl. Like my Annie."

"No," she manages. "You've got it all wrong. You're my first." Her bones twist, snapping the rawhide like candy floss. Another deep breath, and this time she tastes iron, sweat, and fear. The horses squeal, eyes wide and rolling. Rearing, they break their highline and bolt. She runs her tongue over her too-long teeth.

Canines. All the better to eat you with, my dear.

She swings her shaggy head away from the fire, searching for Maman and Grandpère. She howls, and two wolves answer. She knows they're there, watching. But this is her Harvest Moon.

A blessing of red in the woods. And no one will hear the screams.

LEHUA PARKER writes speculative fiction for kids and adults often set in her native Hawaii. Her published works include the award-winning Niuhi Shark Saga trilogy and *Sharks in an Inland Sea.* Her short stories have appeared in *Va: Stories by Women of the Mona, Bamboo Ridge,* and *Dialogue.* An advocate of indigenous voices in media and a graduate of The Kamehameha Schools, she is a frequent speaker at conferences, symposiums, and schools.

Connect with her at LehuapParker.com.

Which Wolf Will You Feed?
Tanya Hales

As I stood in line to gather my daily ration of star shards, the wolves in my mind let out soft whines of excitement. I could sense the three of them running around on eager paws and roughhousing. Despite my anxiety at what awaited me later today, I smiled.

Ahead of me, the other female trainees moved through the white, marble hallway and into the feeding room. I lagged behind, happy to be last. If I was lucky, there'd be an extra shard left, and the guards would be too busy chatting to see me take it. It was unlikely, but not impossible. And it would make the difference between hungry wolves and happy wolves.

Rena bumped her hip into mine. "Kimi! Have you finally decided which wolf you'll choose tonight?"

Like me—and all the initiates at the facility—Rena was seventeen years old, on the cusp of adulthood. We both wore the standard-issue brown tunics with black pants and boots. Apparently the director had decided at one point that no one here would ever look stylish.

I gave her what I hoped was a mysterious smile. "I think I'll leave it a surprise."

Rena groaned. "That'd better not mean you still haven't decided. Your time is up!"

Rena, of course, would choose the wolf of Creativity. She'd talked about it for years. She planned to become an artist like her mother.

Luckily for me, she pranced off to interrogate Victoria next.

I sighed in relief. No one knew I still had three wolves within me. We were supposed to only have two by now, and during the ceremony tonight, each initiate would choose the single wolf who would remain with them for the rest of their life, shaping their personality and talents.

But I had other plans.

I entered the feeding room behind the other girls. A channel of ankle-deep water flowed down the middle, and catching on the sides or the grate at the far end were glowing, white crystals that came from the peak of the Sacred Mountain.

Young men entered the room from the other side, closer to where their rooms were. Most initiates finished quickly, grabbing a star shard in each hand, the light vanishing as they fed the wolves in their minds.

As the other initiates left, I moved slowly, kneeling by the channel and trailing my fingers in the water. There were still a few people left, and I had to make sure everyone else was gone before trying to grab an extra shard for my secret wolf. Stealing shards was a criminal offense, and the guards at the door watched with sharp eyes and swords and bows, not distracted by conversation today.

I sighed. Picking up a cool, glowing crystal in each hand, I closed my eyes and entered my headspace. Although my physical body didn't move, I found myself in a white room within my own mind. My three wolves bounded over, tongues lolling, to press their shaggy, gray bodies against me. Or more accurately, against my soul.

"Took you long enough," Dominion said in his deep voice, sniffing at the shard in my hand.

"Manners, Dominion," I told him with a smile, lifting my hand out of reach. He let out a huff and sat, eyes still on the shard.

Compassion nuzzled my thigh. "He's only hungry." Though I could tell she meant all three of them were.

Reason seemed more distracted than the others, pacing anxiously. "There's no time to think about today's food when the meals for the rest of our lives are on the line."

That made them all go still and quiet.

"Do you know what will happen when you announce you won't be sacrificing any of us?" Compassion asked quietly.

I shook my head. As far as I knew, no one had ever broken the rules this way. We'd always been taught that a person could only live their adult life with a single wolf within them.

One master. One wolf. Balance.

All children started with eight wolves in their mind: Compassion, Curiosity, Honor, Reason, Dominion, Serenity, Creativity, and Grace. But wolves fed on the magic contained in star shards, and not enough flowed from the Sacred Mountain for everyone in the city to feed eight wolves. So before a child was even five years old, the majority of wolves were usually gone, consumed by the starving survivors.

My remaining wolves claimed to have been too young during that time to remember much of it, but I could sense their distress when I brought it up. They didn't like thinking about what they'd done to their brothers and sisters.

I remembered almost nothing of the wolves I'd lost, though when I meditated, I could feel the lack of them, like holes in my personality. Wolves were both their own beings and a part of their master. I mourned the loss of certain wolves in particular, like Curiosity, especially during classes where I felt bored and disinterested. I felt there was a spark missing within me that could make me more excited to learn.

I didn't want to lose any more sparks.

I put both shards in one hand so I could pet Compassion's head. "I don't care what Director Keldan says when I say I'm keeping all three of you. I refuse to become a fraction of myself. I refuse to become like my parents."

My father, with his wolf of Dominion, was loud and over-bearing. His punishments were harsh because he was always right, and he knew what was best for everyone else.

My mother, with her wolf of Serenity, was so perfectly at peace that any external conflict made her withdraw into herself, shutting out the rest of the world, including me, so she could maintain her sense of harmony.

I'd been at the choosing facility for almost a whole year, as was tradition, but I suspected my family was still just as dysfunctional now as it had been when I'd left.

Choosing a single wolf was supposed to give you purpose, passion, focus, and a specific function in society. And yet ...

"I don't want to become just a piece of a person," I said softly.

My wolves looked at each other.

"We won't let that happen," Compassion told me.

"I'll lend you my power and commanding presence," Dominion said. "No one will be able to force you to choose."

"And even if we never get enough food again," Reason added, "we'll take turns eating. We'll remain in balance. I'll quicken your mind so you can figure out a plan."

I could sense his anxiety beneath his conviction. I knelt to scratch him behind his ears, and he closed his golden eyes, trying to relax.

I tried to gather up my own conviction as well. "Thank you. I'll protect the three of you too. Even if I'm punished for my choice, it'll be worth it."

As they leaned into me, I could feel the strength of their talents brushing against my soul. It felt warm. Comforting. Right.

At the same time, I couldn't help but pull my soul back from them, hiding it deeper within myself. My soul wanted to shine, but I knew better than to let it.

Wolves were drawn to souls as well as star shards. They could feed upon either to regain strength, and hungry wolves with less self-discipline than mine had been known to eat their master's souls.

I knew I could never truly hide my soul from them. Even if I didn't enter my headspace, it would be possible for them to reach it and devour it. I trusted my wolves, but I couldn't help the sliver of fear tucked away in my core.

What if things didn't work out, and my announcement led to rejection and punishment?

What if I was really forced to choose only one of them?

I couldn't let my wolves know about these questions. Failure wasn't supposed to be an option. So I kept those thoughts buried deep within my soul where they couldn't see.

Once, there hadn't been a shortage of star shards. Once, they had been so abundant that everyone could keep eight wolves, and wolves even gave their masters the ability to use magic.

But those stories belonged in history books now.

"About that food," Dominion said. "Today's my turn to go hungry."

I nodded. I held out the two small star shards to Reason and Compassion, who eagerly snapped them up in their jaws, gulping them down. Dominion watched with longing in his eyes. He saw himself as the pack leader, the protector, but I knew watching the others eat while he went hungry for a day wasn't any easier for him than it was for the others.

A voice broke into my headspace, pulling me out of my reverie.

"You must care about your wolves."

I opened my eyes to see the feeding room was empty of all initiates except for a young man kneeling across the channel from me. It was Lev; someone my eyes had been lingering on a bit more than typical lately.

I blinked, trying to pull my focus back to the external world, and I felt my face flush. "What?"

"You spend a lot of time with them in your headspace. I've seen you do it other days too." He ran a hand through his black hair, his smile self-conscious. "That sounded a little too much like 'I've been watching you' to be suave."

I laughed, my pulse quickening. I realized my fingers were still trailing in the water, so I pulled them out and dried them on my pants, wondering too late if that was unladylike.

Trying to control my anxiety, I stared at the reflections on the water. "You probably figured out which wolf to keep ages ago."

His reflection cocked its head. "Reason was one of the first wolves I lost as a child." I glanced up to see him wink. "I may be less organized and decisive than you think."

I smiled, my gaze moving over his features. As always, Lev looked tired but handsome, somehow in control in a way the other young men didn't seem to be.

His green eyes locked with mine for a moment before he looked away. "Sometimes it doesn't seem right, you know?"

I nodded slowly. "Choosing which part of yourself to throw away?"

"If there wasn't such a limited supply of star shards ..." He glanced at the guards before continuing softly, "Maybe there could be another way."

I pressed my lips together. For the first time, I found myself wanting to tell someone my crazy plan, yet I didn't know if I could trust him.

I sensed my wolves waiting anxiously to see what I would do. They could see and hear everything I could, and they feared I'd give us away, ruin our plan.

I needed to let this go. Lev would find out soon enough when I revealed it at the ceremony.

But in that moment, I was glad.

Glad I wasn't the only one who didn't want to let any of my wolves die.

Glad I wasn't the only one who didn't want to be forced to choose.

I walked down the hall toward the auditorium amidst a flood of chattering initiates, glad no one tried to talk to me. In minutes, I'd stand in front of everyone at the choosing ceremony and reveal that I was rejecting the safe path.

I felt sick to my stomach.

A silver-haired man with a short beard approached, putting a hand on my shoulder so I'd stop walking. Director Keldan, the man in charge of the facility. My mentor.

He smiled at me, his blue eyes twinkling. "Ready?"

I nodded, hoping my smile didn't look as fake as it felt.

"I'm excited to see your choice," he went on. "Have you considered my offer?"

I bit my lip. Based on subtle remarks he'd made while mentoring me on leadership, I knew he wanted me to choose

Reason and become his apprentice at the choosing facility instead of returning to my family after the ceremony.

"What if you don't like my choice?" I asked softly.

He smiled, but his eyes looked sad. He waited until most of the initiates passed us, then told me softly, "I already know what you'll choose."

My heart squeezed in my chest. Did he really know, or did he just think he did?

The smile fell from his face, his eyes becoming grave. "I'm sorry to say that, earlier today, Lev Tommilson was found dead in his room."

His words hit me like a sledgehammer to the face.

Lev. Dead.

My mind repeated the words again and again, uncomprehending. My mouth hung open, and my hands, clenched in my tunic, felt as stiff and lifeless as dry tree branches.

In my head, my wolves whined.

"It appears Lev's own wolves turned on him and devoured his soul. I was the only one who knew he'd failed to obey the safety regulation regarding wolves. He had four, not two. They overpowered him. And now he's gone."

I stared blindly at the director, trying to imagine it. *Four wolves?* We'd been limited to a ration of two star shards for six months! They must have been so hungry.

And then they'd turned on him.

My breathing became quick and shallow. I couldn't think straight.

Lev had tried so hard to keep as many wolves as possible. And now he was gone.

"I won't let you make the same mistake," Director Keldan said.

So he did know. My hands shook. I couldn't speak.

"It doesn't matter what happened to another initiate,"

Reason told me. "You aren't him, and we aren't his wolves. We've found balance."

"We promised to always protect each other," Dominion said. "And we'll never change our minds about that."

"Even when we're down to only one star shard a day?" I asked in my mind, my internal voice shrill. "Maybe the hunger was just too much for Lev's wolves."

Compassion reassured me, "We care about each other, and that's why we're different from the other initiates and their wolves."

But I was sure Lev had cared about his wolves too.

What would my wolves do when all three had to share a single star shard? We'd always said we'd make it work, but was that like a wounded man saying, "It's only a cut. All is well," even as he bled out?

Even so, I had to stick with my decision. I had to tell the director I wouldn't choose. I had to hold true to my convictions. Or ...

Or I had to choose just one wolf after all.

I didn't hide my thoughts deep enough in my soul. My wolves sensed them and scrambled around in a frenzy. Their voices jumbled together so I couldn't tell who was speaking.

"You can't!"

"We had a plan!"

I didn't even know which one I should choose when I loved them all. Reason? Just because the director wanted me to?

But I couldn't let any of them die. I would never forgive myself. I would never be whole again.

I stood frozen, torn between my options. A single tear fell down my face. Then I sucked in a deep breath, determination filling me. Nothing had changed. I wouldn't betray my wolves.

"I'm keeping Reason, Compassion, and Dominion," I told

my mentor. "I won't choose which aspect of myself to throw away."

He let out a long, sad sigh, disappointment in his eyes. He didn't say another word, only waved to two guards from down the hall who hastened toward us.

"My wolves and I have found balance," I whispered. "We—"

But the guards gripped my shoulders, cutting me off as they dragged me away.

They locked me in one of the cells of the detention center. The room was nearly as empty as my headspace, except everything was gray, including the dingy, bare mattress.

My wolves were still in an uproar.

"What happened, Kimi?" Reason demanded.

"You almost chose Reason." Dominion snapped. "We all felt it. I thought, after a year of planning, that we had an understanding!"

"I stuck with the plan," I told them weakly, head bowed as I sat on the floor. "I was just—"

"Kimi is right," Compassion growled at the others. "She may have wavered, but she didn't abandon us. She's on our side."

"And if she wavers again?"

My wolves continued to bicker, but I felt too exhausted and empty to defend myself or stop them.

After what felt like eternity, I heard a key turn in the door. It opened, and Director Keldan stepped inside.

He looked down at me with cold, disappointed eyes that made me want to bury my face in shame. Instead, I lifted my chin and met his expression with a hard, defiant one of my own.

My mentor leaned against the wall, his arms folded. "I won't let you do this to yourself, Kimi."

I laughed humorlessly. "You don't get to decide that."

Director Keldan gesticulated, expression fierce. "I told you what happened to poor Lev. I don't want that to happen to you, but if you keep more than one wolf, it's inevitable. Adult wolves need more to eat, and there won't be enough star shards for them. Your soul holds the same energy as the shards, and eventually they'll go after it instead. They will destroy you."

"Can't an exception be made for me?" I pled. "I don't need three star shards each day. We've made it work with only two."

He shook his head firmly. "You cannot join society until you've chosen only one wolf."

"And what if I never choose?" I demanded.

He gave me a sad smile as he turned to go. "You will."

Hours in the cell turned into days. Despite our good intentions, the balance my wolves had shared for so long began fracturing.

Any talking devolved into arguing. Everyone was on edge. And worst of all, I was the only one being fed. Twice a day, a tray of food was shoved through a slot in the door. Each time, I was dismayed to find no star shards included. I yelled at the guards outside, demanding food for my wolves, but they never answered. I pounded on the door. I shouted that my wolves were desperate and hungry. But no one cared.

On the morning of the third day, when a tray containing only oatmeal was shoved in, I silently bowed my head, defeated.

"I won't let us die in here," Dominion snarled, sounding more feral than ever. "We can smash down the door!"

"You have a hairpin, Kimi," Reason whined. "Pick the lock. I can help you. It's just a puzzle."

"But there are guards outside the door," Compassion whimpered.

I squeezed my eyes shut. "We can't escape."

My wolves were frantic. Starving. And I couldn't do anything for them.

Another day passed, and it became more and more clear that my beloved wolves were becoming more like beasts. Their human intelligence slipped away. Instead of arguing or trying to plan, they snarled and snapped at each other, pacing like caged beasts.

When I entered my headspace, I could see the way they looked at me. They stared at the glow of my soul with hungry eyes, their expressions more animalistic than I'd ever seen.

As I tried to fall asleep that night, I couldn't help but wonder if this was how Lev had felt before he'd died. Like he was trapped with beasts that had once been his friends, but who were now closing in on him with destruction in their eyes.

The howl of a wolf woke me.

I sat up on my mattress in a panic, rubbing my eyes in the darkness. Trying to clear my mind of sleep fog, I entered my headspace. Dominion paced in the white room. My other wolves stirred, woken by his sounds.

When Dominion saw me, he snarled. My hair stood on end. He was no longer the brave pack leader. He was a wild animal, and it both broke my heart and squeezed it with fear.

He threw back his head and howled. Compassion and Reason pricked their ears, growing stiff and alert. Their pupils contracted in their golden eyes, making them look even more beastlike than before.

Reason joined the howl, then Compassion. I backed away. I'd never heard them howl like this except in play. And I knew none of them were in a playful mood.

Heart hammering, I gathered up the limited control I had over my headspace. Focusing, I formed a white wall between me and my wolves. I hoped giving them space would help them come to their senses.

A heavy weight slammed into the other side of the wall—once, twice, and then a section smashed open.

Dominion prowled out of the hole, saliva hanging from his fangs. His muscles rippled as he moved forward. The others followed, stalking toward me.

All three wolves fixed their eyes on the glow of my soul. I was prey to be hunted.

I swallowed, stumbling back. "Compassion. Dominion. Reason. We're all friends. Allies."

But all humanity had left their eyes.

Leaving my headspace wouldn't save me. They could still reach my soul with their snapping jaws. There was no way out. They'd finally become what the director had warned.

Dominion lunged, snapping at my feet like he was testing my reflexes, and I leapt back.

My heart pounding, I formed another white wall between us.

But they immediately slammed against it, and I knew it wouldn't last.

I ran.

The room opened up, turning into an endless landscape of white mist. I heard the wolves howling behind me, then a crash. My fear choked me, making my limbs shake. I built walls in the white nothingness, erected doors that led to nowhere, even created pits. But no matter how far I went or how many barricades I formed, I still heard them closing in.

I ran until my legs trembled and my stomach heaved, until the mental exhaustion caught up with me. My barriers were puffing away into wearily drifting mist.

My wolves howled. They were close. I couldn't outrun them any longer.

I crumpled to the ground, tears in my eyes.

I'd tried so hard to do what was right. I'd tried so hard to save them. Now it would be my undoing.

A hazy form coalesced out of the mist beside me. It took me a moment to realize the shape looked like Lev. Perhaps, in my final moments, my brain was throwing memories and regrets at me.

The misty version of Lev looked at me. "I'll admit this wasn't the situation I hoped I'd find you in." His voice echoed distantly. "Chased by starving wolves."

"I messed up," I whispered, head bowed. "I thought I could have everything, that I didn't have to give something up. I was such a fool."

"You're not to blame for this," Lev retorted. "The director is. He forced this by starving your poor wolves. I'm locked up nearby, and he's trying to do the same thing to me. But he doesn't know that I've found the secret."

I looked up, eyes wide. "You're alive?"

He smiled. "He imprisoned me, then told everyone I was dead. He wanted to use me as an example. But that's going to backfire."

"But how are you in my headspace?" I asked, still not believing he was real.

"Magic." He smiled. "The magic from the old stories. The magic of my soul and wolves combined."

"But your wolves ... They didn't turn on you?"

He shook his head. As I watched, the forms of four wolves coalesced in the mist, tongues lolling, looking as friendly and at peace as mine once had.

Lev patted one on the head, and it leaned into him. "We've been told since childhood that we can only keep one piece of ourselves. It makes us one-dimensional, easier to control. The director wants to maintain the status quo. Everyone in power wants it maintained. But a revolution is coming."

Lev grinned broadly. "You and I aren't the only initiates who didn't choose one wolf. There are others. A dozen of us. We never planned to announce that we were keeping multiple wolves. We were going to keep it secret and fight back from the shadows. But I was discovered."

He stretched his arms to the sides. "The others are creating a distraction at this very moment so that we can bust out of here."

He knelt beside me, trying to rest a hand on my shoulder, though the mist passed through me. "We've discovered how to use the ancient magic of our wolves. It isn't gone. We can win, and you can join us." He said softly, "You were right all along. You don't have to choose to become only a fraction of yourself."

An unbidden tear fell down my cheek as I heard another howl not far away. "It's too late for me. My wolves are starving. My only chance is to get them to turn on each other. If I don't, they'll destroy me."

Lev reached for my hands with his, and this time, I was sure I could feel him. "That's the secret, though. The one I discovered. It's not you versus them. They *are* you. We never truly needed the star shards. We already have what we need inside of us, and we always have." He looked deep into my eyes. "If you let your wolves—those different aspects of yourself— partake freely of your soul ... That's how you find freedom."

I swallowed hard. "So I just let them eat me?"

He shook his head. "You *feed* them. You've withheld your soul because everyone told you that you had to. This time, give them your entire self. Become whole again."

My mind raced over his words, but my time was up. I could hear my wolves' ragged breathing and racing paws as they approached through the white mist of my headspace.

Lev's form grew hazier. I knew he couldn't save me.

So I stood and faced my wolves as they rounded my last, crumbling barrier and prowled toward me.

My chest tightened. I could hardly breathe.

I was pretty sure I could still appeal to Reason and Compassion, that I could convince them to turn on Dominion. It was in their natures to listen to me, side with me, their logical and relatable master.

But, for the first time, I didn't think of what I'd do in the case of failure. I didn't tuck my worries away or let my fear freeze me.

Instead, I stepped forward and bared my soul to them. I let my inner light shine out, blinding and bright.

My wolves broke into a sprint, jaws open.

I stood firm. I refused to close my eyes.

"You are mine, and I am yours," I told them moments before their jaws closed on me.

But instead of pain, I felt like I'd been hit by a wave of water. My wolves were absorbed into my light. Even as I felt them use up a part of me, they filled it again, and I sensed their energy zinging within me, expanding my awareness and sense of self.

I felt powerful. Expansive. Whole. Right.

Compassion's voice reverberated through my head. "We are united now. This is how it was always meant to be."

"Are you sure you want to make this choice?" Reason

asked. "You'll need to feed us from your own soul if we're all to remain with you."

"Yes," I told them. "This is what I want."

I could tell now that I had enough to share with them, because their energy fed me as well. This was connection. Magic. And it was a magic that wouldn't run out.

My wolves emerged from the light of my soul, stepping out onto the ground with shining fur and bright, smiling eyes. Their tails wagged. Reason and Compassion pranced around each other, playful and delighted. Dominion looked at me, then sat by my feet.

"I am sorry for what I became in the end." He stared down at his paws. "Thank you for not abandoning me."

"I love you," I told Dominion, pressing my forehead to his. My heart swelled, every inch of me filled with light. This was trust. Self-love.

Balance.

I looked back to Lev, beaming. He still had his four wolves surrounding him, but for the first time, I saw the hazy form of four more wolf pups at his feet. He had eight wolves again, just as he was meant to.

Just as I sensed I could one day have.

I grinned at him. "Let's go start a revolution."

When Tanya Hales was a baby, she enjoyed books by chewing them to pieces before eventually moving on to the higher art of reading. Tanya splits her time between her work as a writer, an illustrator, and a mother, all of which she loves intensely. She lives in Utah with her family, daydreaming constantly about imaginary worlds.

Wolfskin
Brenda Carre

Lupina followed the wolves through the snow-bright, winter-crisp night. Only by becoming a wolf and living with them for a time could she convince them to prey on the wild things only.

Not on her people's precious goats.

It had taken three nights to transform. Three nights now, the wolf howls had called her away into the winter cold, giving over the care of her small nursing babe to her sister. Transformation was not just about being a person in a pelt but also gaining the knowledge that came through it.

Knowing the ways of wolves through the minds of their prey was a shaman's way to know both.

The first night, banded raccoon and white mink had clothed her like sinuous nocturnal partners. She watched and waited, drinking in their fears and their hopes to elude a pack on the prowl. Last night, beaver fur had kept her parka-warm while she quested the night. Tonight—the third and most important of all—she was garbed in wolfskin. A woman of eighteen summers, and a shaman since birth.

Fur-clad, her breath like silver mist, Lupina crunched over the paw prints of the pack. They touched her spirit like hands splayed over her heart. She bent to sniff wolf spoor, her haunches no longer human but not yet wolf.

The right way was to tread the line between spirit and fur and to yield to the wolf in her for a time. So her old teacher had taught her. The real battle would be to let go of the wolf and embrace her person again.

Not easy, the longer she stayed in animal form. Four years ago, when she was still Andaloo's apprentice, she'd taken a long winter sleep as a dormouse curled into a ball under the snow. He had summoned her home. Now, with Andaloo gone, to stay trapped in an animal guise was to leave her people without a shaman.

Now, instead of a person to call her home, she marked her return with a memory talisman—the knuckle bone of her littlest finger, carved into her likeness and stuck through her right earlobe. A reminder of who she really was.

Yes, take the pack fierceness within me and their protective nature for each other and weave this into my own threads as a human being and a shaman. Remember ... I am saving them all from starvation and death. They come for us, and we kill them. This is wrong.

The night called her across the snowy barrens, and above her, the lights from a thousand stars branded their way across the great dark seam that divided the cosmos. The high rippled wail of Pack kindled a growl deep in her belly. Across the ghost-white field of ice, a snowshoe hare bolted.

Passion and hunger ripped through Lupina's middle into her breast. Her paws met the snowy crust. The night blurred into hot desire. Her fangs snapped on fur and the taste of hot life.

Use this hare. Use this to find your way into the pack. Feed her young. Follow the calls of Mother Wolf and give her this hare as tribute.

Lupina nosed the ice, hare still in her jaws, and tried to scratch away the itch at her ear. She shook her ruff and whined.

Important. Take your kill, good wolf, and I'll stop itching.

She snorted, and loped onward.

Across her way, lay the scent of Pack. At their forefront was fierce Mother Wolf with her litter of half-grown pups and her warriors fanning out far in the wake of an old caribou. The acid fear and anguish of the sick animal washed over Lupina as she stalked the hunt.

The flesh in her jaws was the hunger of life, but she did not eat. Important to approach Mother Wolf with this hare. Important to become one with Pack.

Do not forget your own pup waits for you. For your daughter you must return. For a time, nourish Mother Wolf's pups and gain her friendship....

Lupina growled deep in her belly, grinding her muzzle into the ice and pawing the Itch.

Ahead in the night, Pack made their kill. The squeals of death lifted her head from the cold ground. Her spirit sang to their yammering cry, a wail to the ocean of light in the sky, and the Itch in her ear fell silent.

Relieved, she loped within sight of Pack and waited. Her night eyes followed the white-gray form of Mother Wolf, the Sister Wolves, and the Wolf-Mate feeding with her. She observed the females who waited and the males who tended the pups. As a lone wolf she waited until all had fed, the small pups pulling shreds from the scrawny carcass.

Once Pack had left, she approached the bones to feed.

No, said the Itch. *Go find Pack.* It got worse the nearer she came to the kill.

Nose down with the hare in her mouth, she left the bones

of the caribou to freeze on the ice. She ran forward and back across the trail of blood, her brush low. Yipping came to her where Pack had gone, and her teats began to tingle.

A pup in distress.

She moaned a low howl, and the lamp of the moon stared its wolf eye at her.

Your pup is cared for, said the Itch at her ear. *Follow the sound of this pup with your tribute and your milk.*

Lupina growled, her ears flat with disquiet. More yelps of pain came from the trail ahead. So, too, came a deep snarl. Her hackles lifted. Her muscles tensed. Her lips bared her fangs.

The squat shadow of Wolf-bear waited on the trail ahead.

Wolverine, said the Itch.

The thick taste of musk washed Lupina's tongue. Her snout crinkled away from her teeth. Against Wolf-bear, a lone wolf was both predator and prey. Its wicked sharp eyes glistened with the bright of the sky dance. The hungry growl changed as it scented her and sprang.

The whole night went bright with the spark of her hatred of Wolf-bear. She sprang, lusting to kill, her jaws parted. The hare flew from her mouth and smacked Wolf-bear in the nose.

Baring wicked teeth, Wolf-bear grabbed the hare in its bloody jaws and fled at a bunching lope, its claws ripping shreds of ice behind it.

Lupina sank to her belly and panted as hatred left her slowly. Claws that could rip a lone wolf to pieces had run from her. She came to her paws, allowing the night wind to stroke her settled ruff and the brush of her tail, and she grinned.

You aren't a wolf. Remember?

She growled, shaking her head at the Itch. She raised her hind leg to scratch at her ear and paused. Down the trail, a wobbling, whimpering form cast a small shadow under the moon.

A pup. A wounded pup with one bent ear.

Bent Ear is a good name for this pup, said the Itch. *Not your pup, but he's bloody, little, and torn. He would have died in the Wolverine's teeth.*

Growling, uneasy at the lingering stink of Wolf-bear coming from Bent Ear, Lupina slunk to the pup. She bit him and licked away Wolf-bear's musk. She licked and rubbed until Bent Ear held her smell and the smell of her milk. He nudged at her belly. Her teats stung with his hunger.

All pups are yours tonight, said the Itch.

Lupina flopped to the ice, and Bent Ear came to her teats.

Somewhere far away came a cry from the place of the No-Pelts, a whole night's run from the ice.

Lupina whuffed in confusion.

All is well, said the Itch at her ear, more of a quieting stroke. *Your own pup is safe. Stay.*

With her teats no longer stinging, Lupina followed the trail toward Pack with the satisfied pup nipping at her heels.

At the edge of the den, Mother Wolf stood and snarled.

Do not show her your belly and throat, warned the Itch. *Stand. Do not threaten. You saved her pup. Stand. Raise your muzzle, enough to show throat, not hackles. She will see and smell the teats on your belly but not maul you.*

Bent Ear wobbled forward to meet Mother Wolf, who bit his ruff, nosed under his tail, nosed all of him, and tumbled him onto his back with his legs in the air.

She smells you on him. Remember what you are. You are here to make a pact with wolves and our people.

The force of Mother Wolf's glare, her weight, her muzzle split wide into fangs. Lupina fought instinct as Mother Wolf leaped at her. Mother Wolf's gray body slammed her down. Huge paws wrapped her, and they rolled as one. Musk on musk. Milk on milk.

Mother Wolf bit onto Lupina's throat, tensed, and let go. The bigger wolf pressed her into the frozen ground, bit at her ruff, at her ears, nosed her from muzzle to tail and glared narrowly at her.

A flick of an ear called Pack to come and sniff and judge.

Body to body with nips and thrusts, Pack buffeted her between them, onto her back, sniffing her everywhere. They howled to the stars, and so did she. They whuffed and licked and bit until they were tired.

With tongues lolling, the smallest pups came where Lupina lay in the snow and took milk.

Days and nights passed. How many didn't matter.

She did everything to shake free of the Itch—as if shaking water. She marked a defiant ring of pee around the place where she slept, yet it didn't stop the Itch from haunting her. Her milk no longer came down, but she had longings for pups of her own.

Hunts and seasons came and went. Content with her place in Pack, she guarded one litter of pups and another. Pack grew and decreased. She fought the Itch into a whisper. Pups grew into young wolves and left Pack to seek their own territory, their own mates. The wounded and sick crept away in the dark.

While Pack hunted, she lived on voles and rabbits, guarding new weanlings with Grandfather Wolf and young brothers One Eye and Bent Ear, who was now a wolf who ran funny. Only when Pack brought goats to the den did a deep belly-worry awaken the Itch at her ear.

You must warn Mother Wolf not to steal our goats. There should be no war between our people and wolves. Convince Mother Wolf and come back to us and your daughter who needs your teaching.

Lupina put down her head against a thorny stick and worried her ear until the pain hurt more than the Itch.

No. Remember. You're not a wolf. You must go home and train an apprentice!

In reply, Lupina ground her ear hard, and the Itch went away. A bone rolled out of her ear. She sniffed it and sneezed. The thing smelled like No-Pelts. Teeth bared, she licked blood from the bone, snapped it into her jaws where it cracked and split and went into her belly. Gone.

Her ear hurt. She sneezed and lay down with a satisfied grin—

Tell Mother Wolf to stay away or we will kill her. Convince her and come home!

She came to her haunches and howled at the Itch in her belly.

I will go away after you warn Mother Wolf to leave us alone and come home.

Lupina rolled on her back, raking her belly as the howls of her brothers and sisters called for the Hunt. She nosed into Pack as they told her where she could go and find fresh meat. Not goat. She bit and teased at Mother Wolf and her sisters, rolled with them and snarled with pleasure when they bit at her belly.

She hunted with them as winter fled away on the hills.

The land turned sweet-flowered. It gave them food, and they did not run to the No-Pelts in the bright silver nights. The young males sniffed at her haunches and rolled with her in the clover. Mother Wolf grew heavy with pups.

The Itch let her rest until one night Mother Wolf rose, belly slung low, and went on the hunt for goat meat.

That was the night everything changed. To no avail, Lupina tried to outrun her belly, but the Itch grew so strong she was forced to ease it by guarding the edge of Pack.

Scrub trees dropped early fruit into the burrows of hares. Familiar night smells filled her nose: moist bitter bog, hard rocky valleys, and water so cold it stung her snout and tasted of bugs. When had she known these places?

Long ago, said the Itch in her belly. *Over that rise is your home. See the light?*

Yes, the light, not just the moon's eye, not just the pricks of shine far above, but something winked over that hill. Memories teased Lupina she couldn't bite at.

A jumble of smells made her pant. Her tongue flooded with saliva and her nose with the scent of goats. Already Mother Wolf and her sisters were over that rise and gone.

Her own hackles rose. She came to the top of the rise and saw the place of the goats. A thing of pointed trees. A yip and a yap broke the night into pieces. These were not wolf-barks. They were Dog. The No-Pelts had Dog.

Too late! Pack is hunted now! She whined and dropped to her haunches, then leaped forward only to retreat. She loped around the noise, siding in, guarding. Warm night broke apart into many smells, many flickers and sounds that cringed her ears.

Whistles. Many No-Pelts, fast and dark, some big, some little. Some held fire in their paws. Too bright, blinding. *Pack breaks, white pain ...*

Quivering with distress, she watched Pack caught at bay by Dog Pack. Everything jumbled through her thinking. She howled as one with Mother Wolf. Sisters and brothers, old and young, ran from the smell of goat and Dog and the No-Pelt ear-hurt whistles.

Silver-gray they bolted past her, Mother Wolf first.

Lupina fled, her ears pricked for pursuit until Dog stopped hunting. She followed Pack back to the river to ease thirst and huddle in a dip. She smelled wolf blood around her. Young Brother and Bent Ear had not joined them. Mother Wolf lay bloody-muzzled with a broken stick in her belly.

Lupina whined and offered her tongue to Mother Wolf's wound. Already, she tasted Mother Wolf's death. Sister and brother wolves moiled and licked their own hurts until Mother Wolf's panting stopped.

This is not Mother Wolf anymore. Her muzzle is empty.

The Itch howled deep in Lupina's belly: a wavering, quavering echo from Pack that rippled all the way to the sky—all the way to hunt elsewhere on this terrible night.

Lupina's dreams were not a wolf's now, Pack Leader though she was. She ran with the wolves, but something deeper lay in her as spring turned to summer.

She twitched and tossed and grew restless and hungry for smells and tastes that belonged to the No-Pelts. Within her dreams, she heard voices and something called *song* and *magic* and *shaman* and *knowledge* and a bone in her belly that would itch until she obeyed its call.

In a rush of surrender she ran, water rushing in spate to urge her on through the shallow hills. She left Pack asleep in the den and loped through the dark. A wolf alone, she came to the Place of the Stick that killed Mother Wolf, and there she found bones glinting white.

She skulked to sniff those bones, her own thickening belly to the sod, and her heavy ruff lifted at whistles from the No-Pelt den far away. A pounding noise thumped through her body.

Songs and drums, not whistles, said the Itch. *Go to them. This is your time. Listen to me and go, and I'll hurt you no more.*

Her ears went flat, but she went.

She'd never come this near to the No-Pelt den, not even that night Mother Wolf had died. She slunk near and quivered as the songs and drums stopped whistling and pounding. A whoof and a growl warned her Dog lurked within.

They're not worried about a wolf alone. Their shaman called you home.

Lupina growled as some worry from long ago came back to her.

The Itch was so strong, she couldn't hold it inside anymore. She wailed in distress, and a similar cry answered her from behind the pointed wood.

"Mama. Mama!"

With a gasp, the Itch claimed her. Memory claimed her. Lupina collapsed to her belly and transformed.

Daughter! No. Oh no!

She howled to the spirits of her ancestors with a voice neither wolf nor human. She'd lived and hunted as a wolf, and her belly was rounding with wolf pups. She still had a pelt, and her feet looked like paws. Unable to lope on all fours, she crawled on new grass toward what had once been her home.

I stuck a bone in my ear to stop this from happening, and it happened anyway. I ate the bone, and I forgot them! For how many years?

A growl of horror rose from her throat.

She crawled to the picket-like spears rammed backward into the earth, a pointed barrier dividing people and dogs from wolves and the wild. With her claws in the ground, she lay lost. A wolf alone, wanting to chew herself dead for betrayal.

"Stay," said a woman to the growl of a dog. A scrape of boots pricked her ears.

"It's her, Auntie," said a smaller voice, one last heard by Lupina as the cry of a nursing babe.

She scrambled back, trapped in her half-pelt, as a latch clicked, and the picket gate opened.

I failed. I went to the wolves to save two Packs and saved none.

"Mama, stay!" said her daughter, Avadera, coming out first. Her wolf-gray hair was braided tight around her little face of five summers. Her earlobe was pierced with a band of silver and on it hung a wolf's claw. She wore a tunic of pelts stitched together. Her necklet held talons, teeth, and bones from every predator on the tundra.

Lupina huddled, muzzle to ground, in anguish. *Five years alone. My child needed teaching. She's my successor, my pupil. What have I done?* Her tail tucked under her. *I forsook them— and her!* She growled at the ground.

"No, Mama, you didn't. I hear you," cried Avadera.

Her daughter's small hand stroked the ear-scar made by scratching out the magic memory bone. "You gave up everything to save us, and you did. I saw you in my dreams. You taught me what you knew. I sang a song to you. We drummed our drums for you. Be a woof, Mama. I be shaman. We do this together."

Avadera tugged on Lupina's ear with her teeth and sniffed her like a wolf. Human teeth done in the wolf way.

Lupina growled with the memory of wolf pups with their milk teeth. With a half-human whoof, she rolled onto her back to yield her fur-clad belly to her daughter's strokes, gray-pelted arms and legs splayed.

With a kindred growl, her daughter climbed onto her belly and nuzzled her throat.

Here was the village shaman—young in years but ancient in vision.

Lupina licked small fingers that tasted of broth and milk. Fingers she could still teach to know the minds of wolves. She rumbled in her belly and grinned past her fangs at her daughter's beloved face. At last, the worrisome Itch in her belly was gone.

Avadera rubbed the claw in her ear—one of Mother Wolf's claws.

Lupina let go of her half-human form and flowed back into a full wolf—except for one thing. She knew the voice she would hear from now until she became bone under the stars would be Avadera's voice. The day would come when her daughter would don a pelt and join her, and another would take up the duty of shaman. A granddaughter perhaps.

Lupina's ear twitched in the language of wolves. *Pack will bring kill to this den when the Hunt goes well.*

"Yes, Mama Wolfskin, when the Hunt goes well," said Avadera, kissing her snout. "Our den will give you scraps when the Hunt isn't good."

Lupina sneezed, and Avadera giggled. "I can tell what I know. When I'm big, I'll have babies. They'll know how to talk to the wolves, and your pups will learn to talk wolf to us humans. You'll be the shaman for wolves and me for us."

Avadera looked up at the woman standing guard. She held a lantern in one hand and the handle of a bucket in the other. Lupina shook her gray ruff and gave a doggish whuff as the woman edged toward her with a bucket filled with soup bones and venison. The smell was delicious.

"You remember Auntie, Mama?"

Lupina yipped and licked her sister's fingers. This was the Sister Mother who had nursed her daughter and would raise her to be a woman.

That is, until the wolves called her out of her skin and into a new awareness.

"There should be no war between people and wolves under these stars, my sister," said Sister Mother as Avadera snugged against her. This was true and would be true.

The stars winked down in their never-ending watch as Lupina devoured her gift of venison and stood with the wolf in her bones and the woman still in her blood.

She'd lived twenty-two years as a shaman, but only five as a wolf. She had years yet before her to race with the wind.

Once she had fed, Lupina stalked forward, ears pricked, to lay her jaw on Avadera's young shoulder. "Protect them, Wolf's Daughter. Something new has been born," she whoofed into her daughter's tight braids.

"Protect them, Wolfskin. Something new has been born," her daughter whoofed back into her mother's ruff.

Lupina stared into yellow eyes like her own and grinned.

I must tell them something new has been born, she thought as she loped into the wind on that star-bright, summer-warm night. As Pack crooned from the hill on the blossoming tundra, Wolf-Daughter's Pack sang to the call of the drums.

BRENDA CARRE is a multi-published author of transformational short fiction and long epic fantasy (brendacarre.com). Brenda's stories can be found in the *Magazine of Fantasy and Science Fiction*, *Pulphouse Fiction Magazine*, *Fiction River Magazine*, and *Pulp Literature Magazine*, to name a few.

Brenda often turns the mystique of the Canadian landscape into fictional myth and magic. It is her delight to honor Dave Farland, mentor and transformational teacher. May his memory forever be a blessing to the contributors of this anthology and to those who read and benefit from its sales.

Peace on the Argent
JJ Lynn Daniels

I lay panting where I had fallen to the floor. Not for the first time in the last two weeks, I was grateful for the coolness of the tiles that some angel had chosen when designing the Training Room. Sweat dripped from my nose, a steady *pat-pat-pat*, further contributing to the puddle forming under my aching body.

"It's not supposed to be easy, Lucas." Master Bowman's voice broke through the sound of my heart pounding in my ears. "If it were, everyone would do it."

"In my world, everyone has done it," I ground out. My arms shook with the effort to push myself upright. "Again," I said.

Master Bowman gave me a steady look. The way his left eyebrow curled incredulously was a criticism in and of itself. I knew what he saw when he looked at me: a pathetic half-breed who would never amount to anything. He'd never say it out loud, but it was what everyone saw when they looked at me.

The alpha son who couldn't shift.

I risked a glance at the mirrored wall across from where I stood. A scrawny youth met my gaze. Arms and legs too long and skinny. Ribs visible beneath the pale skin of my chest. A face that was all sharp angles and scowl lines.

Last week, I'd bleached my hair with some stinging concoction that Laura had smuggled on board. Mom hadn't even reacted when she saw it. It was the most recent in a long line of bold hair choices.

I was bored of it already.

"Again," I repeated.

Master Bowman stepped forward and checked the leads he'd stuck to my chest at the beginning of our training session. Once satisfied they were secure, he returned to the control panel across the room.

"Like we talked about before," Master Bowman said. "Clear your mind. The transformation starts in the mind. The electricity is just to prime your muscles to do what your neurons are telling them. Focus on what you want."

I nodded, but my mind was filling rather than emptying. It always did during these sessions. A wave of fear that I would never fully shift, would never fully become what I was meant to be, washed over me. I could barely breathe under the weight of the thought.

"Ready?" Master Bowman asked.

I gritted my teeth. I wasn't ready. I never was for what came next. But I wouldn't let the Master Wizard know that.

I nodded and squeezed my eyes shut.

I heard the switch flip. It was always the first indication that the inevitable was coming. No stopping it now. I gave a halfhearted attempt to empty my mind, as instructed, but the anticipation of the pain made it impossible to focus. My muscles clenched against the oncoming shock.

Then it hit me.

A strangled cry escaped my lips. Then my jaw seized up, and I fell to the Training Room floor. Again, I blessed the angel who had chosen cool tiles for this room, and then the world went black.

⚶

I escaped the stares and whispers of the people crowding the space station's main hallway and ducked into my family's quarters, grateful to find the room empty. I wasn't in the mood to answer questions.

I'd caught a glimpse of my face as I left the Training Room for the showers. My second attempt at the shift had resulted in a broken nose when I hit the floor. While Master Bowman had reset the bone immediately, the swelling was going to be atrocious for days.

The main receiving room whispered of comfort. A ring of couches encircled a low table where my parents hosted other ambassadors and their families. The scent of lavender puffed happily out of a fragrance pod plugged into the wall, bathing the entire space in feelings of calm and peace. No amount of lavender could touch the frustration I felt.

The main door slid open with a mechanical hiss, and I froze.

"Lucas." My mother's tone was surprised.

I plastered a pleasant expression onto my face before turning around.

"Don't freak out," I said.

My mother didn't even flinch at the sight of my face, though I couldn't say the same for the rest of her entourage. A twittering of shock and discomfort made its way among the half dozen ladies all dressed in my mother's signature baby blue.

Only my cousin, Laura, kept a neutral look. Well, *neutral* was being generous. She grinned at me when my mother wasn't looking. I knew she'd demand the full story from me later.

To my mother's credit, she was an ambassador through and through. She would never let something as simple as a broken nose throw her off her game. The way she stood, regal in blue robes that made her eyes shine and her graying hair appear full and silky, she was the definition of put together. No one would accidentally associate this sophisticated woman with the broken-nosed kid with poorly bleached and spiked hair standing before her.

"I trust you will be joining us for lunch," Mother said.

It wasn't a request. I tried to match her courteous smile without wincing.

"Yes, ma'am," I said.

Laura followed me to my room. As soon as the door closed behind her, she threw off the formal blue robe that covered her normal clothes and tossed it on my bed.

"What did you do to your face?" she demanded, spinning me around.

"Ow, gentle," I said, the centrifugal force of her spinning me making the fresh break smart.

"You look awful," Laura said.

"Thanks."

She squinted her eyes at me, looking me up and down. "I'm digging the hair though."

I pulled away from her and opened the small wardrobe beside my bed. My formal robes hung within, safe from the scattered items of clothing that littered my bedroom floor.

I pulled out the robe I knew my mother expected me to wear: the baby blue of the humans checkered with the dark navy of the wolf shifters. It slid on with all the ease of a well-tailored outfit but hung on my shoulders with a weight of responsibility that I didn't want. I shrugged a few times to be sure it seated properly.

"So who's coming for lunch?" I asked.

Laura's sigh sounded as though it started somewhere deep in her middle and built as it rose. "Clan Koshka."

I threw a grimace at her over my shoulder. Clan Koshka was entirely populated by feline shifters, and, as such, they lacked a formalized hierarchy to their society. At least we wolves had a distinct alpha. You could be sure when you spoke to Father that what you were getting was enforceable. Among the cats, their policies shifted depending on who was in charge on any given day. Negotiating with them was like trying to catch water in your hands.

"I know, I know," Laura said. "I brought a secret weapon in case they get out of line."

My eyes widened at what she pulled from beneath her shirt. A half-moon shape with rounded holes along its length, the perfect size to slide your fingers through to grip it. It could have been jewelry for how innocently it sat in her palm, but the fist that clenched around my heart told me the truth.

It was silver.

"You brought silver knuckles into my father's residence? Are you insane?"

"Aren't they cool?" Laura asked, her brown eyes lighting up. "I was able to hide them in a shipment from Earth. Wanna try them on?"

"Hell no," I said. I retreated until the back of my legs hit the wardrobe, and I felt the robes pressing against my back.

"Don't be a wuss," Laura said, laughing. Before I could dodge, she threw the knuckles at me.

Time seemed to slow down as I watched them arc through the air. They flipped once. Twice. The silver flashed in the artificial lights. A sinister glow. It was hard to believe such a small trinket could murder my family. The poison of silver, once in the bloodstream, was almost always fatal to a shifter.

My hand moved before my brain could give the command. I caught the weapon.

I don't know what I'd expected. The lightning pain of the leads Master Bowman trained me with? A flash of fire as it licked my flesh? Certainly not this numbness. Certainly not this humming in my head as I stared down at the gleaming silver.

"I knew it!" Laura exclaimed.

"Knew *what?*" I croaked. My mouth was dry, like all the moisture had leeched from it when I caught the knuckles.

"You haven't shifted yet," Laura said. "So the silver didn't affect you! You're immune until your first shifting."

"Are you kidding me, Laura! You scared me half to death for one of your *experiments?*"

My cousin shot me a grin. "But I was right!"

"Get out," I growled. I never felt so much like my father as when I was angry.

"Don't be mad," Laura said. "This is great news."

"*Get out.*"

"Shit, fine." Laura snatched up her blue robe and practically flew from the room.

I looked down at the silver in my hands. It mocked me. If I had shifted when I was supposed to, when every other shifter my age had, it would be burning me now. The silver would be burning its way through my skin and flesh, finding its way to my bloodstream for the kill. Instead it stared at me, cold and lifeless. The hand that held the metal might as well have been human.

I dropped the knuckles into the pocket of my robe and resolved to ditch them at the earliest opportunity.

Somewhere *outside* the alpha's cabin.

I was grateful my mother had offered to walk with me to the Council Room. Father was testifying before the Assembly, and he would be insulted if I didn't show up.

Walking the main hallways of the *Argent* would have been agony without my mother's entourage. As it was, I still received the odd look and was the source for some whispered exchanges, but no one approached me. Surrounded as I was by a sea of blue robes, no one had the courage to call me a half-breed to my face. Still, my face burned as I saw a representative from Echelon VI jerk her head in my direction and then whisper to her companion behind an open hand.

I wanted to cast my eyes to the floor. I wanted to turn around and return to our quarters. But I couldn't do that. I was my mother's son. I was my father's son. And I had an image to maintain. I straightened my spine and lengthened my stride, falling into step beside my mother.

I noticed how her face softened when I was near her. She truly deserved a better son than the one I was shaping out to be. The weight of the knuckles in my pocket seemed to grow heavier. The silver that didn't burn.

"What my esteemed colleague is failing to point out is the absolute *lethality* of the weapon in question." The representative from Taurus III spoke with his hands just as much as with his words. He punctuated each point with an arm thrown wildly to the left or the right or even directly into the air. It amused me to watch his fellow representatives ducking out of the path of his wild, waving arguments.

It would have amused me more if he wasn't arguing directly against my father.

"Silver Ionizing Ray Guns were created *specifically* to kill shifters. The fact that a wolf would defend their presence on this space station is unthinkable." The representative was winding down to his conclusion. "I would expect such a defense from a human, but not the wolf she married."

I had always known my father was a well-controlled man. I knew he prided himself on the fact that he wouldn't give in to the fury of shifter stereotypes. The fact that he didn't throw himself across the Assembly to wrap his hands around the representative's throat proved how in control he was.

I doubted, in his shoes, that I would have done the same.

"Representative Mahon," my father began, "your argument is passioned, and I can appreciate the candor you use to defend against what you believe to be a threat to your clan; however, shifters are not the *only* representatives on this station. Ionizing rays have been used in maintenance for centuries! The most effective means of repairing the shell of this space station is the silver ions provided by these ray guns. Forcing our scientists to find another way to protect our station from the wear and tear of orbit will cost an unnecessary amount of time and money. The fact that these tools make you uncomfortable is not a sufficient argument for banning them."

The Assembly erupted into shouts and arguments and counterarguments. I couldn't blame them. The ray guns made *me* uncomfortable. I wanted nothing more than to be able to protect my family. Until I was able to shift, I was useless to them.

I had to go.

I caught my mother's eyes so she would know I was leaving and ducked out of the Council Chamber.

The main hallway that led off from the Council Room was mostly deserted. That was fine by me. I rolled my neck once as I walked, trying to ease the tension that was mounting there. I admired my father. I admired the way he fought for peace in the Assembly. I wanted to be that, I wanted to protect my family. Without the shift ...

"Well, if it isn't the half-breed."

The words drew me up short. A chill spread down my spine. I turned.

There were three of them. All at least two years older than I was. All well past their first shift. From the colors they wore, they belonged to Clan Koshka.

"Ah, the half-breed can hear," the shifter in front said.

I recognized his voice as the one who had first spoken. He stood a half head taller than I did. Dark hair and dark eyes gave his face a sinister feel. His voice was gravelly, jarring against my already heightened nerves.

I thought of what my father would say. How he could dispel violence with a word and smooth over tensions with a joke.

"I'm just trying to get home," I said. "No trouble here."

"Your father speaks out of turn," the Koshkan said. "Someone ought to teach him a lesson."

My heart dropped to somewhere below my navel. I felt hollowed out. The feline to the left of the speaker shifted into hybrid form, fur sprouting over his face, canines lengthening.

"I told you, I don't want any trouble," I tried again. My voice sounded weak to my own ears. A rushing sound took over my hearing. I thrust a hand into the pocket of my robe, searching for my communicator to contact the *Argent* authorities. But instead the weight of the silver knuckles met my fingers. I took a deep breath. I was out of options.

I slipped the knuckles onto my hand.

"That's a shame," the Koshkan said. "Trouble is exactly what abominations like you were bred for."

My vision narrowed as the hybrid feline lunged forward. I couldn't hear the sound his steps made as he crossed the short distance between us. Impossibly sharp claws filled my vision as he raised a hand toward me. Then I was stepping forward myself. Bringing my hand up. The weight of the knuckles felt like a feather as adrenaline took over.

The hybrid reeled back from the force of my blow, a silent scream tearing from his throat. His hands came up to his jaw, and I could see smoke escaping between his fingers.

Shit, the silver was eating through his face.

"He has silver!" the Koshkan who had been taunting me shouted. That I heard.

The other two shifters turned tail and ran, leaving the hybrid on the floor, screaming and flailing.

I heard the distinct sound of boots pounding up the hall. Help was coming for him.

A part of me knew I should stay. I should make sure he was okay. Explain myself, maybe. But a hand of dread gripped my heart.

I turned and ran.

Master Bowman found me in the Training Room ten minutes later. I sat cross-legged on the floor, directly below the glass ceiling. Only dark sky visible above me. During the first-shift ritual, the moon would shine full and bright down into this room, but not tonight. Tonight it was as dark as my thoughts.

Those Koshkans were right. I was a half-breed. An abomination.

A spawn of human and werewolf. I would never be able to shift. I would forever be in between. It wasn't my fault I couldn't shift. Couldn't defend my family. It was my genetics. The human side of me holding me back. Forcing me into weakness.

"Oh good, you're practicing clearing your thoughts," Master Bowman said.

I didn't correct him.

"Your mind must be completely empty before the shift can take place."

An unexpected snort escaped me.

The Master Wizard was beside me in an instant. "Need a tissue?"

I looked up into his face. The words had been pleasant, but there was a fire in his eyes. The wizard did not like to be mocked.

"This is ridiculous," I said finally. "Clear your mind, really? Have you ever tried to clear your mind with an electrical current primed to run through your torso? Have you ever tried to clear your mind when half the space station is waiting for you to fail?"

"Then don't," the wizard said.

"What?"

"Don't clear your mind. Don't do what I say." Master Bowman shrugged. "Don't make the shift. It's no skin off my nose either way."

"Why can't you fix me?" I demanded. My voice came out a strangled cry. I hated that. "Isn't that what my parents are paying you so handsomely for? To fix their defective kid?"

Master Bowman laughed, and the harsh sound stabbed through the hole in my chest.

"Hell no. I'd fix a defective werewolf for free." He leaned in closer, his hot breath washing over my face. "Your parents are paying me handsomely to put up with your asshat attitude while I do it."

I tried to keep a straight face, but he was right. I was an absolute asshat.

"I'm sorry," I said finally. "You don't deserve that."

"Neither do your parents," Master Bowman said gently. "You should go talk to them."

I winced.

I slowly extricated my legs from the position they were in, nearly groaning as they protested the movement.

Master Bowman gave me a sage nod as I walked from the Training Room. It was the closest to respect I'd ever gotten from him.

Outside the Training Room, I was met by my brothers, full-blooded werewolves in the navy-blue robes of our father's house. They escorted me back to our family's quarters. None of my escorts would have been caught dead missing their first shift. Just me. Their half brother. The half-blooded screwup.

My brothers were dismissed almost as soon as we arrived in the receiving room. I tried not to stare too openly at my father. His face rippled with the rage he worked to get under control. It was because of me. He was going to lose his cool because of me. My cheeks burned.

It started with yelling. The rushing sound in my ears made it almost impossible to make out his exact words. Then my mother's soft voice was calming him, drawing him back the way only she could whenever some Assembly member had pushed him too far.

"Do you want us to take away your trainings with Master Bowman?" My father's voice finally broke through my numbness.

"No," I whispered.

"Moonrise is in thirty hours," my mother said to my father. "Don't take this from him now. Give him a chance."

"We've been giving him a chance for the last year!" My father's voice rose again, and I winced.

"He's not broken." My mother's words were a staccato beat in my chest. "He just needs some extra help. With all the practice he's been getting, he'll be able to shift with the moonrise. I know it.

"The Koshkan will be fine," my mother continued. "The security tapes showed that the feline attacked first. This will all go away."

My father, an imposing figure even without his navy-blue robes, seemed to deflate at my mother's words. His shoulders dropped, and he sat heavily on the couch across from me.

"I shouldn't have yelled," he said finally.

"I deserved it," I said, not daring to meet his gaze.

"Silver knuckles?"

I nodded.

"They didn't burn you?"

I shook my head.

"Interesting."

I looked up then. My father studied my face. His eyes were sharp enough to pierce my skin and see the answers underneath.

"Laura thinks it's because I haven't shifted yet," I said. "She thinks that if the shift happens, I'll be just as vulnerable to silver as the rest of us."

"When," my mother said firmly. "*When* the shift happens."

I nodded.

"We should take a break." Master Bowman's voice broke through my panting breath.

"We should go again," I said, pushing myself upright on shaking legs.

Master Bowman threw me a look. "Your mind is not in it. You're not clearing your head."

"I'm trying!" I yelled. My voice echoed across the Training Room floor and came back to my ears, hollow.

"You're not trying," Master Bowman said. "You're thinking of all the reasons why this *won't* work. That is not trying."

I remained silent. He was right.

"Maybe I'm prompting you wrong," Master Bowman said thoughtfully. "It's not that your mind needs to be completely empty. It's—" He searched for the right word. "Peace. Your mind needs to make peace with what you want. If you're in a tumult inside, if you are filled with fear over what might or might not happen, you'll never get the transformation you want."

I pondered his words. Peace? How could I find peace when this moonrise was my last chance to shift? After this, I'd be too old. The window would be closed. I'd never be able to protect my family the way my brothers did.

"You need to decide what it is you want, more than anything," Master Bowman said. "What will bring you peace."

I stared at my hands.

"Take a break," Master Bowman said. "Moonrise is tomorrow. We'll try again then."

My mind was restless. Peace was a joke. It was some kind of cruel joke that wizards played on wolves before first shifts. It had to be. No way did Master Bowman actually believe I'd find peace or be able to sleep the last night before my final chance. He'd probably laughed to himself as he went to bed. *He* was probably sleeping like a rock wearing pink-striped pajamas and sparing no further thoughts for a werewolf in distress.

I heard a sound from the hall outside my room. I squinted at the clock beside me. I wasn't the only one up at 0300? An image filled my head of my mother sitting in the kitchen, drinking hot cocoa, and worrying about me. I couldn't let her worry alone. I slipped a jacket on over my light pajamas and padded to the hall.

The first clue that something was wrong was the sound. More importantly, the *lack* of sound. Usually there was a humming that filled the residence, a comforting sound that let us know that the security system was primed and ready to alert us to any breach of our doors. The quiet was oppressive. A weight that only added to the dread that clung heavy to my chest.

The door that led from the hall to our receiving room was cracked open.

Someone had broken in.

Without a thought, I smacked the panic button on the wall. The *Argent*'s authorities had a response time of three minutes on this side of the space station, which was fast, but not fast enough if someone was already in your residence. Already threatening your family.

I turned on my heel and raced up the hall.

My brothers' rooms lined the hallway, and I banged on each door as I passed, waking them with desperate cries. My parents' bedroom was at the end of the hall. I was sure the intruder was headed there.

My father had plenty of enemies, but we were supposed to be safe on the **SS** *Argent*. There was an agreement, a treaty on an embassy space craft.

I shoved my way into my parents' bedroom and drew up short at the sight before me.

My mother huddled on their bed, blankets drawn up to her chin, her eyes wide. My father stood before her, shielding her body with his. Across the room stood a dark figure dressed all in black, a mask hiding his face. In his hand, he held a metal object, shining in the low light from the hallway. A Silver Ionizing Ray Gun.

I could hear my brothers shouting behind me. I should have waited for them to arrive. I should have let them use their wolf forms to protect our parents. But that SIRG could hurt them. It could kill them.

I didn't waste another moment in thought.

I launched myself across the room.

I woke in the *Argent*'s infirmary. Bright lights stared down at me; I fought the urge to squint at them. Pain screamed from my right arm. I knew I'd gotten hit. I knew wrestling for the SIRG was a risk, but damn, it smarted.

"Mom?" I asked. It wasn't my most badass moment —sue me.

My mother was there, though. Her hand cool on mine. My father, his warmth hard to ignore, stood beside her.

"What were you thinking, Lucas?" his deep voice rumbled.

I squeezed my eyes shut, and a tear ran hot down my cheek. "I just wanted to keep you safe. I've only ever wanted to keep us safe."

"You did, Lucas." My mother's gentle tone enveloped me. Eased the ache in my chest.

"Who was it?" I asked.

"Some gun for hire," my father said, his voice filled with disgust. "We were able to take him into custody alive. I'm sure the *Argent*'s authorities will get to the bottom of it. I will act surprised and horrified when we find that Taurus III is behind it."

"Regulus," my mother chided.

"Well, I'll try. I've never been a good actor."

"What time is it?" I asked. "Did I miss—"

My mother made a hushing noise. "You didn't miss anything. Moonrise is in two hours. The doctors want to keep an eye on you a little longer."

I shook my head and tried to push myself up, wincing at the pain in my arm.

"But"—my father's eyes danced with amusement—"I think we can cause enough of a distraction to sneak you out."

I stood still, gazing up at the glass above my head. The Training Room was darkened for the shifting, the moon the only light streaming in from the ceiling. A chill passed over me as I stood half naked before the crowd.

Master Bowman had placed the leads back onto my chest without a word. A slight squeeze on my shoulder the only encouragement he gave. There would be no yelled instructions from the control panel. No reminders to clear my mind. It would be just me and the moon this time.

My parents stood at the front of the crowd. They'd donned their formal robes for the occasion. I recognized my brothers' forms behind them and Laura standing beside them.

Master Bowman awaited my signal. I was in control this time. I would be the one to tell him when to throw the switch. I felt a burning in my chest behind my breastbone. Was this what other wolves felt before their first shift? Was this the signal I had been waiting for?

I looked at my parents, the pride I saw shining on their faces in the moonlight. If I hadn't been a half-breed, if I had shifted earlier, they may not be here tonight. They may very well have been killed last night.

I took a steadying breath.

I knew what I had to do.

My family didn't need another wolf.

My family needed me.

With a brush of my hand, I tore the leads from my chest.

A gasp sounded through the assembled crowd.

I gestured to Master Bowman, and I saw a flash of a smile before he closed the blast doors above me, shutting off the light from the moon.

The artificial lights came on, and I walked off the Training Room floor.

I'd made my decision.

And for the first time, I felt peace.

Growing up as a voracious reader in a desert in Southern California, JJ beat the heat to pursue her author dreams within view of the Rocky Mountains.

When not working as a registered nurse, raising three little girls, or chasing her German Shepherd rescue dog, JJ enjoys writing stories that connect with the souls of her readers and explore the themes that affect us all.

Twilight Bargain
Ken Bebelle and Julia Vee

The pads of my paws scraped against the broken concrete of the narrow maze of streets and alleys at the top of Queen Hill. Yelps and growls of Alexiano's wolf pack bounced off the ruined brick and stone buildings that made up this section of the zoo, following me as I bled and ran, searching for sanctuary.

But there was no sanctuary to be found in the zoo, where survival of the fittest was the first law every shifter obeyed. I put on a burst of speed when I saw the faded green house with white trim. I sprinted through the backyards, jumping over dilapidated fencing. The breath of my pursuers blew hot on the scruff of my neck.

Above me, the moon was a faded queen behind the haze of Seattle's perpetual twilight.

I heard her call, but she did not rule me.

Not here.

Here, I had greater control over my wolf, and we had reached an accord. We did not want to get killed by the pack.

I worried at the back door of the green house with my

forepaws, wedging the rain-swollen door open. It cost precious seconds, but it was worth it. Alexiano, the alpha, smashed through the decaying wood fence at the back of the yard, his jaws wide and teeth glistening wet. The vigorous run across Queen Hill had only inflamed him. He spotted me at the back door of the house and moved faster, cornering me, his prey.

Fear warred with elation as I set my trap.

I'd hidden in this house before, and I knew the front door was jammed shut, the wood swollen grotesquely from the humidity, and the windows were boarded up. The house was a death trap.

Unless you were small.

Which I was. I was the smallest werewolf in the Americas. It was my bane and my problem. But today it would save my furry butt.

The back door slammed open, and howls and musk filled the house. Scratching claws skittered across the kitchen tiles, and a half dozen timber wolves slewed into the front room, yellow eyes glowing in the Twilight gloom. They slowed as they found me huddled behind a rotting couch. The wolves spread out, surrounding me, each one twice my size.

I edged my muzzle past the corner of the couch. "Good chase, right? Time to call it a night?"

Alexiano roared and pounced. Martin followed suit, his jaws menacingly wide.

I turned and jumped through the hole behind me. I hit my target perfectly, getting my head and forepaws through the window with barely room to spare. My hind legs clawed at the plasterboard below the window and slipped, shredding the rotting wood.

A huge weight slammed into my rump, and red-hot lines of pain raked across my haunches. I yelped and kicked, my legs finding purchase on someone's muzzle before I squirted through the window. I tumbled to the warped floorboards of the porch.

They would have to backtrack through the house to get out, buying me time. I ran, pain lighting up my legs with every step.

I nearly made it to Market.

This was the second law for shifters—Market Freedom. The Market only happened when the tide sank low enough to reveal the muddy land bridge to Bell. On those days, enterprising Fae and vampire merchants braved the sucking mud and tangles of stinging jelly weed to come to Queen Hill.

The edge of the Market, marked by strings of hanging lanterns, was just a few blocks ahead when the howls of Alexiano's pack caught me. I was exhausted, and my rear legs were nearly numb from pain. The tantalizing scents of cook fires and sizzling fat touched the edge of my senses as Alexiano's claws sank into my side.

The impact took us both off our feet, skidding through muddy ruts left by the merchant wagons. I went limp and snapped with my own, pitiful jaws, trying to grab an ear or maybe his tail. The world spun, lights flashed, and I landed on my back. Alexiano slashed his claws across my chest. I kicked, trying to reach him, trying to keep him away. It was useless.

"Alexiano."

The alpha paused. From behind him, the voice came again, a calm counterpoint to Alexiano's bloodthirsty rage.

"He's had enough."

Alexiano turned, giving me a view of the grizzled black wolf behind him. The alpha grinned, his sharp fangs glistening wet. "Is that a challenge, Paolo? Over this runt, old man?"

Paolo ducked his head. He knew he had no chance against Alexiano. The old wolf snuck me a bite of food here and there, but a challenge would get him killed.

Alexiano leaned close to me, saliva dripping from his panting tongue. "I'll say when the runt's had enough."

I snapped at his muzzle. Resentment fired in my bones and made my tone hard. "Vai pentear macacos!"

Alexiano roared, and his jaws opened wide. Telling him to go comb monkeys hadn't been wise, but I was long past wisdom. I would pay for it now. He slammed his forelegs down on me, pinning my head into the mud, exposing my neck.

All my time in Seattle had led up to this moment. This pack had never truly accepted me. Alexiano was the alpha, and the pack followed a hierarchy. I was the omega. I knew my place. I let them chase me and helped the pack blow off steam. I was supposed to have a place. But Alexiano never acknowledged me, and now he was going to kill me.

Paolo coughed. "Alexiano."

Alexiano whirled, his eyes blazing. "What?"

Paolo looked up. I looked up as well and found the string of twinkling Fae lights that marked the border of Market hanging above Alexiano's head. I also noticed that the Market sounds had stopped, and Queen Hill was as quiet as I had ever heard it.

A low growl started in the distance, and a troop of Kodiak bears shouldered their way into the clearing. Grandma, a fearsome, brown-and-gray bear at the head of the pack stopped just short of our little fracas and simply stared at us, her eyes bright with annoyance.

Alexiano snapped at me, his jaws closing just shy of my nose. He turned away in a huff. "Desgraça!"

The rest of the pack turned and followed.

The Kodiaks held their position for a moment longer before breaking up and making their way back into the heart of the Market.

Around me, business resumed, and the sounds of

commerce danced like the rushing waters of a river. Through that river of market activity strode a tall, muscular witch with dark skin, dressed in a long robe of saffron-yellow, rough-spun cloth. Her dark hair was tied into long braids and wrapped with a knot of red. A shield half as tall as she was rode on her back, and she carried a walking stick of gnarled, polished wood that squelched in the mud with her steps.

The woman stopped and knelt in front of me. She gave a long sigh.

I hated the pity I saw in her dark eyes. I pushed myself up and turned away. Maybe I could find some scraps at the edge of the Market, enough to shift and heal.

Before I'd made it even five feet, the rich tang of fresh blood grabbed me by the nose. I froze, willing myself to turn slowly. I couldn't show desperation.

The witch held an open package of waxed paper in her hand, revealing a fresh cut of red meat. Blood ran in dark rivulets down the creases of the paper and dripped into the mud. The scent set my breath to panting, and I struggled to keep the whine out of my breathing.

She chuckled, but the laughter didn't sound mean. "Need some food if you're going to shift, don't you?"

Now the whine came out, and I hated myself for it. But I did need the food. The witch smiled and stood, wrapping the meat back up. "Follow me."

She turned and walked away, tucking the package into her robe.

I scanned the Market, considering my chances of finding anything to eat. After another moment, I lapped up the blood in the puddles and set off at a limping trot after the witch.

Heading north of Market meant leaving the safety zone. I didn't worry about Alexiano. I knew him, and he'd spend the rest of the night soothing his own ego. And the warrior woman before me moved with purpose and assurance—and carried a really big stick.

As I trailed behind her, I caught the scent of sweet orange and crushed bark from her skin. Her steps were quick, and the noise of the Market faded, leaving only the quiet of dark roads and tall trees.

We walked like this for miles before arriving at an arboretum. The crushed leaves and cones beneath my paws felt like a sanctuary of its own. The witch stopped in a clearing and knelt in front of a small arrangement of stones. She swept off the leaves and gestured to me.

"Come."

I moved closer. The largest stone was a rectangular slab with a pattern chiseled into it. My wolf eyes were keen, and even in the dim twilight filtering through the trees, I could make out the shape of a stag with a large crown of antlers. Above the antlers, a curved bow pointed upward like a half sun, a nocked arrow at its center.

Alone, the stag didn't mean much. But together with the bow and arrow and here in this forest, a stillness came over me. An offering stone to Oxóssi.

He was the provider, spirit of the hunt and the forest. He was my Orixás.

I bent my head in respect. Wonder filled my heart to find him here, so far from my homeland. I turned back to the witch and studied her bold features and knowing gaze. Was she a priestess?

As if sensing my question, she shook her head. "No, he is not mine. But I saw that he is yours."

She set the package of meat on the grass and opened it.

Now, when I bent my head to eat, it no longer felt like charity but rather a shared offering before Oxóssi.

All too soon, the meat was gone. A comfortable lethargy stole over me as my belly swelled full for the first time in days. I thanked Oxóssi for my good fortune, then sat on my haunches and regarded the witch, who had so far been silent.

She didn't look at me but studied the trees around us as she spoke.

"When I crossed the Veil, I began to see many things. Things I could only get flashes of before. My gift was faint, but here my eye opened, and I perceived the true shape of things."

Now she turned to stare at me, her dark eyes searching and patient.

I tilted my head, ears twitching. I knew what I was. A shaggy gray werewolf, my head too big and my frame too lean. Always hungry, always an outcast.

"I did a lot of searching to find my true shape, learn my true nature."

She spread her arms wide, and one of her sleeves fell back, revealing a delicate tattoo of tracing vines and leaves twined around a pierced heart perched atop a coiled serpent. The Witch's Veve. "I am Yvonne, and I practice in the House of Wisdom."

My respect for her rose again. Here in the Twilight, the covens were many. They were secretive and powerful, charging exorbitant amounts of silver for their healing, spells, and charms. The House of Wisdom was more secretive than most, and that was saying something. The big question for tonight was: what did a witch from the House of Wisdom want with me?

"I have been watching you, Dario. You struggle to survive amongst those stronger than you."

I licked my lips, savoring the last traces of salt and blood on my tongue. "And?"

"I can see your true shape. It is the thing you are looking for."

"I'm not looking for anything other than food."

Her eyes twinkled in amusement. "You can lie to me, but you can't lie to yourself. Yours is a hunger that cannot be sated with food. You want to challenge an alpha and win. I will show you your true shape, and in return, you will swear to bring me a werewolf's canine."

I didn't know what to say.

This sounded like one of those Fae bargains that I knew to avoid. But the idea that my malformed wolf might not be me was enticing. If she had a true vision of my wolf, I wanted it. I needed it.

But I knew a witch's working was a dangerous thing, and crossing the pack was a death sentence.

I shuddered to imagine what she could do with a fang from Alexiano. Would she have power over his bloodline?

Memories of Alexiano's abuse chilled my gut. The way he didn't let me eat. The way the beta, Martin, had clawed my hind leg to the bone last month. It had taken many shifts to heal that.

By rights, I was entitled to eat after the rest of the pack. But they always left me nothing. Tonight I had darted in and stolen a bite of their kill, a fat doe that had wandered too far down from the grassy hills. My theft had kicked off tonight's breakneck chase. Bitter resentment rose in me, and suddenly I didn't care what the witch wanted to do with the werewolf fang. I would give it to her happily.

"If what you say is true, and I shift into a more powerful form, then I will honor this bargain."

A soft wind swirled above us, and I heard the rustle of

leaves, as if all of the grass and trees had heard and witnessed my words.

Yvonne reached into her satchel and pulled out a dark-brown bottle. Uncorking it, she held it up, then tipped it three times. Once to the left, once to her right, and then once between us. The sweet scent of rum filled the air, and though it was a chilly evening, my body warmed as if I had taken a swig.

She began to hum a pleasing tune. Familiar, yet just out of reach of memory.

I curled up on the grass, suddenly sleepy. My eyelids drifted low. The rum tickled my snout, and I sank heavily into the earth. The night wind and rustling leaves vanished, replaced by a vibrating pulse of drums beneath me.

The drumbeats grew louder. Hypnotic. In a breath, I was back in Brazil listening to the thrum of the atabaque, its tall form of jacaranda wood. Invisible strong hands beat on the taut calfskin, the rhythm pounding in my blood and growing louder than my own heartbeat.

I swayed, an involuntary dance, but my spirit longed to move more, to fling myself into wild abandon. Here in these beats, I was safe, surrounded by flames and drums. My claws retracted, and then I was only a man. The heat from the flames seared my skin, and sweat poured down my back. I danced, bare feet striking the earth.

A stag leapt over the flames, gleaming white. The antlers flamed red and gold, sharp and menacing. It was an emissary from Oxóssi, and I flung myself to the ground before him.

"Rise!"

I did as he bade, and the stag charged me.

There was no time to shift, to dodge.

The antlers pierced me to my spine. Pain ripped through my senses, and even in this in-between place, I knew I could die.

The stag tossed me off his antlers, flinging me to the dirt. Blood poured from my wounds, drenching the earth. I coughed, and blood sprayed from my lips. I reached for my wolf form, praying the shift would heal me, but my wolf wasn't there.

I struggled now, desperate, calling my wolf again. He and I had always had a difficult relationship, but he had never hesitated to rise before.

The stag loomed over me, bending his massive head low. "Rise."

Oxóssi commanded me, but I couldn't obey. My legs twitched and grew numb. Despite the flames surrounding us, my teeth chattered, and I shivered in the soil wet with my blood.

"Rise."

The stag's head moved closer, and I didn't have the strength to crawl away. Was it here to finish me? In moments, it wouldn't matter.

Its dark eyes were luminous, the flames reflected within. I watched in a daze and felt warmth trickle over my forehead. The stag was crying. I blinked in confusion.

The stag's tears bathed my face, and my shivering ceased. The pain receded.

I looked for my wolf again. Sensation returned, and I felt tension release in my spine and hips. The wound in my belly gaped open, ragged and bleeding. My intestines roiled and shifted, something moving within. I watched in horror as a bulbous head pushed out from my belly, a bloody forked tongue tasting the night air.

In the smoke-ridden darkness, the rest of the serpent's body followed, slick with my blood. It slithered out of me, as long as my arm.

My blood slid off its golden scales, its triangular head and scale pattern proclaiming it to be the lancehead viper. Venomous. Deadly.

The viper's jaws extended, poised to strike, and on instinct, I grabbed its head, squeezing it into submission. The coils fell limp, and I yanked it the rest of the way out of my body. Where the tail should have curved to a smooth taper, it was bent and deformed.

It looked wrong.

Like me. It should be powerful. It should be menacing. But beyond its fangs, it looked weak.

Rage flushed my face and coursed through my veins. I lifted the serpent high and bit down, spitting out the broken end. The serpent thrashed in my hand, and instead of blood, golden light poured out from the wound. The end lengthened before my eyes, thickening until impossibly, a second head emerged.

It swayed, and continued to stretch and grow, until it had doubled in size. It coiled back on itself, twisting into an undulating helix.

This was my true wolf.

The snakes twined tightly around each other and dove back into the gaping hole in my gut. Golden light seared the wound, and my skin knit together, ragged edges smoothing without a scar.

This time when I called my wolf, his strength surged through me, burning away my fear. His howl echoed in the night. Pain ripped through me, the change coming fast. I whimpered as my bones shattered and re-knit. I rode the surging waves of the agony of transformation.

Familiar and yet excruciating anew.

When the change finished, I rose on four legs, and the flames faded. The stag was gone. There was only the warrior witch drinking rum. The scent of leaves replaced the smoke. I looked down on Yvonne from my new vantage point.

She tilted her head up to me and a slow smile spread across her broad face. "Not so small now."

I lifted a paw. It was the size of the rum jug. I arched my back, howling to the moon. The sound rolled out from deep in my wide chest. My monstrous jaws flexed, and I felt strong enough to bite through stone.

I ran through the muddy forest that covered much of the zoo and Queen Hill. My long legs propelled me through thick underbrush. Blood thundered through me, hot and quick. My chest expanded and drew deeply of the damp night air. A myriad of scents bombarded me, singing of fresh-churned earth, cowering prey, and monsters on the hunt.

I jumped over a felled tree. My claws raked into the rotting wood, and I angled toward the sound of howling wolves. Ahead of the pack, an elk darted between the trees, its scent heavy with the tang of fear.

In seconds, I was abreast of the pack's laggards, the slower wolves who often ended up fighting for scraps amongst themselves. I bounded past them and left them behind.

The middle of the pack was larger, young pups jockeying for position, trying to make a show of themselves to gain the beta's notice. I ran alongside them for a moment and marveled. I had feared them just yesterday. Now I could see they were only bickering puppies.

Paolo, the pack's third, was nowhere in sight. Anger burned in my belly when I realized Alexiano had excluded him from the hunt as punishment for speaking up for me.

Martin was next, his tongue lolling as he ran just behind Alexiano.

Yesterday, Alexiano's jaws had looked monstrous, fearsome, as he had threatened to bite out my throat. For months now, he had towered over me, never letting me forget my place or my weakness. Now he just looked petty and small, a weak leader who kept his pack from getting stronger in order to appease his own ego.

I did not miss how Martin kept his eyes on Alexiano instead of the elk as they ran. Martin seemed hungry for something other than tonight's prey.

The elk put on a final burst of speed. Alexiano was lagging, his breath coming in great gasps. If he didn't slow the elk down, the rest of the pack would never catch up to add their fangs and claws to the fight. It had never occurred to me before that Alexiano wasn't strong enough to kill our prey without the pack's help.

I kicked off with my hind legs and launched myself up. I bounded off a low branch and landed between Alexiano and Martin. My larger body pushed the two of them off-balance like they were mere rabbits. Yelps of confusion filled the air as the alpha and beta crashed to a halt.

I ignored them and leapt forward again, stretching out the full length of my body, claws extended. My forepaws found the elk's haunch, and my claws sank home, drawing a bleat of pain from the animal. I flexed my body and brought my hind legs up to tackle the elk to the forest floor.

We tumbled through wet leaves and mud. The elk arched, trying to impale me with its antlers. I opened my massive jaws and found the elk's neck. The elk screamed, and boiling-hot carotid blood ejected into my mouth, rich with the animal's fear.

The animal bucked again, but its life energy was already

draining into my gullet. I held it down and tightened my grip. I twisted again, the elk's neck cracked, and then it lay still.

Alexiano caught up, his hackles up and eyes blazing. "Who dares?"

Martin arrived a half second later, his eyes still on the alpha.

I lifted my head from the elk, my muzzle running with blood and gore. More hot blood ran out of the elk's neck and soaked into the forest floor, but neither Alexiano or Martin made a move toward me. I raised my snout and howled, and the sound shook the trees. The middle of the pack skidded to a stop, and several wolves instinctively ducked their tails and whined at the tenor of my howl.

Alexiano growled and snapped at me. I cuffed him across the nose, tearing the soft tissue. He jerked back and whimpered.

I planted my feet in the earth and addressed the pack. "I took down this kill for you!"

Martin lunged at me. I snapped at him and tore off an ear. He gave a yelp and rolled away.

The entire pack waited quietly, their ears twitching and tails down, except for Alexiano, who tried to give a menacing growl around his torn nose. It was pathetic.

I walked up to him, holding his gaze the entire way. Only when I was within range to cuff him again did he finally whimper and lie down in the mud. I stood over him, blood dripping from my jaws to spatter across his eyes. "Doesn't feel good to be looked down on, does it?"

Alexiano huffed. "I don't—"

I growled and swung again. My paw connected with his head, and the impact flung him into a tree. His head hit with a bone-shattering crack. "Don't you, desgraça?"

Alexiano had never been known for his intellect. It was Martin who figured it out, his voice a whine. "Dario?"

I crossed over to the defeated alpha and shifted. My fur melted away, and my limbs shortened. My paws shrank, and my claws disappeared until I was left with soft, human fingers. I would not be as strong in human form, but I needed Alexiano and Martin to know I had no fear of either of them.

I knelt at Alexiano's side and grabbed him by the neck. His tongue lolled out, and his eyes rolled back. Blood seeped from his mouth where he had struck the tree.

One wet eye found me, and he rasped, "Do it, runt. Kill me."

It was my right. I had challenged the pack's alpha and won. Our laws said his life was mine. I looked down at the broken wolf in my hand, who had terrorized me for the last year, and felt ... nothing.

I wormed my hand into his mouth and grabbed his canine. Alexiano didn't even whimper as I ripped the tooth from his jaw. I let go, and he dropped to the forest floor in a heap.

Martin approached, keeping his belly low on the ground, half his head bloody from the missing ear. "Alpha—"

I snarled, and he shut up. Yesterday, they had been a towering pack of frightening werewolves, and I had only lived on scraps of their charity. Tonight, they were cowering tail tuckers. I turned my back on Martin and went back to the elk.

When I called my wolf this time, the shift was smooth, like pouring water from one container to another. The bone-deep pain was satisfying. My fangs ripped open the carcass, spilling steaming organs out. I slurped down the liver in one gulp and snapped up the heart. I savored the choice parts of the kill as was my right, staring down the pack. No one moved, but their eyes moved hungrily over the bloody elk. They would eat after I left.

I wanted one other to eat before they did.

With a snap of my jaws, I ripped off a large portion of the elk's haunch. I padded away from the carcass and the pack, leaving them in silence. I didn't look back.

I found Paolo at his shed. He was out front working on a bike repair. His human form was tall and lean, brown-skinned and hard with corded muscle. His salt-and-pepper hair was the same tone as his fur. His head jerked up as the wind shifted and brought my scent to him. Paolo froze when he saw me. After a moment's pause, he ducked his head slightly.

It was strange, the old wolf deferring to me. I dropped the bloody chunk of elk at his feet.

"Paolo."

His face creased with confusion, and his eyes traveled over my new form. His nostrils flared as he took in my scent again, and his bushy eyebrows crawled up his head.

"Dario?"

I grinned, baring my new fangs. "Hello, old-timer."

"Moon above, boy, what have you done?"

"I finally found myself."

Soft footsteps sounded behind me, and we both turned. Yvonne came around the corner and stood a ways off from us, her walking stick planted in the ground. "He had a little help."

Paolo growled at the witch. "Dario, is this some enchantment?"

I shook my head. "I was always meant to be like this."

Yvonne shrugged, a careless move of her broad shoulders. "I was merely his guide."

Paolo grunted, unappeased. "Bad idea, bargaining with witches."

I would have agreed with him before. But my wolf and I were finally in alignment, and I owed Yvonne for showing us the way. I shifted, a blur of movement and magic.

I tossed Alexiano's fang to the witch.

In an easy motion, she caught it in her fist. She held the bloody tooth between her fingers. "Dario the dire wolf. Has a nice ring to it."

And then with a twirl of her walking stick, she left us, her saffron robes swaying.

Paolo picked up the elk meat and sniffed appreciatively. "I guess I'm calling you alpha, now?"

A day ago, I would have said yes. A day ago, I was weak and starving and subject to the whims of the pack. I would have done anything to become an alpha.

"I'd prefer if you'd call me a friend."

Paolo bit off a chunk of meat and nodded as he chewed. "You're that already, Dario."

"Good."

I hesitated. Part of me wanted to stay and make sure the old wolf was okay, and Paolo seemed to sense my conflict.

He smiled and dipped his head. "Well, I better get back to work. Thanks for the food, friend."

Tears pricked my eyes. "Yeah. See you around, Paolo."

I didn't need a pack to hunt with anymore. For the first time in my life, I didn't need anyone. I turned and headed south. There was enough time before high tide to use the land bridge to Seattle. Yvonne had helped me find my wolf. Now it was time for me to find out who I really was.

JULIA VEE writes stories about monsters and food. Julia attended UC Berkeley and majored in Asian Studies. She is a graduate of Viable Paradise.

KEN BEBELLE studied Cybernetics at UCLA and has practiced prosthetics for over twenty years, specializing in upper limb prosthetics. He writes science fiction and fantasy with his coauthor, Julia Vee.

Their debut novel, *Ebony Gate*, an Asian-inspired urban fantasy, will be published by TOR in summer 2023.

IF–Wolf

Mike Jack Stoumbos

D o we need to talk about addiction?" Mindy asked the man digging through the company fridge on the other side of the break room counter.

Her coworker, Derek Latimer, didn't make eye contact with her. "Addiction is only a problem worth addressing if it's unduly interfering with someone's work," he recited, his voice both crisp and flat. He grabbed the brown paper sack with *DL* printed in Sharpie and pivoted back to the counter, letting the magnetic door close behind him.

"Or with their life. What I mean is ..." She trailed off, suddenly distracted by the sight of Derek tearing through the sandwich's biodegradable wrapper with one hand to take a larger bite than could realistically fit in his tight mouth and small jaw.

Mindy brought her fingertips to her own lips—empathetic reaction—even though she wasn't the one chewing. Then, keeping her composure, she said, "How long has it been since you've eaten?"

"Since before I logged in," Derek said through a full mouth.

Mindy's eyes flicked to the window, which looked like a mirror at this late hour. "Okay, see, that's a problem." She positioned herself directly across from Derek and leaned forward onto one elbow, close enough to be in spittle range, a risk she was willing to take to achieve eye contact. "You were under for ten hours this time. Were you in your avatar the whole time? Did you surface at all? How many thought-prints did you take?"

Few of the immersive developers at Glove Enterprises still said "going under," given that the fully immersive virtual-reality interface was a conscious process with many user-controlled checks. She wasn't surprised when Derek glared in response, either critical of her word choice or for the renewed argument.

"I didn't leave the woods for an interrogation."

Mindy knew he left "the woods" for necessary bodily functions. The unshaved, unwashed look didn't concern her nearly as much as the deep-set marks on his forehead or the bags under his eyes, lack of sleep compounded by excessive thought-prints. "You know, hunting in VR doesn't actually provide nutrients."

Derek grunted something around a mouthful that sounded like, "It should."

"You need to take breaks. Regardless of how you feel, Mr. Sarsaparilla wants us to maintain—"

"Listen, Mindy," Derek said, after a quick swallow, "if Colin had a problem with the work I was doing, he'd tell me. You're neither the boss nor my mother, so it's not your business."

As rude as the remark was, Mindy couldn't dispute its accuracy. While they'd worked side by side on several immersive VR projects in the last decade, neither had been project manager lead over the other in quite some time. In fact, since

Glove had started the InterFace-World initiative, or "IF-World," both parties had been placed in a creative-freedom think tank, which had such a good track record that no one needed middle management bosses. Outside of the basic HR guidelines, the only suggestions they had to follow were delivered by the department director, Colin Sarsaparilla, and often only when major shareholder interests were in play.

Having effectively inhaled his sandwich, Derek balled up the wrapper in one fist. "Let me ask you something—how are we doing on funding?"

"Glove Enterprises is committed to full-body immersion research."

Derek shook his head. "I'm not asking that."

They both knew their jobs weren't in jeopardy. Glove would continue to employ both programmers, no matter how lofty their dreams of IF-World grew. In fact, the loftier the better. There were rumors about steps toward long-term and even permanent interfacing on the foreseeable horizon. Consumers already spent massive chunks of their waking and sleeping lives in Glove's virtual worlds, and all projections showed growth.

"I mean our project," Derek said. "Adaptive AI in the virtual wildlife preserve. Are you one hundred percent sure they're committed to that?"

Mindy scrunched her lips together. "No."

It had been a noble effort, but with this week's report on the cost of in-world AI—not just money, but time and memory space—the board wasn't likely to vote in their favor, not when cheap NPCs and old documentary footage were so much easier.

"Right." A few unspoken truths hung in the air between them, silent as the smoggy night air outside. "Now, I have three business days 'til the proof-of-concept demonstration. Five with the weekend."

Mindy sighed. If only there were more people working on their floor after hours, someone else could try to talk sense into Derek. "You might have to let this one slide. Look, we did good work, but we can't rewrite reality. They're going to rule that bots are cheaper and move us to another project."

Derek jabbed a thumb at his own chest. "Not if I can prove Adaptive AI is worth the value."

Mindy finally unfolded her arms. She didn't say that she was working late on the same goals or that she was running feasibility projections and would keep doing so until the project was officially shut down. Instead, she tapped her knuckles on the countertop and said, "Take breaks."

Derek watched her go.

Mindy Ellwood had a few years and about six inches on him, but, like most short programmers in gray hoodies, Derek disdained being talked down to. Not when it came to high ideals and moral imperatives for wildlife preservation—and not when coworkers changed tune and started giving up.

Alone in the break room, Derek slurped down a faux-gurt supplement then took his focus meds with a concentrated energy-drink shot. He knew he exceeded dosage recommendations, but that was temporary. Besides, that wasn't the addiction Mindy was worried about.

Derek quickly sorted his recycling from compost, avoiding looking up at the window that would reflect his few-days'-old stubble and maybe even the bruises on his temples.

He strode stiffly on two legs, though four would've been more comfortable, more natural. He wound through the tight corridors to Test Room Delta and scanned his wrist device to open the door. Delta auto-illuminated with faint, blue glow strips, and the frosted gel around the LEDs provided a relaxing, wintery feel. Though the hallways on this floor were narrow, test rooms could easily fit fifteen observers to crowd around the two tanks or stare at the dozens of monitoring screens.

If allowed, Derek would install a mini fridge and locker here. Hell, he could go for a toilet and shower within two steps of the tank.

Derek pulled off his hoodie and hung it on the wall hook under the label Delta Interface Tank 1. Next were his flip-flops and undershirt. He left on the mesh shorts, which breathed a little too well and maintained little appreciable body heat. Willpower prevented Derek from shivering as he input his access code and opened the tank. Mind over matter. That was important when interfacing.

The tanks were horizontal beds, more like high-tech coffins or those oval-shaped sensory deprivation chambers. Conductive gelofoam coated the interior, ready to relay signals to muscles and nerves.

Derek slid onto the foam on his back, positioning his spine along the most sensitive receptors. He donned the visor and reached up to pull the lid of the tank closed, without checking any other settings. It could take somebody hours to configure an Interface Tank to their specific size, shape, and sensitivities. For weeks now, Derek had de facto claimed Delta Interface Tank 1. Most shared with a coworker or two—preferably of similar height and build—but nobody tried to horn in on Derek's territory anymore.

The visor supplied prompts for Derek's left eye, asking him to flex certain muscles, blink his eyelids, imagine specific shapes and colors.

"Calibration achieved," the system reported, then projected

a high-fidelity percentage. "Welcome, Derek Latimer. Do you approve full immersion, within established safety limits?"

A test, to see if he could answer it with thought, which he did.

Yes. Eagerly, consumingly, yes.

A jolt shocked the base of his skull as Derek fully synced.

Derek let his thoughts go blank, kept his eyes closed while he resettled into his new skin and fur.

The visor offered an interface, but Derek kept his eyes closed and thought the interface away. Real animals didn't need alerts or messages popping up; they didn't need to know their coordinates in a virtual plane, so neither did he. He had his other senses—sharper now than those from the body in the tank. His ears, nose, and nerves were already working overtime to once again adjust to the forest.

Before even opening his eyes, Derek shook himself off, starting with his shoulders and cascading down to his tail. His fur wasn't wet, but he needed to let it fluff and then settle on its own. The exact pattern of the fur had been programmed with understood likelihoods of how it should sit, not actualities. So whenever he emerged in IF-World, Derek shook back to what he now knew as normal. He didn't need a mirror to know how his wolf avatar appeared, the majestic gray patterns with the silver-white patch on his upper back—a mark reminiscent of family leaders from species much longer extinct than even the wolves.

The air smelled cold and metallic. Low humidity, frost on the ground. No cinematic snowfalls, but the crunching shift underfoot as pebbles unstuck themselves.

His ears perked up and ever so slightly angled forward.

Known trail, past prey, home, all within range. Derek's personalized instinct package filtered through his body—or, rather, his wolf avatar.

He began to run.

The wind pressed eyelids open, held ears erect, streamed in waves down his back, rippling toward the tip of his tail. His paws barely felt individual impact at a rolling gait, easy distribution of pressure propelling him forward. An urge manifested in his throat and filled his mouth like the beginning of a cough, but it came out as a bark. A raggedy sound, less graceful and majestic than documentary depictions but more accurate.

Derek scented and heard Diana before she emerged from their cave. Her breathing changed—programmed response, shifting from curiosity and potential alarm to a calm reception and fondness.

Diana pointed her nose at him and walked in a quarter circle but didn't trot to meet him halfway. Instead, she made a whining sound, not actually in distress but longing, waiting. Her digital directives forbade her from venturing too far from the cave these days.

Diana was built similarly to Derek but female and with many more brown striations along her fur, especially her shoulders. Derek had designed her directly from a real specimen, whose omnidirectionally recorded images were still less than a decade old and compatible with interface-generating software.

Even at immediate proximity, Derek couldn't tell Diana was a series of rendered images instead of a fur-and-blood living creature. Maybe a real arctic wolf could tell the difference—if any of them were left—but not a human observer. Diana was the most intricately programmed Adaptive AI ever created, physically and behaviorally.

Her expression made him feel guilty for even the minor absence. She licked his snout and nipped the tufts of fur on the sides of his face, then turned away to go back inside, where other voices sounded eager to greet him.

Deeper in the den were six of Derek's newest creations: AI

pups, emulated to appear about eight weeks old, but on a fast early growth rate and generated individually over only the last two weeks.

They recognized their father and rushed toward him, jumping on each other in their efforts to be the first to reach him—that was entirely emergent, not directly programmed. That was both the secret and the challenge, and his pups would never know how instrumental their growth was in saving the project.

In the den, he taught by example, and their responses and emotions seemed as real as Derek's. As far as the programmer was concerned, the only difference lay in the fact that his emotions were triggered by impulses of an organic brain. The pups, with their gray, black, and brown-speckled faces and unpredictable energy, had memory databases in InterFace-World systems. Newly learned memories impacted future decisions, which impacted experiences, new memories, and more decisions. That was the theory.

Either way, the joy they brought Derek was very real.

Without leaving his avatar, Derek had the monitoring system scan and record his current thought-print, which he knew would give his human body a headache. Fortunately, he'd muted that sensation while interfacing.

Falling asleep in the tank wasn't strange for Derek.

On Friday morning, he stumbled downstairs to the cafeteria and packed two lunches for the day before rushing back upstairs to continue working.

Many of his coworkers wore casual attire, but most had been home to change between workdays. Mindy Ellwood sported a different cardigan. The fellow next to her—Colin

Sarsaparilla—wore a tailored suit, expertly maintained silver hair, and a smile that had seen at least five-figures of fine-tuning surgery.

It wasn't a coincidence the two of them were standing in a cramped hallway near Test Room Delta.

"Mr. Latimer," Colin said in that friendly casual manner that belied his seriousness. "It sounds like you've been logging a lot of overtime without enough downtime. Are you doing okay?"

Derek gritted his teeth, biting down a comment that Glove should be happy when salaried employees put in overtime without expecting bonuses. "I'm fine. Making sure the newest intelligences are ready for review."

"That sounds all well and good, but I want to make sure. We don't want to risk you burning out."

People still said "burn out" when referring to overworked employees, but it was also a growing term for brain damage, dissociation, and paralysis from unsafe interfacing. Still, the most dangerous sensory-overload cases had involved teens stuck in high-stimulation games with constant thrill or agony. Derek had only heard of Glove employees suffering long-lasting effects from burnout years ago, before the advent of full-body immersion in Interface tanks.

The risk might have been minimal, but Colin, who handled the payroll and insurance claims, was willing to address it if given warning by a nosy coworker.

Derek avoided looking at Mindy. "Sir, I'm confident I can get back to a sustainable rhythm after the upcoming demonstration. For now, I need to make sure the AI program is supported enough to perform optimally."

"Yes, your emergent behavior experiments. Very exciting. I heard you recently programmed new Adaptive AI."

"Not exactly, sir." Derek shifted uncomfortably, knowing

that the cost of each AI generation was precisely why the wildlife preservation project was likely to go under. "Using my avatar and one previously programmed AI, I developed an algorithm to produce six viable pups, who are learning from experience rather than me—or anyone else—installing individual subroutines. They're genuine learning AI, and therefore unique personalities. Not as directly programmed but able to grow up through a life cycle."

Colin nodded. "Intriguing, Mr. Latimer. So you think this 'genuine learning' intelligence is repeatable?"

"Yes." Derek tried to stand straighter, to show more confidence than he usually felt. After all, the pups were taking on behaviors observed from their parents quite effectively, even if they weren't quite ready to demonstrate. Once properly begun, Derek believed any animal—no matter how bizarre or long-extinct—could behave like a living creature, or at least as the closest approximation humans would ever be able to experience.

"Pardon me, sir," Mindy said, literally stepping in and tightening the three-person triangle. "Not to take away from Mr. Latimer's accomplishments, but we can't prove his amount of tank time is safe. Even if we could—"

"Sir," interjected Derek, "I am confident that when shareholders or board members enter the program to run with the wolves, experience their hunts, my method will make it completely real to them. It is the kind of thing everyone has wanted to experience and will keep coming back for. But to get the project approved and funded, I need to show non-programmers that what I'm doing works. It's true that we don't have any data for this amount of interfacing, but I have a handle on it."

Colin looked between the two of them, and his gaze settled on the disheveled programmer with a growing reputation for wolf obsession.

"You only have two more business days," Colin said, with a raised eyebrow that read like the opening clause of the contract and full unspoken awareness of the coming weekend. "Then, succeed or fail, your hours return to normal."

"Yes, sir." Derek didn't imagine *normal* was accurate, but things would certainly change. Once he had proven his process, Derek would have teams of people working under him, carrying on his research with other animals, while he tended his pack in much lower stakes.

"I can get behind that. I'm willing to trust your judgment for the moment, Mr. Latimer." Colin Sarsaparilla then pivoted to Mindy, whose eyes flicked back and forth between the other two as if she were watching a ping-pong match. "Thank you, Ms. Ellwood, for raising the question. I'm inclined to aim at optimism for now. And, Mr. Latimer, I'd like to see you get paid for the overtime you're putting in. Please formally log it, and I'll make sure it's reflected in your pay." Colin bid them "Happy Friday," and left.

Derek's heart thudded in his ears.

Mindy spoke first. "Look, Derek, I'm not rooting against you. I'm just concerned."

His attempt at neutral came out brusque. "Noted."

"I'm serious; Adaptive AI is too difficult. Forget the shareholders—it's too costly for the programmers. Why do you think everyone else is backing off the project? Even you can't turn it around by yourself in this kind of time."

Derek had some choice words for those who had given up, including Mindy. Instead, he said, "I have two more business days and a weekend."

"It's not worth what you're putting yourself through."

"It is if I succeed."

Mindy's posture shifted. She stepped back, giving Derek physical unfettered access to the test room. As he passed, she said, "Be careful." Not a threat but a request for his own well-being.

Derek couldn't be dissuaded by fears or concerns.

He had won.

It didn't matter if others thought him crazy. Colin Sarsaparilla was the only vote that mattered right now, and that one vote of confidence would get him the others.

A young boy wore a puffy orange jacket and aimed a rifle that was a little too big for him. He trembled slightly as his thumb hovered over the safety, while the predator stared him right in the eye.

"Down, Derek," a soft voice said, and a much steadier hand reached forward to guide the gun down and away from the arctic wolf.

Derek's father, an older Mr. Latimer, sank to a slow crouch beside his son. Mr. Latimer had soft, gray-blue eyes that contrasted against his frequently stubbled, sharp jawbone.

Young Derek knew to take cues from those eyes and—after making sure the safety was still on—settled onto one knee. He felt the cold forest floor creep into his kneecap through the denim.

"He won't hurt us." Mr. Latimer's own gun rested easily in the crook of one arm. "We're just going to take a moment.... It's a rare treat, these days. To see one in the wild." His father let out a sad, slow exhale. "Soon, there won't be any left."

They didn't hunt anymore that day, because Mr. Latimer said they shouldn't interfere with an endangered predator's feeding ground.

Derek remembered looking back at the animal, strong and

majestic in some ways, but with a broken spirit. Had the wolf known its legacy was doomed?

The old wolf continued to watch the two humans retreat, until the bright puffy jacket was obscured by bare trees and wisps of snow.

The young pup, its head only reaching its father's knee, asked, "Why didn't we hunt them?"

The adult wolf, a silver-gray diamond on his back between the shoulder blades, replied, "Because, son, soon there won't be any of them left on the surface. They'll all be in tanks."

Derek thrashed awake, his neck sore from craning to one side against his arm, his ribs uncomfortably compressed while slumped over a desk. The dual monitors at the workstation both showed standby screens. The Delta Interface Tank lay open to his right.

He had not planned on sleeping, couldn't afford to sleep, and he began hyperventilating when he saw it was past noon. He had no active wake-up alarms on Saturdays, so his body had kept sleeping, trying to catch up, though his brain didn't want it to.

Derek had already felt horribly behind schedule, even with the pups' accelerated growth programming—which reinforced findings that developing AI was too hard.

"No!" he yelled at no one. Standing, Derek mumbled to himself, "I can still do this. I can make this work."

He had his meds and caffeine. If he limited, or eliminated, the transitions into and out of the tank, if he pre-programmed the scanners for ongoing, active thought-prints—he'd have a headache the next time he resurfaced, but they were faster than typing out reports—he might still have time.

Before he went under again, though, he had to leave the right message.

⚰

"People want what they can't have, Ms. Ellwood," Colin said, his determined face lit by frosted-blue light. "With IF-World, we make those things available. Most people have never seen an open wilderness with white snow in person. They've only seen a moose or deer in a zoo, and they have certainly never seen an arctic wolf. Not for twenty years."

"Even so ..." Mindy knew commenting on Derek's safety didn't speak to the dollar signs in Colin's head. "Even if he makes them perfect, how could a pack of wolves really make the difference? Why does it need to be now instead of ten years from now? Why not something easier or still living, like moose or eagles or endangered fish?"

"Because nobody cares about fish, Ms. Ellwood."

The comment stung, but Mindy knew Colin wasn't speaking about the real-world biosphere or the sustainability of the food chain. It wasn't even his own opinion. Just data from the masses.

"Nobody wants to spend time *as* or *with* the prey animals. If someone wants to be an eagle, it's because they want to fly, not because they care about a group eagle experience. Now, running with wolves? Ms. Ellwood, that is a top fantasy. The number one desired spirit animal or RPG animal companion is, was, and will always be a wolf. People see snow falling, they want to run on all fours, howl at the moon, and eat the damn moose side by side with real, four-legged, furry companions. Hell, *I* want to."

He turned away and paced, curling his shoulders forward

as he drew a vape pen from his jacket pocket, but he put it away again without a single drag.

"As for 'why now?' Call me cynical, but I don't know if there will be another opportunity." He gestured out the window at the smoggy, gray-orange sky. "Current shareholders still remember what it meant to go for walks in the woods. But as the outside world goes extinct and more people move inside, I don't know if the next generation's majority voters will remember enough to care.

"I was rooting for the project—still am—regardless of why people got involved. Some wanted to preserve an environment for posterity, some to honor the animals, some to one day assist in cloning and repopulating.

"I also know that thousands of consumers would pay thousands of dollars to travel with a wolf they believed was real—as real as the urban-regulation terrier they've got at home. And if Derek convinces the board it's good enough for *millions* of consumers, then the project has a shot, and everyone wins."

"Even Derek?" Mindy asked.

She turned again to the main monitor in Test Room Delta, whose standby had been programmed with a single, signed statement: *Do not wake me.*

Applause echoed through the chamber, bouncing off the shells of both Delta Interface Tanks. Tank 2 opened to reveal an elderly investor wearing a snug-fitting conductive suit and too elated to be embarrassed.

"It was real." She laughed as Colin Sarsaparilla offered a hand to help her sit up. "My God, it was real. I was a wolf, and I ran with the pack!"

Cheers and robust congratulatory remarks joined the clapping. They had just watched, on clear wallscreens or their own observer headsets, a pack of wolves, each with distinct, individual patterns and personalities, in the clean, reimagined Yukon, hunting down a moose. Six wolves were still yearlings, but led by a proud mother and father who took the head of the pack.

Nobody rooted for the moose.

"Incredible, Colin!" repeated one man with hair whiter than any of the animals. He seized and shook the boss's hand. "You say you can duplicate this level of believability?"

"Of course, with the data and methodology of pioneer Derek Latimer"—Colin gestured to the other Delta Interface Tank, still sealed shut—"we can train the initial generation of any group of animals, making them as real and recognizable as any witnessed in the wild."

Applause continued. Whether the investors were excited to build a fortune, to preserve wildlife, even in a virtual sense, or because they personally wanted to live out a childhood dream, they were all hooked.

They accepted that Mr. Latimer, author of the entire endeavor, had to be logged in before they arrived and would remain so after they left, so no one questioned when a technician crouched beside Derek's tank, plugged in a scanner, and made some adjustments.

There were more than enough tubes and wires in the room to easily mask the IV lines that kept Derek hydrated.

The investors trickled out, some to raise a glass of champagne in the break room, others to immediately spread the news.

One programmer remained in the room. She examined the available data, not of the AI's viability, but the subconscious of the human user who still controlled the lead wolf.

When the door opened behind her, she tensed but didn't turn.

"Congratulations to you too, Ms. Ellwood."

"Was it worth it?"

"People like to ask that." Colin Sarsaparilla took deliberate steps closer to Mindy but paused by the tank. "Unfortunately, the answers are quite relative. After we confirm Mr. Latimer's condition with an on-site doctor, I'm sure the shareholders will still say yes. And, though I didn't know the man as well as I'd like, I'm confident Mr. Latimer himself was very willing to make the investment."

Mindy refrained from sneering or snarling. "He shouldn't have needed to make this sacrifice."

"We can't give up yet, Ms. Ellwood. We may yet be able to revive him."

Present data said otherwise. Mindy knew that, by now, Derek's consciousness was too divorced from his human body, too scrambled by the machine, too split between multiple AI's, each repurposed thought-print a small shard of his soul.

Colin stepped directly behind Mindy, close enough to put a comforting hand on her shoulder, which she neither asked for nor welcomed. "Until then, you can carry on his work, which, it's not any stretch of the imagination to say, is what he would've wanted."

It wasn't any stretch of the imagination to say that Colin would use this opportunity to research long-term and permanent interfacing. The possibilities in the virtual world spanned ahead for Colin's daring ambition, unlocked by an ideal test subject who had signed his life to that effect. Coma patients, people physically paralyzed, the elderly, and even prisoners serving life sentences would benefit from continued studies.

Meanwhile, pieces of Derek's mind and all his research

would be available to build—and teach—artificial intelligences for other high-demand animals.

"Do you like horses, Ms. Ellwood?" Colin asked.

Derek shook himself from shoulders to tail, the tremor along his body fluffing his fur before it settled again. As he shed the water drops to avoid taking them into the warm, dry den, he had a vague memory of a similar shake during another kind of entrance.

An affectionate whine from within, however, pulled his attention. Happily, he trotted toward the smell of his mate, Diana, and the excited noises of their new pups, while six yearlings continued to drag their fresh kill toward the den behind him.

MIKE JACK STOUMBOS is an author and educator, best known for his space opera novel series, This Fine Crew. He is a first-place winner of the Writers of the Future contest with a story in Volume 38, alongside the late David Farland. Mike Jack's first professional fiction publication appeared in the *Dragon Writers* anthology, which also featured a story by Farland, and it was through this community that Mike Jack got started as a science fiction author. He continues to teach writing craft and mindset workshops for aspiring authors.

You can find him at MikeJackStoumbos.com or @MJStoumbos on Twitter.

The Journey Within
William Joseph Roberts

It was just another useless battle in an already pointless war. I hate to admit it, but my father was right. The bickering and gerrymandering of old-world politics was no place for Americans. But here I was. A sergeant of the British Second Division under the command of Brigadier General Pennefather, thousands of miles from home in the middle of the Crimean War.

I admit now that the level of stupidity I will go to out of sheer spite and stubbornness is a personal flaw that has on occasion landed me in less than desirable situations. The consequences of my previous encounters paled in comparison to this one, even when combined.

If my father, Thaddeus Blackmoore, had had the opportunity to lecture me before my departure, I was sure I would have been as unresponsive as a log. His lecture would have undoubtedly consisted of phrases such as, *"You have your own affairs to attend to here at home, Caleb,"* or *"Why do you insist on needlessly risking your life?"*

As with the rest of my brothers-in-arms, I was cold, hungry, and beyond exhausted when our new orders were announced. Without so much as a hot meal, we'd marched hard to claim and establish an outpost on Home Ridge. Shortly thereafter, on Pennefather's orders, we fixed bayonets and marched blindly downhill through fog so thick you could barely see the man in front of you. The only good thing about the situation was the glowing hint of dawn to the east.

Sergeant Samuel Bowthorpe, the one individual in this entire war I considered a friend, marched shoulder to shoulder with me as we charged into oblivion.

Gunfire resounded, and a flash of light illuminated the fog to our right. Cannons roared to life from the ridge opposite us, briefly lighting the top of Shell Hill, where it had been rumored the Russian heavy artillery was positioned. It looked like the intelligence was correct after all.

"Glory and honor be with us in our hour of need," Samuel said before quickly kissing the cross pendant he wore around his neck and placing it against his forehead. "Blessed be the Father Almighty," he whispered, then tucked the cross back into his shirt.

I grunted a laugh. There was no glory or honor in this war. It was a war of semantics and pride.

A musket ball sizzled between the two of us past my right ear.

I crouched low, continuing downhill. "You can keep your glory and honor, Samuel. I just want to survive this idiocy long enough to return home."

On our left, numerous muskets fired in succession into what I assumed was the enemy line. Flashes of fire erupted sporadically, illuminating the heavy fog in such a discordant pattern that my stomach began to churn.

Samuel stopped, throwing his arm wide to halt my movement, then crouched low. "Ready yourself, my friend."

I knelt beside him as he shouldered his rifle.

A branch cracked ahead.

"Our moment of honor is upon us, Caleb," he whispered, then pulled the trigger. The percussion lock of his issued Minié rifle struck and ignited the charge. The conflagration radiated throughout the surrounding fog for a brief moment, highlighting the shadowy forms of the enemy ahead.

Samuel roared and charged forward toward the nearest man-shaped shadow. His bayonet sank deep into Russian flesh.

I followed close behind.

Another Russian appeared to his left and fired almost point-blank into Samuel's chest. Following his fall to the ground, the Russian buried his bayonet deep into my friend's neck.

I fired and charged forward. Swinging my rifle like a club, I knocked the Russian's blood-soaked bayonet away before he could bring it to bear on me. Drawing down my rifle as if it were a great spear, I leapt forward and plunged my bayonet into the Russian's chest. The soldier's heavy winter coat put up little resistance.

Two more quick thrusts, and the stunned Russian slumped backward.

From the chilly shroud of fog, the rifled bore of a barrel appeared, guided by the unsteady hands of a young Russian soldier.

I dove to the left.

He fired.

The hot musket ball seared flesh, tearing through my left side. The pain of the wound cut through me like lightning. Sulfurous infusions of spent powder blanketed my senses, burning my eyes and nostrils.

The young soldier's eyes went wide when I roared and charged at him.

He stumbled backward, tripping as he backpedaled down-hill. The tip of my bayonet had barely grazed the young soldier's woolen coat when it was knocked away by the butt of another rifle.

Bringing my own rifle around, I swung blindly in the direction of my new assailant. The force of the swing pulled at my wound. I felt the popping of broken ribs and doubled over in pain.

My new attacker fully emerged from the fog.

He towered over me. Even in the dim light of dawn, I could make out the heavy muscles beneath his thick winter coat. With a mighty sweep of his Cossack sabre, he sent my rifle soaring out of my hands as I thrust forward in attack.

Drawing my Colt Dragoon revolver, I cocked the hammer and fired into the Russian's torso. He stopped, taking a slight step back. Confused anger danced across the dark lines of his heavily bearded face.

I caught a glimpse of the young soldier staring up at the larger man, stunned by the large Russian's ferocity. Once the young soldier saw my notice, he began to scramble away. I cocked the hammer again and fired at him before he could escape or retaliate.

A heavy boot brought my hand and pistol to the ground. The massive Russian smiled down at me. A coppery scent tinged the air.

I stared down at the beautifully etched curves of the Cossack sword that had found its way into my midsection.

The large Russian muttered something under his breath in his mother tongue, a prayer I could not comprehend.

He jerked the blade free and stepped over to straddle me. Gripping the blade with both hands, he drew it above his head, ready to strike the killing blow.

"We like our blades just as much in Kentucky," I said.

Drawing the Bowie fighting knife strapped to my left thigh, I sliced the back of the Russian's right knee.

He collapsed on top of me, driving the tip of his sabre into the earth beside me.

The blade of my Bowie bit deep into his side.

Blood-tinged curses filled the air as the Russian struggled for advantage. Shifting himself, his massive hands locked around my throat.

Darkness encroached at the edges of my vision. My lungs burned, screaming for the slightest breath.

Over and over again, I drove my blade deep into his side.

The large Russian reared back, pulling me off the ground as he let out a bestial roar that echoed across the valley. Again, I drove the blade deep into his torso, desperation fueling my efforts.

Perhaps it was the excitement of the moment or just the imagination of a dying man, but when I blinked, fighting against the onrush of unconsciousness, I saw his thick black beard transform into fluffy white fur.

Feline features rose and fell, rippling across the Russian's face. His eyes shifted, spreading wider, taking on the gleam of a cat's eye. Whiskers sprouted around his nose, and fangs grew in his mouth.

He rose up and let out another roar. Paws, not hands, slipped away from my throat.

I could breathe again.

The great Siberian tiger struck, sinking its teeth deep into my right shoulder.

I thrust my blade into the beast's neck and sawed upward, striking the tiger's spine as I worked the blade. It convulsed, biting deeper, almost chewing before it exhaled and its massive girth went limp, blanketing me.

Its warmth permeated my cold flesh even as I fought

against the exhaustion and loss of blood from my own wounds. Pain became as irrelevant as time, as both ceased to exist at this precipice of reality.

Whispered prayers hung in seemingly silent verse. Man-shaped shadows grew closer between each stilted breath, shifting through the foggy morning light. Pleading cries of wounded men drifted over the valley, some barely audible over the constant din of distant gunfire. One of the shadow men loomed over me. Between forced breaths, I watched it move along the edges of the darkness, examining me.

A calm, fatherly voice spoke. I could not understand the words, though they eased me. The tone of the voice was kind and caring.

I felt as if I had been lifted from the mortal confines of my body. Warmth enveloped me, and the frigid bite of winter lessened, the pain of war fading to a long distant memory. I thought the Almighty Himself had come to bring me home.

Pain engulfed me, pulsing with each beat of my heart.

"You are one of the lucky ones," said a voice from the darkness. Her tone was kind, even if laced with a harsh Slavic accent.

"There will no doubt be scarring," she said, "but that is to be expected with war, is it not?" She let out a knowing grunt under her breath.

Soothing coolness dabbed at my face.

"Can you tell me your name?"

I opened my eyes. Bright light streamed in through two

arched windows set in a stone wall. The hand-blown glass set into each portal distorted the clarity of the world beyond with ripples and waves of color.

A comely young woman sat on a stool beside the bed I lay on. She wore her dark hair in a double braid pulled to one side and decorated with small sunflowers along its length. Her gaze held aspects of both innocent curiosity and matronly scorn. She swirled a cloth about in a large bowl of melting snow, then wrung it out. The trickle of water into the basin resonated within the small stone room like groundwater seepage in a cavern.

"Have you forgotten your name?" That matronly glare rose to the forefront of her visage as she dabbed the cloth across my face and neck again.

"Caleb," I said hoarsely.

She compacted a small amount of melting snow and placed it against my lips. I raised up and suckled slowly at the offered comfort before laying my head back on the pillow.

"Both I and my dry throat thank you, mistress."

She let out another knowing grunt with a nod and wrung out the cloth.

"How long have I been here?"

"Little more than a week," she replied. "We thought for sure the fever would take you as it has so many others." She continued to dab at my face. "Father David said he'd heard you call out to the Almighty and found you already in the grip of the fever. I'm sure that if you hadn't called out, he'd have left you for the crows."

"I am blessed and thankful that he did not." I smiled, then forced myself up onto my elbows to more properly address her. I grunted as pain shot through my shoulder and side. My shirt was missing, replaced by bandages. That look of matronly scorn returned. "And whom do I have the pleasure of thanking for such tender care? Surely only a goddess could bring me back from death's doorstep."

She looked away, the slightest hint of a smile appeared at the edges of her lips, disrupting her stern gaze. Color climbed her neck, turning her small pale ears pink.

"I am Kateryna," she said matter-of-factly through her blushing smile.

"Kateryna," I said in a whisper. "Such a pretty name for a pretty lady."

I glanced around the small room. It was cozy and simple. Cut and mortared stones made up the floor and walls, with the afore-mentioned windows set into the stonework being the most interesting things about the room. Otherwise, a small shelf with a candle occupied the wall beside a closed wooden door. The bed that I lay upon made up the majority of furniture in the room, accompanied by the chair that Kateryna occupied and a simple bedside table.

"Where am I?"

"You are in the Saint Clement monastery near the village of Inkerman."

She packed another small portion of snow for me and placed it against my lips, which I gladly accepted.

My head swam. A flush of heat washed over me. Feeling my stomach begin to churn, I lowered myself and laid my head back against the pillow. Perspiration rose in beads and ran down the sides of my face.

Kateryna wrung out the cloth once more then dabbed it across my face. "I am afraid your fever is worse than when you arrived." She pulled back the bandages on my right shoulder and winced. The overwhelming scent of fetid flesh assaulted my senses.

Folding the pus-covered dressing, she pressed the clean side against my shoulder. Pain shot down my arm to the tips of my fingers. The muscles of my arm involuntarily flexed and contracted. Heat radiated up my neck and across the right side of my face.

"Blahoslovenna maty Mariya," Kateryna whispered under her breath. She stood and shouted "Otche! Otche, Davyd!" before sprinting from the room.

Sharp, stabbing pain raced across the side of my head. My right eye throbbed, and my vision distorted, skewed of clarity and color. My arm jerked again, the muscles contracting with more force than I imagined possible. I tried to flex and stretch my hand to relieve the cramping, but it curled, nearly doubling over to touch my forearm. Veins bulged along the back of my hand. My flesh pulsed and contorted, taking on a new shape. Patches of thick black fur sprouted then receded, shifting to gray, then a fox-like red.

"Nekhay Boh pomyluye vashu dushu," a voice said in a panicked whisper.

My vision swam as I turned to look in the direction of the voice. In the doorway stood a gray-haired man dressed in the simple woolen robes of a monk.

Clutching at his rosary, he approached and gently took my hand in his before lowering himself into the chair beside my bed. He examined the transmogrifying appendage as it shifted color, shape, and texture. His focus moved from my hand to my face, staring at me for a long moment. His piercing blue gaze held a calm, almost serene quality to it.

"English?"

I nodded through another spasm that ran down my right side into my leg.

"Kateryna," he said calmly, continuing his assessment. "Please retrieve the kit bag from my quarters."

Fighting through the pain, I gasped for breath.

"Yes, Father David," the girl said before she disappeared into the darkness beyond the doorway.

"Try to relax, my son. Take slow, even breaths when you can."

"What is happening to me, Father?" I asked through gritted teeth.

He looked away from my wounds and drew in a slow, contemplative breath.

The pain subsided long enough for me to catch my breath. "Am I dying?"

He patted the back of my changed hand and laid it across my chest. "Tell me, my son. Did you see anything strange or out of the ordinary during the battle?" He cleared his throat and glanced uncomfortably about the room, as if searching his memory for the right words. "Something perhaps ... supernatural?"

My expression only must have confirmed his suspicions because he nodded then turned in his seat and yelled down the corridor. I recognized Kateryna's name, but nothing else.

Fire suddenly lit every fiber in my being. My muscles contracted and contorted against my will.

Father David crossed himself and prayed in a low whisper, "Protect and deliver us from evil."

Kateryna reappeared with a leather-wrapped bundle in hand which she immediately passed off to Father David then removed the bowl of melting snow.

Father David unfurled the bundle on the side table, revealing a number of vials and instruments I had seen in a number of surgeon's kits, as well as the oddities of a wooden stake, a compact wheel lock pistol, and a powder flask. He removed a small glass vial and, after pulling out the small cork, sniffed at the contents.

"Drink this down, my son," he said, placing the vial to my lips.

I drank back the bitter concoction as instructed and coughed, choking on the awful flavor.

"What is that?" I shook my head as if to dispel the lingering taste. "Please, Father, for the love of all that is holy, kill me first before inflicting that upon me again."

Father David let out a brief laugh. "Laudanum. It will help take the edge off the transformation."

I shook my head in confusion. "Transformation? What do you mean, Father?"

With a nervous smile toward me, he turned to Kateryna and took her hand in his. "You may go, my child. Please, bar the door behind yourself. You and the others know what to do should he become more than I can manage."

Kateryna nodded, gave me a concerned glance, then left the room, closing the door as instructed.

Father David looked back to me, then to the wheel lock pistol. With practiced ease, he uncorked the powder flask and poured a measure into the pistol. After replacing the flask, he retrieved a large caliber ball that gleamed silver in the room's limited light. He dropped it into the end of the barrel with a wadding material and ramrodded it home.

Setting the pistol to the side, he examined my shoulder and nodded, grunting under his breath. "I fear that this"—he poked at my wound—"is the result of an encounter with a Wilkołak. An individual who has been attacked by one carries the curse of the beast."

Spasms raced across my shoulder where he pressed against my skin.

He quickly grabbed a leather bit from his bundle and held it to my mouth between his thumb and forefinger. "Bite down, my son. It will help with the pain of the transformation."

I did as he instructed and was almost immediately struck by the pain of a full-body convulsion.

Father David held my hand between both of his and said a quiet prayer. "The only advice I can truly offer is to say that you cannot fight off this affliction."

"What is happening to me, Father?" I mumbled around the bit.

"Transformation, my son."

"I don't understand—" Another bout of seizures struck me. Flashes of light and dark raced through my mind's eye. Visions of desert cliffs, forests, swamps, and snow-covered tundra invaded my memories as if they were my own, yet they remained foreign and unfamiliar to me.

"The curse of the Wilkołak is to either become the eternal beast or to become one with your spiritual reflection of the beast. It does not matter what sort of beast or beast-man inflicted your wounds. That is only the transmission of the curse. What matters is what beast is an inner reflection of yourself. The transformation will cause the manifestation of this reflection.

"In the end, it will either consume you, and you will become the beast, or you will learn to master it as with anything else one may do in life. But you must truly want such mastery. You must pursue it as with any passion, wholeheartedly and to the fullest extent of your abilities."

Father David released my hand and pulled back the sleeve of his robe. His arm and hand transmuted from pale pink flesh to a heavily muscled forearm and massive paw covered in thick brown fur. He smiled and let out a lighthearted chuckle.

"Trust me. I have been down this path as well."

Muscle spasms erupted, and pain rippled throughout my being. My extremities burned as if they had been too close to an open flame. My vision flashed in and out of existence, shifting colors. Shadows tunnel-visioned in front of me.

Father David gripped my hand and held it so both it and his face were within my narrow view.

"Focus on your inner self and the sound of my voice," he softly directed. "Focus on those aspects of your being that are most important to you. Those things that you inherently put into everything you do."

My flesh mutated, shifting from skin to feather, from fur to scales, and back. New sensations pummeled my senses, overwhelming me. Flushes of fevered sweat trickled down to soak into the bedsheets. Sharp pricks of frostbitten pain threatened to consume me.

My mind pulsed with new images and sensations.

"Remember, you have to want, heart and soul, to achieve your goal." Father David's haunting voice felt like a dream.

It felt as if my entire being had suddenly dissolved into nothing and dissipated among the stars.

"This is not an easy path to take, my son. Only those truly committed to the goal may succeed."

Writhing in the cursed throws of change as I was, Father David's words were calm and reassuring like a minuscule beacon in the dark chaos of eternity.

"You cannot take this on with half-measures," Father David continued. "Focus on what matters most to you, on what makes you who you are. That is how I was able to survive the curse. My brothers were not so lucky."

The tumult of colors and forms began to coalesce. Familiar figures emerged, taking shape from the storm of unrealized ideas surrounding me. First my father, Thaddeus Blackmoore, then members of the Cherokee tribe my father rescued, giving them sanctuary on the estate. Other members of the extended family appeared—young, old, still living, and those who had passed away long ago.

Family. My family. Being there for them in their time of need. Taking care of those who relied on me. That was my driving force. To help those who couldn't help themselves. Just as my father had always done, and his father before him.

To care for others, nurture them, and guide them onto their own paths. I'd never thought of that as being my passion or fuel for life, until now. Standing there, the whole of my extended family staring back at me, the warm, comforting sensation of home engulfed me.

One by one, the faces and forms faded away into a misty fog that replaced the chaos of visions, encapsulating me.

Calm silence settled over my small gray bubble of existence. The turbid clouds thickened, their chaos smoothed into a laminar flow as if I were at the center of a vortex and the dark infinity of the universe loomed overhead. My breaths came in long, controlled pulses.

I steadied myself, focusing on the calm ripples forming in the clouds with each exhalation. Two slow, lingering swirls hung ahead of me. They changed, shifting from idea to reality in a brief moment of thought.

Two fierce yellow eyes stared back at me. They moved and swayed with the cadence of a protective hunter. From the wall of unimagined reality the form emerged, and a large red wolf stood before me. I could feel those yellow eyes on me, judging me, as if weighing my soul against a lifetime of actions and deeds.

Its intense gaze drew my focus. I could hear the calm beat of its heart, the steady rhythm of each breath. Those eyes, ever vigilant, were alert, but tired. The burden of the protector settled on me. The anxiety of the position was a sudden weight on my heart.

"The spirit of protection has found you worthy, I see," Father David said, chuckling.

At the sound of the Father's words, the misty darkness beyond those yellow eyes thinned, revealing the old man's form. His features were bright, sharper than they had seemed before. Instead of looking up at him from the flat of my back, we were nearly at eye level with one another. He still sat on the chair by my bed.

I sat back on my haunches, staring at the old priest. His features were sharp with a distinguished presence about him. His eyes glowed with a primal fire.

A feral rage for dominance welled up within me. I craved to sink my teeth deep into flesh, to taste blood on my lips. I licked them and let out a low growl.

The old man would do.

He curiously stared at me, unmoving. "Congratulations, my son." Father David smiled wide. "The worst of it is over. You have survived the transformation, but now you must decide, and decide quickly, where your place will be. Know that if you give in to the beast, you will remain a beast for the rest of your days. If you stay the course and focus on what you hold most dear, you can push through these urges and achieve your goal. You can once again walk among the world of men."

I stared at him for a long moment. That nurturing look in his eyes reminded me of my grandfather; he was welcoming, willing to help anyone on their path, whatever it may be. Father David's features slowly dulled. He once again looked like the warm, compassionate individual who had sat at my side to care for me. His eyes lost that feral gleam. The sharp-edged tone of his voice smoothed to that of a watchful grandfather. Besides a dull ache that lingered from my transformation, I felt nearly myself again.

Father David chuckled. A caring smile flashed across his

face. "I am glad that you have chosen to return to yourself, but you still have much to learn about this curse," he said, guiding me to lay back on the bed. He hummed a soothing tune as he tucked me in, as a father would to calm a child after a nightmare. "It will take much time to learn to live side by side with your other self."

My eyes grew heavy at his soothing tone. I yawned and stretched. He patted the back of my hand as he stood. "I will guide you through this next stage of your journey. There is a balance that must be struck, and I will teach you all that I know. But for now, rest, my son. Your journey has only begun."

In a previous lifetime, WILLIAM JOSEPH ROBERTS was an F-15 mechanic and Staff Sergeant in the United States Air Force.

Since his enlistment ended, he has pursued careers as an industrial and architectural designer, design engineer, eclectic writer of science fiction, fantasy, and post-apocalyptic stories. He is the lead publisher/editor with Three Ravens Publishing.

William Joseph Roberts currently resides in the quaint southern town of Chickamauga, Georgia, with his loving wife, three freaky-smart nerd children, and a small pack of fur babies.

Of Wolves and Wives
Mel Todd

There was no smoke rising from the chimney to welcome him home as Divad approached the small cottage. Perhaps Helia had gotten busy and forgot dinner again. It happened when his wife was entranced with a new project. Divad shrugged and headed in.

"Helia, I'm home," he called out as he stepped through the door. Their cozy, three-room thatched cottage wasn't fancy and proved he wasn't a high-ranking wizard, but it kept them safe and warm. What more could they ask for?

He pulled off his wizard robes, the animals embroidered along the hem identifying his magic, and hung them by the door. Helia hated having her den out of order, and he liked to make her happy. The heather he'd brought with him would help brighten her day. She loved the smell and the flower.

"Helia?" he called out again as he set the flowers on the table. Usually she was home this time of day.

A whimper came from the back bedroom, and he headed there, his leather shoes quiet on their wooden floor. Divad pushed open the door to find an empty room. Frowning, he looked around and was about to step out when a scared whimper caught his attention. He kneeled and peered under the bed. His wife was curled up in a tight ball, her blue dress almost black in the shadows.

"Helia, what are you doing?" His voice held a hint of laughter. She would never be like human women, but her actions always made sense when viewed through her experiences.

Her head jerked up, and amber eyes latched onto his. "Divad!" She scrambled from beneath their bed. The blanket she'd made while learning to sew covered the mattress with colors of the forest. With a cry of relief, she slammed into him, trembling.

"My dearest, what is wrong?" He held her tight and petted her hair with soft strokes, something that always soothed her when societal rules confused her.

"I couldn't get out. They trapped me. There were no openings to let me out," she stammered, holding on to him so tight he thought he heard his bones creak.

Confused, he looked at the door and the shuttered window. "The door was right there."

She looked up, amber eyes dark with worry, and shook her head. "It was gone. I couldn't get out."

Something seemed off, but then other wizards or sprites— even fae—could play mean tricks. "I'll ward the house. Are you ready for dinner?"

"Dinner!" She sprang up and rushed to the stove, lifting the lid off the pot sitting on it. "Fire, take it. It didn't cook because the fire went out. We are having cold bread and meat today," she muttered, looking up at him with sorrow.

"How long were you trapped?" he asked slowly. The stove normally stayed stoked all day as long as it was fed wood, but then the chimney had been smokeless.

She glanced up at the sky. "Since the sun was not yet at its height." She wrapped her long, strong arms around her stomach. "I don't remember why I went in there." She glanced back at the bedroom, eyes dark with wariness.

"Do not worry, my heart. Bread and meat sounds delicious."

He watched her the rest of the evening as they ate and talked about his day; he spent most of his time tending various animals and working to convince wild animals to not invade gardens. Talking to an animal didn't carry much prestige—or pay very well—but it was consistent money and goods.

The next few days, he relaxed as Helia seemed to return to her normal smiling self, delighting in the oddness that was life. They walked into town on market day, looking at various items up for offer, the bright colors catching her eye. She always wanted to see what colors were popular to work on dyes to match them.

"Divad, Helia," a friendly voice called out, and Divad turned to see Nevik walking toward them, his staff shining. A master wizard, he traveled through their small town on occasion and would often stay for dinner. It was a delight to talk to another wizard, and over the years, he had become a dear friend.

"Nevik, how are you this day?" Divad started to say more when he felt a tug at his robes. He turned to see Helia hiding behind him, a wild look in her eyes. "Helia, what's wrong?"

"Who is that? Is he a hunter? We should run." Her eyes were wild, and she was breathing fast, nearly panting, her body tense, ready to flee.

"This is Nevik," he said slowly, icy worry climbing his throat. "He has been our friend for years. He had dinner with us a few months ago." Divad left it that. He did not mention that Nevik had eaten with them four or five times a year for decades. Or that Nevik had been at their wedding.

She shook her head, looking at him. "He has demon eyes. We need to run."

"Helia!" he snapped, glancing back at his friend in worry. Nevik had been born with one blue eye and one brown—a sign of his magic—but it was a sensitive topic for him. But there was no anger on his face, just concern.

"I'll let you two be. I'll swing by later?"

Divad nodded abstractly, staring at Helia, who whispered, "I need to go home. Too exposed here. Too many hunters."

"Yes, my heart," he murmured and led her home.

She relaxed once she was back in the house she had slowly created and molded over the years. The joy she'd found in learning how to do things like humans did made her creations even more precious to him.

"How do you feel now?"

"I am fine. I don't know why I was so upset. There are no hunters here, and even if there were, why would they hunt me?" She wandered over to the stove and stood looking at it.

"They wouldn't. What is wrong?" He moved closer, trying to figure out what she was looking at.

"What is that?"

Divad scanned the oven, trying to figure out what she was referring to.

She frowned and poked at the kettle. The one they had bought four years ago. The one she used almost daily.

"This?" he asked, his mouth dry. "It's a kettle. We use it to heat up water."

"Hot water. I like that." She wandered around their house, and for a moment, it felt like the years vanished and it was back to the days after she had changed into a human. Asking what everything was, how you used it. Back when she was shifting from a wild creature he cared for to the woman he didn't know how to live without.

"Helia, why don't you lay down? I'll get dinner ready." Fear battled to control his voice, but he kept it calm. Years of dealing with animals had taught him how to control his tone.

"Nap. Yes," she murmured and wandered into the bedroom, shutting the door.

Divad stood there, staring at the door. His chest ached, and eyes burned, but he turned and started a simple stew. He slipped the bread that she had made that morning into the oven.

A low whistle caught his attention, and he stepped outside to see Nevik standing by a tree a little way from their cottage.

"I didn't want to startle her by knocking. How is she?" he asked, his voice low. Divad had left the door open; shutting it made too much noise.

"She didn't know what a kettle was when we returned." Divad leaned his head against the bark of the tree, the roughness biting into his forehead. It had been a long time since he'd felt so useless. "What is going on?"

"Have you scanned her for curses or poisons? There are some that could cause this." Nevik's voice was hesitant, unsure.

"I'm an animal mage, remember? I can't do that. Can you?"

Nevik nodded. "But I'll need to see her."

Divad straightened. "I'll take care of it. Come in." His voice held the hard note of someone doing something unpleasant. And this would be.

He walked in, trying to keep his stride casual. Helia had always been very sensitive to body language. He knocked on the bedroom door, then pushed it open.

She lifted her head to look at him. For a minute, he remembered the young woman she had been. When he'd finally given in to her pleas to change her to human. He'd been so sure it would end in heartache. He'd never imagined the years of joy and love that had transpired from that moment of weakness.

Divad's hand shook as he petted her hair, the rich color reminding him of the pelt she once wore. "Helia, I need you to come talk to someone."

It took Helia a moment, then a smile bloomed across her face. "Of course. Is it Nevik? Would he like to stay for dinner?" She made as if to get up. His heart eased. Maybe it was a temporary thing. People sometimes got brainstorms that created holes in their memory for a while. He'd have thought she was too young for that, but he'd seen stranger.

Nevik walked into the room as Divad sat, holding her hand. "Ready? He's just going to make sure no one cast something on you as revenge."

She nodded. People didn't always like his answers, or assumed his magic was greater than it was, and people had lashed out before. He squeezed her hand, smiling at her as he thought through his magic.

Had he done this? Was there a spell he'd tried that might have come back on her? He wasn't much of a wizard; the spell to shift her from wolf to human had taken almost all of his magic, then cost him a week of recovery.

He smiled and squeezed her hand. It had been worth it. He couldn't have imagined how well she fit into his life or how empty it would have been without her.

The chanting ceased, and he looked up at Nevik, who shook his head slightly. Divad fought not to sigh. A curse or a hex would have been something he could fix. Maybe poison? He'd have to ask the animals around the house if there was anything amiss.

"Would you check on the stew for us, my heart? I think the flatbread is ready."

"Of course. Are you staying, Nevik? We haven't seen you in so long." She rose as she talked, her body still strong and lithe even though she had spent thirty seasons with him.

"Not this time. Though I thank you for the offer. Though if Divad will walk me to the lane?"

"Do stop by and see us next time? I'll try to make some blackberry preserves for you later this year."

Nevik nodded and waved as he and Divad walked down the path from the small cottage. The sun was setting, and in the distance, the soft sound of a wolf echoed over the hills. The sound used to make him smile, but now Divad frowned in worry.

"There was nothing on her. I don't know why she is having these attacks. Have there been more?"

Divad explained how he'd found her "trapped" in the bedroom, and Nevik looked at him with worry. "I was going to stay for a day or two, but I think I shall continue to the king's seat and avail myself of the wizards at the Tower. Perhaps one of them might have helpful information."

Divad fought to keep his knees from buckling. Was he relieved or devastated? He had no idea. But it meant that door had been closed. What was this? Poison, disease, sickness? What was wrong with his wife?

"Thank you. Anything you need to do that?"

Nevik paused. "Could I get some of her hair—fresh? It would help those who might research it."

Divad nodded. "Yes, one moment." He headed back in and found Helia at the fireplace, stirring food in the pot. "Dearest, may I have a few strands of hair?"

She cast him a bemused look, so familiar every time she ran into something new and weird from humans. "If you wish."

He tugged three strands loose from her thick hair, ignoring the flicker of confusion on her face as he pressed a kiss to her cheek. "I'll be back in a moment."

With that, he headed back out the door to Nevik and handed him the strands of hair. "I'm still hoping this is fixable."

But the fear niggling at the back of his mind wouldn't be assuaged.

"Me too. I'll let you know." Nevik looked toward the house, and his face became serious, worried. "Go. Love her. You never know how much time you have left." With a swirl of his cloak he was gone, leaving Divad standing alone with his heart wrapped in brambles.

Divad turned to go back to the cottage, only to see Helia standing in the open doorway, a stricken look on her face. He quickened his pace to reach her.

"What's wrong?" he asked as he got closer.

"Did I do something wrong? I seem to remember ..." She trailed off and looked around, her brows furrowed.

Bittersweet pain slashed at his heart. The question was so like what she had asked when first in the world of humans. But this ... this was worse.

"Nothing at all, my wild one." He tilted her face up and dropped a kiss on her lips. "I think you're just sick."

A sigh escaped her. "Oh, good. So I'll get better and remember." She paused, biting her lip, then leaned close to him and whispered, "What is that big tub in the corner for? Do we cook with it?"

Divad wanted to close his eyes as he felt a part of his heart die, but he smiled instead. "No. It is where we take baths. Would you like one?"

"Ew, get all wet and cold? That sounds very unpleasant." Her nose wrinkled up, and she pulled back, frowning at him.

A laugh forced its way out of him. That had been her comment the first time, so many years ago, when he'd tried to convince her she reeked. At least this repeat would be fun.

"Do you trust me?"

A wary look caused a lump of fear to lodge in his throat, then a slow nod. "Yes?"

"Come on. Let me show you."

After dinner, with lots of reassurance, Divad carefully introduced her to the wonders of a hot bath. Charms on the tub let him fill it with water from the well and heat it. Her laughter and amazement brought smiles and tears to his eyes. He fought down one, not the other.

Every day when he left for work, he reminded her he'd be home at dusk. She would smile, sometimes with love, sometimes with confusion.

He only worked at what had to be done—contracted jobs, routine ones—and put off anything not an actual emergency. The rest of his time he spent seeking a cure, or at least an idea as to what had happened to his wife. He visited witches, mages, wizards, seers. Anyone with even a wisp of power he asked, begged them, for help. They tried, but none had any answers.

Each evening, he approached home with a mix of joy and fear. On good days, she was laughing and smiling, food was ready, and she'd worked on her sought-after dyes. Her forest skills knew no parallel, and she could find the herbs and plants to create bright, vibrant, colorful dyes that lasted years. Her goal had been to find a red so rich it looked like blood that didn't run or fade.

On bad days, the stove was cold, the provisions chewed on, and he'd find her in a room with wild, fearful eyes. Those days he read to her of kings and dragons, of the gods and land. Slowly she would calm down, and they would sleep with her wrapped around him, holding onto him for life. His arms were just as tight around her as he tried to hold onto the woman he loved.

Then one day he came home and found her naked under the bed, snarling and snapping at him like a cornered wolf.

"Helia?" His voice shook as he kneeled beside the bed, staring into amber eyes that showed no awareness of him.

The low, inhuman sound that rose from her throat didn't scare him, but it shattered his heart, and he bowed to inevitability. There was no cure. He couldn't fix her. Piece by piece, he was losing the woman he loved. His chest hurt, and a stab of pain raced down his left side as he fought his grief.

"I'll be back, my love."

Reluctantly he rose to his feet, ignoring the growls from under the bed. He brought in chucks of seared meat and cold water, then shut the door behind him.

Divad ate a cold dinner, waiting until the sun had disappeared and the moon shed her silvery light across the land. He pulled on his cloak and, after triple-checking the fire was banked, he set out to a glade they had visited often through the decades.

Once there, he tilted his head back and howled, a long, sad sound that echoed across the mountains and down the little valley. Then he sat down to wait. He tried not to fret about Helia being alone.

The moon had barely moved when there was an answering series of howls that came back, sharper and stronger than his, a chorus of many voices.

Silvery moonlight rippled across the land as wolves streamed through the trees, racing toward him. Divad exposed his neck as the largest of them approached him. The wolf's shoulders would have met Divad's waist had the man been standing.

A low growl, ending in a yip and sniff. "You called? Where is Helia? I do not see my sister."

Pushing through the grief and worry, Divad lowered his head. "She is not well. That is why I came. I must beg help for your sister." For all that Bartok, the leader of this pack, had approved of Helia's request to leave and become human, she would always be his sister, never Divad's mate.

The wolf sat back as the others of the pack paced around them in a large circle. Divad could see Bartok's mate, his cubs, and others he had met over the years.

"What is wrong?" the wolf asked.

Each word he spoke felt like a stab to the heart and a betrayal. "Helia is losing her ability to interact with humans. Today, she couldn't remember how to speak to me."

Bartok tilted his head then turned to look behind to the gathered pack. "Bring Tyria." There was a ruffle through the pack, then a young wolf with light-blue eyes came forward. Her ears were down, and her tail tucked between her legs.

"Yes, alpha?" They weren't words, but to Divad, they might as well have been. For him, the language was rich and complex, more than those who slaughtered the wolves would ever guess. Until lately, he'd always loved his magic. Now he hated that it was useless in helping Helia.

"Search the songs. Is there anything about Helia's choice and consequences?"

The young wolf's ears flicked up, and she sat back, a low crooning rising from her throat, the tone changing up and down. Divad listened as she sped through all the songs she knew, passed down from song keeper to song keeper.

As the other wolves darted off to hunt, explore, or just race through the woods, Divad watched the moon and wondered if he'd get to sit beneath its light with Helia one more time.

"There is one," the young wolf spoke, startling Divad, who had slipped into a light trance. "It is very old and much has been lost."

"Speak," Bartok ordered.

Tyria straightened and began to sing.

Human skin is thin, though fingers nimble.
Speech to all, but not the people.

Worlds explore, but time is fleeting.
Two-legs' minds are wild and dangerous
Too soon will your soul retreat
Two-legs best as prey, for tongue
Will fade, then back the wolf comes.

Divad bent his head, allowing the tears that welled in his eyes to fall.

"You had your time. We will take her back." Bartok stood in front of him, not as an enemy, but also not a friend.

"Will you? Will you protect her? Remind her of who I am? Keep her healthy?" Divad wanted to beg, plead for any other option, but he had feared this ending all along. Animals didn't make good humans. It was a sign of Helia's intelligence she had done as well as she had. After all, he'd been blessed with her longer than many he knew.

"She is of the pack. She will run with us until the day she dies." With that, Bartok and the rest melted into the night.

Divad dried his tears and made his way home. He opened the door to find his wife curled up on the bed, still naked, food gone, water spilled.

"Helia?" he whispered, hoping that maybe she would open her eyes and everything would be fine.

She whimpered and curled tighter. "Don't hurt. Want home. Don't hurt. Too big. No smell home. Want fur." She sobbed that last part.

Divad reached to wipe tears off her face, but she shied away from his touch. That hurt more than anything he'd ever felt.

"It's okay. You ready to become a wolf?" He had no idea if she would understand or how much, but he wouldn't change her without her permission.

"Wolf? Want wolf."

"Yes, my love." He stood back and pulled in his magic, gathering and channeling it into something he'd only done once before. Animal magic was tricky, and the subject had to be willing.

Power swirled around him, pulsing in time with his breaking heart. Like a swarm of bees, the magic hummed and pulsed, and he kept pulling in more. He used magic to heal, to communicate. But to change someone required more than he'd ever used before, except once.

His magic thrummed in the air, the pressure hurting as much as his heart, and he gave his assent.

Magic flowed over Helia, who had cowered away from him, arms over her head, a swarm of swirling rainbows sinking into her body.

Divad watched with an odd sense of relief and horrific guilt as Helia changed. Her hair shortened, her skin sprouted fur, her bones shifted, and a tail appeared. In a matter of moments, and over a lifetime, she became wolf again. Her pelt was the same rich brown he remembered, but there was gray on her muzzle, and she moved slower when she jumped off the bed. But it was her.

"Man? Why am I here?" He flinched at that; it was the same thing she had called him so long ago.

He sidestepped the question. How did he answer that? How did he touch on the years where he loved her? He had planned to grow even older with her. The desire to rail and scream at the cruelty of it all clawed at his insides, but he just smiled. "Are you ready to see your brother?"

"Yes!" The word burst out of her, and she headed to the door.

Past exhausted, but knowing this was the only way to keep her safe, he pulled on his cloak and let her out. He walked the long walk to the clearing once more. This time when he called for the pack, they raced out of the shadows. They had been waiting for her.

"Bartok," she yipped and bared her throat to her brother. "Why was I with this man? Why don't I know so many pack members?" Helia sniffed in confusion at the wolves, pulling back. "Who are these interlopers? Where have I been?"

Divad choked down a sob. Those wolves were all new members that they had met during their regular visits to her family as a human. Bartok nibbled her throat and licked her face. "This man is friend of pack. We trust him."

At any other time, Divad might have laughed in joy at finally earning Bartok's trust, but now it was salt on a raw wound.

Helia came over and sniffed Divad. "You smell familiar. Of home and comfort. But why?"

"It doesn't matter." Divad scratched her ears and ran a finger over her brow ridges. "Go with your brother. He will watch over you. I will come here every week to see you." The words were directed more to Bartok than her, and Divad was relieved when the alpha nodded his permission.

"Very well," Helia said. "I will see you then." She turned and followed the pack, though she moved slower than the others and seemed unsure of her way.

Bartok nodded at him again then disappeared through the trees.

Divad made it back to the house as the sun came up. He drank two bottles of wine that day, but the headache didn't make the pain in his heart go away.

Every week, Divad loaded up treats and tidbits for Helia and a brush so he could tend to her coat. The pressure in his chest was just grief. He had lost his incredible Helia, but she wasn't in pain and seemed content. He would be fine.

On each visit, he sat at the base of the tree, waiting until full dark fell and the wolves appeared. He brushed her coat, scratched her ears, let her babble about the rabbits and deer the pack had chased. He offered her treats and convinced himself the licks across his face meant that somewhere deep inside, she remembered his love.

Only after the wolves left did he let himself cry, then headed back to his empty house.

This night, Divad lowered himself to the base of the tree with difficulty. His chest hurt, and he'd been having trouble breathing all day. He just ached and wasn't sure why. All of that flashed away as Helia came over to him. She walked slowly, not trotted. Her muzzle had gotten whiter. It hurt to see that when Bartok, who had to be years older than Helia, still moved and acted like a wolf in his prime.

"Man. You came again. Do you have the brush?" Occasionally she recognized him, but most of the time, she focused on the treats and the brush. It hurt, but at least she sought him out. The others watched from a distance, but they never intruded on their time.

"Always. You know I love to brush you."

She slowly lowered herself to the ground and put her head on his lap, and he began to brush her. She fell asleep in his lap, and when his hand stilled and his eyes closed, she didn't move.

His hand buried in her fur as his heart stopped. Her last breath hissed out on a soft sigh.

A month later, Nevik came to the house. The door was ajar, and rodents had moved in. Concerned, he cast his magic to find Divad's last location. The trail of magic led him into the woods, deeper than he normally went. The bright ribbon led him to a clearing. Nevik stopped and looked where the light hovered.

At the base of a tree was Divad, his face at peace. Next to him was a wolf with its head in his lap.

Nevik approached, but he could tell immediately they had been dead for a few weeks. He looked around, and out of the shadows of the trees a massive wolf in his prime walked, staring at him. Nevik nodded once to the guardian.

The wolf nodded back, then disappeared into the trees.

Nevik buried Divad and Helia under the tree, together. He planted heather and red sage, using his magic to make them grow healthy and strong. With a silent nod to his friend, Nevik slipped from the clearing, leaving behind the memory of a wolf who loved a man enough to become human and the man who loved a woman enough to let her go.

MEL TODD has more than twenty stories out, including her urban science fiction Kaylid Chronicles, the Blood War series, and her bestselling Twisted Luck series. Owner of Bad Ash Publishing, she is working to create a place for excellent stories and great authors. With over two million words published, she is aiming for another million in the next two years. With one coauthor and more books in the works, Mel and her stories can be found on Amazon and other retailers.

Just Another Pinball Wizard
Robert J. McCarter

I spotted him as soon as he came into the place.

He was tall and lanky, like teenage boys who get their growth spurt late are, all limbs that he didn't know what to do with. His eyes were a sharp blue, and his hair was a wavy, dark-brown tussle that fell into those eyes and let him feel like he could hide behind it.

He wasn't a regular at the diner; I would have known him if he was. The way his sharp eyes roamed over the half-filled booths and the scattered tables made that clear. He was looking for someone. He nodded at a table stuffed with four other teenage boys and made a step toward them but then stopped.

He was looking at the sole pinball machine on one side of the restaurant next to the soda machine and the busing station. He didn't look there long—maybe a second or so—before he walked to the table with his friends, but most kids his age were enamored with their phones and wouldn't give a relic like a pinball machine a second look.

Maybe his old man had one in the garage. Maybe he had seen one in an old movie and was curious. Maybe he had a thing for wolves, and the image of the howling wolf on the back of it made him feel his own wild nature.

Whatever it was didn't matter none to me. I knew what to do. I had done it a dozen times before. Didn't matter if he had played pinball lots or not at all, it wouldn't be hard to get him hooked. Not hard at all. It never was.

⁂

"What can I getcha, hun?" I asked as I walked up to the table with the newly seated, lanky, blue-eyed teen.

He had nice eyes, intense eyes, even though he hid them behind those overlong bangs. Right then and there I decided that he wasn't the one, that I would let him be.

He looked me up and down like many of the teenage boys do. I have curves, and I ain't afraid to show them seeing how it helps with tips, but his gaze flicked away when he saw my face.

"Umm. Just water, thanks," he said.

If I was twenty, he would have given me a hopeful smile, thinking he had a chance. If I was thirty, he would have given me a slightly embarrassed smile, maybe those cheeks of his flushing a touch red. But seeing how I was north of forty, all I ever got from this lot was eyes flicking away when they saw a not-young face attached to those curves.

Pisses me off. A woman's worth is not diminished by age. It is the opposite.

"Sure thing, hun," I said with a smile that hid my anger. "Seein' as you are new, feel free to try the pinball machine. It's on me." I fished two tokens out from my apron pocket and plunked them down in front of him. "Looks like you're the type that likes to howl at the moon."

His friends chuckled, and those cheeks of his did flush red for a moment.

The diner ain't much, not as these things go. It's been in operation for over seventy years, and it shows. The off-white linoleum floor is scarred, the lights are fluorescent, and the blue vinyl of the high-back booth seats has seen better days, but the walls are painted a cheery pastel blue, and local art decorates the walls.

I know it all too well. I could walk between the tables with my eyes closed. I smell that strange, greasy amalgam of scents in my dreams. I hear the murmur of voices and the clanking of silverware on porcelain and especially the pongs and beeps of that pinball machine even when things are silent.

And while I said earlier that I was north of forty years old, the truth is I'm closing in on fifty, which brings up the obvious question of what the hell am I still doing waiting tables?

I walked into this diner when I was a teenager. It's only five blocks from the high school, and I was meeting some friends much like the lanky boy. These were the popular girls, and I was nervous. Did my brown hair look too mousy in its ponytail? Were my brown eyes too plain? Was my clothing too cheap? Was my makeup applied with proper deftness and the correct proportions?

Back then, the walls were a dingy gray and there wasn't local artwork hanging, but the layout was the same. Booths against one wall, tables staggered across the floor, and that damn pinball machine against the wall near the soda fountain and the busing station.

Well ... it wasn't the same pinball machine but strikingly similar. It had Wolf Pack blazoned across the front and a wolf painted on it that looked so real, like it was leaping out of the pinball machine, its eerie yellow eyes looking right at me.

"Abigale," Jenny Walters called. "We're over here." She was blonde and beautiful and the head cheerleader.

I tore my eyes away from those yellow wolf eyes and went over to the table trying to shake the chill that had just run up and down my spine.

Later, the waitress, who looked so old to my young eyes, gave me a few tokens to try out the game. Damn her.

Today, the pinball machine has Wolf World emblazoned on it, and the wolf that is out in front of the pack, that seems so real, is just standing there—its teeth bared, and its amber eyes glowing with intensity.

The lanky teen with the overlong bangs and sharp blue eyes is playing it, of course. Just like I did. Just like the others have. If those wolf eyes connect with yours, if the offer is made, you can't refuse.

I watched him from across the diner as I cleaned a table and put the condiments back in their holder. He was lean, but there was a coiled energy to him. He'd be a good runner if he wasn't one already. You might call that energy "wolfish." Or I might. Or I could just be fooling myself, so I don't feel so bad about the path I just led him down.

He had artfully faded jeans on, his skinny hips swinging as he played, his lips curling almost into a snarl when the shiny metal ball slipped past his flippers.

I haven't played this version of the game. I want to, with every fiber of my being, I want to. But that would be bad. The only one I ever played was Wolf Pack, and that's what got me into this mess.

I smiled and sighed, feeling like I just drank a good cup of coffee. The machine liked him. The machine was happy. And

God, Jesus, and the devil himself knew we wanted to keep the damnable machine happy.

The kid wasn't very good; he was almost through with the tokens I'd given him. I served pancakes to a four-top, and, on my way back to the kitchen, I took another token out of my apron and placed it on the glass of the pinball machine.

He didn't even notice me, a full-on snarl and then a low curse escaping him as he lost another ball.

Back in the kitchen, the cook, Clint, eyed me with those watery gray eyes of his. "Found one, huh?" he asked with a nod. He was a big guy with a shaved head and a dingy apron strapped over his T-shirt and shorts. He looked more like a bouncer than a cook.

"You can feel it?" I asked.

He bit his lip and nodded, taking a deep breath and shaking his head, a feral grin lighting up his face. "Oh, yeah. It's been a while since we had one."

The kitchen was hot, small, and crowded with the big gas stove, stainless-steel sinks, and prep tables. It smelled like the grease that covers everything in here, stale and cloying.

"Can't feed it too much," I said.

"I know," he said, his face puckering for a moment. "Still, feels good."

I grabbed some BLTs and walked out. I didn't want Clint to see the frown on my face. It did feel good, and it felt terrible too, if you know what I mean. Life has plenty of things that feel that way. Too many if you ask me.

The old owner of the diner, a tall, skeletal-looking man named Winston, knew where the first wolf pinball machine came from, but he's dead. Rumor has it that it goes back to the fifties when some traveling salesman talked the original owner into buying it for a price that seemed too good to be true.

It was.

That first wolf pinball machine was called the Howler, and it was hungry for more than just quarters.

But I still owed Winston. He stopped me from … well, you'll see in due time. It was late on a Saturday night, and I was playing the Wolf Pack pinball machine. I was good at it. One quarter and I could play for an hour. I had set the top score many times.

I could see the layout of the machine with my eyes closed. I knew that the right flipper was a touch sluggish, so it had to be hit earlier than the left. I knew every bumper, every trick, every bonus, every square inch, and I knew how to make it howl.

If you shot the ball up the ramp into the dark forest on the second level, and then bounced it off the bumper that pictured that rival pack, and then back down to the lower level to knock down all the chits that represented the hunters, the machine would howl.

The sound the machine made was a little reedy, but to me it felt like I was a wolf and I was howling. Even at my skill level with the machine, getting it to howl wasn't easy, but it was the best thing. And I mean that, it was literally the best moments of my life. Or, at least, it felt that way.

The place was closed, the waitress who had gotten me hooked was still cleaning up, and I was lost in the game trying to get the steel ball up the ramp to the dark forest to start the howl sequence.

"You're a real pinball wizard, aren't you?" Winston asked. He was wearing his ever-present gray slacks and button-down white shirt with the sleeves rolled up exactly twice. He had a too-lean face with slicked back salt-and-pepper hair and a caterpillar of a mustache.

I knew the song, of course, so I just nodded and smiled.

"You ever find it strange that you always play pinball here and that this is the only pinball machine you play?" he asked, his tone odd, like the speech was rehearsed.

I knocked the ball up into the dark forest and glanced at him. His face was pockmarked, and his cheeks sunk in. Half the fluorescents were off, which gave him a more skeletal look than usual.

Winston liked to look at me, that much was clear. I had the curves and I had youth, and being looked at was something I was just starting to get used to. And even though Winston was a strange guy, he seemed harmless.

"Life is strange," I said. My mother had just run off with her boss, and my father was fumbling along trying to raise a teenage girl.

He chuckled; it was as dry as the desert wind. "That's true enough. But your attachment to this machine is strange, don't you think?"

"I like to hear it howl," I said, and it seemed that simple to me.

God, I was so young.

"We all do," he said, and there was something in his voice that made me look at him. He was paler than usual, his eyes wide, and his mouth open a bit like he was winding up to scream.

"Shit!" I said as the ball snuck past me because I was distracted.

"You need to stop playing," he said, his tone flat but with an underlying urgency.

I shook my head. "I've got another ball left."

"I like you, Abigale," he said, and my heart started pounding because I thought he meant *like*. "You're a good kid. I'd hate to see you end up like the others."

He walked to the back of the machine and pulled the plug, the Wolf Pack machine giving what sounded like a truncated growl before going dark and quiet. My stomach twisted. The machine being off seemed wholly unnatural.

"Hey! I wasn't done with my quarter."

When Winston stood up, it looked like he was in pain, and his hair looked like it had more salt than usual, but, innocent as I was, I figured it was a trick of the light.

He pulled a quarter out his pocket and placed it on the glass of the machine near the plunger and walked away.

"I don't want a quarter. I want my game!"

Winston walked to the diner's glass door and held it open. "We are closed. You have to leave now."

I said some things, some more things I shouldn't have, and some words I definitely shouldn't have. Winston flinched a couple of times in the face of my verbal assault, but he held firm and locked the door behind me as soon as I left.

When he walked back into the restaurant, he looked stooped and old, and I felt this strange incompleteness, like something was very, very wrong with the world.

But why? It was just a damn game.

Out on the street, I paced in front of the diner for a while, fuming, crazy to get back to the pinball machine.

I didn't know it then, but Winston saved my life that night. And it cost him—boy, did it cost him.

Wolf World is not the same game as Wolf Pack, but it is the same game, if you know what I mean. Sure, the graphics are different, and the layout is different, but it still howls, and it still has its dark purpose in the world.

The lanky, mop-haired, teenager's name was Tommy,

which I learned on his third visit. By his fifth visit, I didn't have to feed him tokens anymore; he came with quarters and beelined to the game to start playing.

He stayed attached to that machine until he ran out of quarters or it was past closing time and I cut him off.

Tommy used to be in the band, played the tuba for God's sake, and had been in a few plays. He got decent grades, considering his family situation with just his mom now since his father ODed.

He had flair too. He'd bump the machine with his skinny teenager hips and deftly alter the path of the ball, especially when he was on the hunt for the howl. He didn't even tilt it anymore.

He also had an odd grunting language as he played. One type of grunt was happy, another one was scared, and a third one was the grunt of defeat. At first, they all sounded the same, but after a while, I picked up on the meaning.

He was tall, so he often stood with his knees slight bent and his tongue sticking out a little to the right as he concentrated.

The machine definitely had its claws in him. He was a goner, no doubt. It would take an intervention to stop him and likely even that wouldn't be enough. It would probably take his mother dragging him far away from this crappy little town.

"Here you go," I said, handing him a glass of water right after a ball snuck past the flippers and he had cursed under his breath.

"Thanks," he said, gulping the water, handing the glass back, and wiping the sweat off his brow.

"I used to play you know," I said, nodding at the pinball machine.

"Yeah?" he asked, his eyes actually meeting mine for a moment.

"Not this particular machine, but one called Wolf Pack.

Back when I was your age. I was damn good. Could make it howl every time."

His eyes widened, and he looked me up and down real quick like we hadn't met before.

"Why'd ya stop?" he asked.

"Wasn't good for my health," I said. "Was hell on my grades. And someone cared enough to stop me."

He blinked like the thought was a new one and his brain had to reset to process it.

"Wasn't ..." he mumbled like he wasn't sure what I had said.

"Wasn't good for my health," I said again slowly. "I had to quit. Cold turkey." That was a lie, of course. I had quit playing, but I hadn't quit the machine.

He really looked at me now, maybe finally looking past the age on my face and seeing me. Maybe. I wasn't Winston, I wasn't about to do what he did and pay the price, but I did like the kid and thought he deserved a chance.

"There's a hellova price to being a pinball wizard," I said. "And that's the truest thing I know."

"Yeah," he said, shaking his head like he was trying to wake up. "Thanks for the water." His eyes went back to the machine, and it was like I had never been there.

He pulled back the plunger, and the steel ball shot up to the top of the track and started bouncing around, the machine making bleeps and blurps, like that was its language and it was celebrating its victim.

When I went back into the hot kitchen, Clint caught my eye and said, "You tried."

I nodded and stood there for a moment and took a few deep

breaths. The kid was on the hunt for the howl; I knew the noises of the machine well enough to know he was getting close.

"I'm no Winston," I said. I wasn't really talking to Clint, it was just words that needed to be said.

"Poor bastard," Clint said, and my stomach clenched. "You found him, didn't you?"

I nodded. "Yeah."

All those years ago, I came back to the diner, repeatedly, desperate to play Wolf Pack, but Winston wouldn't let me. I screamed. I yelled. I hit him, but he wouldn't budge. He'd lock me out. He'd unplug the pinball machine. He did whatever it took. And even though he suddenly seemed old and frail, Winston still managed to stop me from playing.

I didn't know it then, but I was in withdrawal. I was jonesing.

I was at the diner so much, Winston eventually put me to work as a waitress. My dad was pleased I had gotten a job, and I started hovering around the machine as others played it.

None of them were true players like Tommy and me, none of them were pinball wizards, and the machine wasn't taking much from them, but I started to feel a little better.

Winston taught me the twelve steps and explained that although that damn machine wasn't a drink or a pill, we were addicts as sure as anything.

"One day at a time," he said to me early one morning before we opened. The pepper was pretty much gone from his hair, and his face was more skeletal than ever. His voice was thin and reedy, and I swear he was getting older every single day.

But I still wanted to play Wolf Pack. I needed to play. It was everything that was right in the world, even though I knew it was so very wrong.

"We'll find someone else," he said. "You'll still want to play, you'll never *not* want to play, but it will get better. I promise."

Winston looked like an old man now and felt more like a father to me than my own. "Okay," I said with a sigh and got back to work.

It wasn't bad when I was working, there's always so much to do in a diner like ours, but before the doors opened and after they closed, it was hell.

Winston did find someone else, a paunchy middle-aged man with sad eyes. He gave the guy a token just like the other waitress had given me one and just like I gave Tommy one.

And it did get easier as the man got attached, as he started coming in to play every day, as he no longer needed tokens and mastered the machine, making it howl every single time.

Except this time, Winston didn't unplug the machine and save him. He let it happen. He took care of the aftermath.

A week later, I came in to open up and noticed it wasn't Wolf Pack anymore. The pinball machine was brand-new and emblazoned with Lone Wolf. This time, the big wolf had green eyes like the middle-aged guy who had been obsessed with it.

I found Winston on the greasy floor of the kitchen. His eyes were pale like all the brown had drained out of them, and his white shirt with the rolled-up sleeves hung on him like it was two sizes too large.

"It's done," he said, his voice sounding like the rustling of leaves in the middle of a graveyard. "The Wolf Pack is gone. If you don't play again, you will be free."

I knew he was lying. I knew what it was like to feel someone play the game. I knew I was still an addict, and I could never leave this diner and that game. But I didn't say anything. I took his hand, and the skin was soft and seemed so thin.

"Thank you, Winston. Thank you."

Then he told me that he'd been the one. He'd been the original owner of the diner who let that traveling salesman sell him the pinball machine for too cheap a price seventy years ago. He told me all the secrets that he knew. He told me how the machine had slowed down his aging process. He told me he was paying the price for defying the machine.

"Why?" I asked him. "Why did you do it? Why me?"

He tried to smile, but with his now truly skeletal face, it was terrifying. I smiled back anyway. "You remind me of my daughter," he said.

I had never known he had a family, but he didn't have to tell me how he lost them. That damn machine.

I left him and called 911, but it was too late. By the time I got back, he was gone, and I was the one left with the terrible secret.

Tommy, our current, reigning, pinball wizard, kept coming in and making Wolf World howl on the regular. I made a couple more attempts to reach him, but he was too far gone, and I knew it was my fault.

If I hadn't slipped him that token, he probably would have escaped. He would have had confusing, troubling, and often boring teenage years just like everyone else. He would have grown up and become someone.

I didn't create the machine, but it's not like I've ever had the guts to get a sledgehammer and destroy it. Don't know what would happen, but someone ought to try it.

"You're almost there," I said to Tommy. It was late, the diner was closed, the blinds shut, but he was getting close to the howl, and all of us wanted to feel it. We wanted more than the howl.

"Yup," he said. It was barely more than a grunt, his eyes never leaving the ball.

"You're almost there," I said again, but I wasn't talking to Tommy.

Wolf World was looking old and dingy, but soon it wouldn't. Soon it would be something different. I thought of slipping him a token to make sure it happened tonight, but he was at one with the machine and was a true pinball wizard.

I went back to closing the place up. I was in the kitchen with Clint when the machine howled. Our eyes met, and we couldn't help but smile. It was a smile of ecstasy, but it wasn't a pretty smile. It was feral and filled with teeth. It was sick, and I hated it and loved it at the same time.

I could feel it coming, so I sent the other waiter home and told Clint to leave by the back way when he was done.

Then I went out into the diner, poured myself a soda, and sat and watched Tommy.

I owed them this. If I was going to keep feeding the beast, the least I could do was witness what happened to them.

I didn't have to wait long. Soon Tommy was howling, and the machine was howling, and the energy ripping through the place made me think I would never have to sleep again.

Tommy wasn't looking at the machine anymore. His back was arched, his head high as he howled, and yet he never let the ball escape. He was now the pinball wizard from that old song, playing completely by feel.

Even though I was sitting to his side, the feral light in his sharp blue eyes was too much. I looked away, just for a moment, and when I looked back, it was happening.

Tommy's hips had changed. They weren't skinny teenager hips anymore; they were squarer and sharper, smoother. His hips were part of the machine now, and yet he still played.

The machine was making strange noises, happy noises,

predatorial noises. The kind of noises that would scare the hell out of you if you heard then in the middle of the night out in the forest. The kind of noises that would make you run for your life.

But I stayed there, sipped on my soda, and watched. Hungry for it and hating it at the same time.

The pinball machine was changing too. It was less hard and square. It was getting a bit smaller, it was making way, it was transforming, but Tommy still managed to play it as his legs got skinny, as his torso flattened and elongated, as he bent himself over, until he was arched over the now-smaller machine.

And still the pinball wizard played. And still he howled.

I don't know how to describe what happened next. Not really. Tommy became the machine and then the machine that was Tommy consumed the old machine.

It was mechanical and biological at the same time. It was terrifying and exhilarating. It made me think of Winston, knowing that he saved me from this at the cost of his own life.

It sounded like flesh rending, like metal screeching, all accompanied by the blips and beeps of a pinball machine and the triumphant howls of a wolf.

I drank my soda and watched, my heart pounding in my chest like I had done all the cocaine in the world.

After it was done, we had what looked like a brand-new pinball machine. The Wolf's Way. This time the wolf on it had sharp blue eyes. They looked real. They looked like they were watching me, because they were.

I got a mop and some Windex and some rags and did my duty. There were bits of clothing that had shredded away, and I gathered them into a garbage bag. There was a vaguely biological substance on the floor with a few metal oddities in it that I mopped up. And the machine itself, while looking new, was sticky and smelled like a cross between oil and fresh blood.

I took my time. I did it right. And when I was done, the Wolf's Way looked perfect and new. A one-of-a-kind pinball machine waiting for the next pinball wizard.

It was late when I finished, and as I stood there, staring at the new machine, I wanted to play. God help me, I wanted to play.

In the reflection of the chrome, I saw myself, and I looked different. I would say "younger," but it was more complicated than that. There was still age on my face, but there was enough energy to counteract it, make it not matter, and I knew that Clint and all the other old-timers who had danced with the machine but had not gone as far as Tommy, felt the same thing.

You see, I lied earlier. It's true that I look like I'm about forty, but it's not true that I'm closer to fifty. It's a lot more than that. I feed the machine, and the machine feeds me. I hate it, and I love it. The machine transforms us all in one way or another.

Later, when I burned the remnants of Tommy's clothing outside of town where teenagers sometimes gathered to have parties, I tried to picture the lanky teenager with the too-long hair that fell in front of his sharp blue eyes, but I couldn't see him. Not really.

All I could picture in my mind was the blue-eyed wolf emblazoned on the new pinball machine in the old diner, hungry for its next victim.

ROBERT J. MCCARTER is the author of more than ten novels and over a hundred short stories. He is a regular contributor to *Pulphouse Fiction Magazine,* and his short fiction has also appeared in *The Saturday Evening Post, Andromeda Space-*

ways Inflight Magazine, Everyday Fiction, and numerous anthologies.

Robert writes in a variety of genres, and his diverse background—including a career in software engineering, growing up on a ranch riding horses and acting—colors the stories he tells.

He lives in the mountains of Arizona with his amazing wife and his ridiculously adorable dogs.

Find out more at RobertJMcCarter.com.

Barbarians

David Farland

The smell of guts and dust and horseflesh told the tale: running steeds at dusk, a tight corner on a narrow mountain road, a carriage rolling over the cliff.

Dval stepped to the margin of the rutted dirt road and stood beneath a sprawling live oak. In the gloaming darkness he spotted wreckage a hundred yards downslope: a fine black carriage rested on its side without a door, so that it opened like the nest of a weaver bird. The carriage was of barbaric make—Mystarrian. They were a clever people, but did not understand the ways of true humans.

Instantly Dval crouched low, lest any survivors spot him, and pulled his dagger from its hip sheath. The handle of his obsidian blade felt comfortably familiar in his hand.

Near the carriage, trunks had tumbled open, spilling dresses and undergarments, while a pair of mangled horses lay broken over boulders. One animal struggled to breathe, while the other had given up the fight.

The driver had been thrown far downhill and lay wrapped around a tree, preternaturally still. Dval wondered what treasure they might have left behind. He knew that he should run and tell his uncle what had happened, for he was the leader of their tribe.

But the lure of treasure called. Dval bounded down the hillside, his leather moccasins whispering through dry grasses. The only sounds were the songs of cicadas among the scrub oak, and the distant screech of a burrow owl. Overhead, stars glimmered dully in a smoke-filled sky.

The smell of smoke worried him.

On the plains in the distance, crimson flames burned in a crescent, as if fire itself had shaped a scythe to harvest the fields to the Mystarrians. Winds from the sea swept the scythe steadily westward.

The sight of flames filled Dval with foreboding. He had not yet heard of the "gray fleet" that had been sighted near the Courts of Tide. He had not heard of the inhuman "toth" and their strange ways. Yet all the events that would shape his destiny had been set in motion that day.

When he reached the wagon, Dval checked on the surviving horse; its cavernous breaths thundered in and out. Its back was broken, and it could barely lift its head, but it smelled him and stirred, a whinny that was part scream, then turned enough to see him. Dval rested one hand on the horse's chest to calm the poor creature. As its breathing eased, Dval studied the fine carriage—black lacquered wood without any markings. He found a door on the ground. Silver inlay outlined a man's face with a beard and hair made of oak leaves: the symbol of the king of Mystarria.

He found a guardsman near the wreck—a young knight in fishmail and helm. The fine steel would be worth a fortune, and the soldier wore a gold ring. Dval worked the ring free from the man's fingers, put it on.

Farther downhill laid another woman, a young matron,

with glazed eyes peering up into the stars, as if to ponder eternity.

Dval smiled. *Keep pondering, woman.*

The wounded horse cried. Dval loved horses, so he drew the knight's bastard sword from its sheath. The blade was made of strange metal—a dull silver, neither northern steel nor brass. It was extraordinarily light. Runes inlaid along its length were like nothing made by men. The strange geometric shapes gleamed like silver fire in the starlight. This was a duskin blade, at least four thousand years old. He tested the blade's edge with a thumb. It pricked like a wasp sting. Blood throbbed out.

Dval wondered where the blade had come from. Duskin blades were usually found at least a mile underground in ancient tunnels.

He addressed the dead knight. "You're a lucky man to have such a fine blade." Then he saw how the man's tongue hung out between his teeth. "Well, not *that* lucky."

He strode to the horse, plunged the blade in its neck.

The horse lay down its head wearily, as if in relief, and the scent of copper filled the woods as it bled out.

He imagined its spirit galloping away in fields of dreams.

Hoping for more treasure, Dval went to the overturned carriage, climbed the axletree, and peered inside.

At the bottom lay a girl, cradling an injured arm. She looked up and gasped. Deep-red hair framed a heart-shaped face, cheeks stained with tears. Like some northerners of legend, she had brown speckles on her face. He'd never seen freckles before. Her large green eyes engulfed him, pupils wide and black, filled with terror. She was a daylighter—one who could not see in the dark. She could not have been more than nine, two years his junior, perhaps three. Her left leg lay askew, badly bruised, possibly broken.

"Weir bisth dua?" she asked, trembling.

Dval did not speak the uncouth tongue of Mystarria, but guessed at the question.

"Dval," he said, pointing at his chest.

She tried to repeat it, using one of her own words. "Val?"

Close enough. He nodded.

She pointed to her own chest: "Avahn."

If I crush her skull, he realized, *they will think she died in the wreck. I can take their treasure.*

He peered around for witnesses. Everyone else from the wreck seemed to be dead. He did not see any reason why she shouldn't die too. Their people had been at war since before either of them had been born.

But he felt guilty. He was in their territory. One of his uncle's blood mares had been high on the mountain slopes, grazing in the lush alpine grass, but had "wandered" down into the hills, as they did to give birth.

When he'd told his uncle that the horse was gone, he'd said, "Are we not poor enough? Go find the mare, you fool." Always that sneer in his voice.

Dval hadn't expected the horse to wander far from camp, but moccasin prints suggested that his cousin had actually driven the mare away as a prank.

He was trespassing in this land; the penalty for getting caught was death.

A cool wind blew down from the ice caps above, whispering over him, raising goose pimples on his arms.

A mournful howl arose from the woods downhill—a low moaning sound that ululated, then tapered off. It was the hunting cry of a dire wolf. The wolves in the Alcair Mountains were as large as ponies, each weighing as much as three hundred pounds. In winter they followed herds of shaggy elephants that roamed the Kakolar Plains, but in the summers they often foraged into the hills to hunt for elk.

Sometimes their cries were filled only with ravening hunger, but this wolf was telling others that it tasted the scent of blood.

Dval crouched, frozen in indecision. If he left the girl and kept searching for his uncle's lost blood mount, the wolves would finish her. He could simply come back and plunder the wreck later.

A deep growl sounded nearby in the oak forest, not more than a hundred yards away. There was no time to climb a tree.

Dval scrambled into the carriage for safety. The girl shrieked and shrank away. He was Inkarran after all, with skin and hair as white as aspen bark, and ice-green eyes that could see in the night.

He knew a few words in her tongue. "Gud," he said, pointing at himself. "I gud."

She nodded, and tried to rise, but startled at a low growl outside.

They froze, trapped inside the carriage, while wolves began racing around it, panting, heavy paws mincing dry grass. A wolf howled, high and eager, inviting others to the feast.

Dval raised a finger to his lips, begging the girl to keep silent. She nodded, then gently laid back down on the floor. Though she stiffened when her arm moved, she did not cry out.

There was only one entrance into the carriage—the broken door above. Dval stood with sword raised upward, prepared to thrust.

For long minutes dire wolves growled and ripped at the dead outside, sometimes snarling at one another. He could hear padded feet circling the carriage. Dozens of them.

Let there be enough to feed them all, Dval silently prayed to his ancestors.

He gripped the hilt of the unfamiliar sword so tightly that it felt as if his muscles melded with it. Long after he ached with fatigue, he stood, peering up.

To relax vigilance is to die, he heard his uncle's warning.

The girl hardly breathed.

Suddenly heavy paws scrabbled against the frame of the carriage above, and Dval was unprepared for the wolf that leapt through—a large black beast with grizzled hair turned to mist by starlight.

Dval stabbed upward blindly.

The girl shrieked. The dire wolf yelped in pain, scrabbled backward, and blood rained down. The girl kept screaming.

Did I kill it? he wondered. But the blow had not been deep. The beast would probably only be wounded.

An injured dire wolf would attack again, he knew, if only to prove its fierceness.

Outside, other wolves growled and yipped excitedly. Some sniffed at the carriage while others circled.

A second wolf put its paws up on the carriage and whined, sniffing at the opening. Dval jumped and lunged hard, taking it beneath the throat. It leapt away.

Wolves danced about the carriage and growled in a frenzy. The girl shrieked some more.

"Shut up!" he shouted. "Fear draws them!" But the girl did not understand.

He slapped her face, shocking her into silence. "A rabbit screams like that when it wants to die." He explained, but she did not know the ways of the forest.

Sometimes, when one faces a bear, the best thing to do is to sing. It confuses the animal and shows that one is not afraid. So Dval shoved the girl and sang now, an old battle dirge:

I was born to blood and war,
Like my fathers were a thousand years before.
Sound the horn. Strike a blow.

Down to death or glory go!

Wolves whimpered. One barked at the carriage.

Faster than a serpent, a wolf leapt up into the doorframe. Dval lunged with his blade; the wolf bit it. Blood spattered, but the blade twisted in Dval's hand. He lunged, struck the wolf's leg, but the beast growled and snapped. Fangs sank into Dval's shoulder, close to the neck, crushing more than piercing.

Dval shoved the blade up with all his might, driving the creature away. His vision blanked; he stood blinking, blood in his eyes.

At his side, the little girl began to sing in her own crude tongue. Her voice caught with fear at first. It was not a battle song, but a lullaby, such as a mother might sing to a child to frighten away imaginary wights. As she sang, her voice grew in strength.

Sometimes, a song does not just show courage, it lends it, Dval realized.

He wiped spatter from his eyes. Thick blood ran from his shoulder. He feared that it would only attract wolves, or that he would pass out.

The girl continued to sing, struggling to her feet. She put her right hand around his, as if to hold hands.

In Dval's land, when a woman took a man's hand, it was a proposal of marriage. Was it the same among her people?

They were both too young, only children.

There was terror in her eyes still, and fierce intelligence. Her lower jaw quivered with determination.

She only seeks comfort, he thought.

She pulled up her skirt, drew an ornate dagger, its silver hilt crusted in gems. It was a pretty weapon, such as a wealthy merchant might carry. She peered at the opening above, as if to do battle.

Avahn waited for the wolves and wondered at her situation.

On sighting the gray fleet, her father had sent Avahn and her mother to safety in the mountains. But safety is an illusion.

Avahn's mother had been thrown out the door during the wreck, and the silence of the woods spoke eloquently of her fate. Avahn didn't want to look outside, see the inevitable. Grief is invisible, but it bears a tremendous weight.

She didn't know where she was, how to get home.

She wished that she were a runelord, that she had an endowment of strength. Her father had suggested that she take one, but ...something always stopped her. Sometimes, the vassal's heart stopped when the facilitators drew his strength away, or he would grow too weak to breathe. She'd never wanted to put someone through that.

Avahn knew little about wolves. The Wizard Goren said that a dire wolf is not afraid of a man. A lone man makes good prey. But he'd once said, "The smell of metal frightens them, especially if more than one man is near."

Avahn and the boy were vastly outnumbered, but she determined to show no fear, even though her heart pounded as if it might break. Perhaps someday, if she grew to become a powerful runelord, she wouldn't be so swayed by fear. Today was not that day.

The boy was bleeding badly. She knew he might not be able to protect her much longer. There was nowhere for her to hide in the carriage.

She studied him. Dval was not huge. Like most Inkarrans, he was lanky and pale in the starlight. Only his calves were dark, for they had been tattooed with a tree, one that bore totems giving the names of his ancestors. He wore little besides his moccasins—a summer kilt, a necklace of wood beads, earrings made of dyed cotton.

Another wolf leapt up on the carriage and peered in; Dval lunged, but it leapt away so fast, it seemed a creature of mist and dreams.

Once, from her mother's castle at Coorm, Avahn had watched a silver fox out in a field on a green morning. There were mice in the field, and the fox danced about tufts of dry grass. Any mouse that stuck its head outside its burrow risked getting eaten.

Their only hope was to stay inside. She thought about the Master of the Hounds, Sir Gwilliam. When given a new litter of wolfhound pups, he'd spanked the largest and explained, "Every pack of dogs has a leader. To control the pack, you must control their leader."

She tried to warn the boy: "Val, we must kill their leader." She jutted her chin up toward the opening. He shook his head, not understanding.

We only have to make it until morning, she thought. *My father will send soldiers to look for us.*

She did the only thing she could. She sang.

Five more times that night, wolves attacked, and Dval managed to strike deeply and drive them away, but with each hour his strength waned, and Avahn didn't know how long he could continue.

Near dawn, a crescent moon climbed overhead, spilling silver light that glistened like a spiderweb.

Avahn worried. The gray ships had come to the Courts of Tide, and she'd seen fires in the valley shortly before dark. She did not know who set them.

All that she could do was keep singing.

When the sky began to brighten and the smell of morning dew filled the air, the leader of the pack came. It was a great wolf, larger than the others. It lunged through the doorframe without preamble, snarling and snapping. So quick was the attack that Dval struggled to repel it, thrusting his blade awkwardly.

Avahn was thrown backward, and the wolf made it halfway into the carriage, shoving Dval to the ground. It focused on the boy, bit him on the head.

Without thought, Avahn lurched forward and plunged her blade deep into the wolf's neck. Its fur was so thick, she wasn't sure how deep the wound was, but hot blood spurted from a vein at its throat, and the wolf yelped and snapped at her, and Dval scrambled away.

The wolf's strength was so great, it whipped its head sideways to bite her and slammed her into the wall of the carriage. She heard wooden struts crack from the impact, even as her ears began to ring.

Unconsciousness came so swiftly and completely, it was like falling into a deep dark bottomless pool. She struggled to remain awake, but struggling was no use.

Dval stabbed at the monster wolf, though he was on the floor. The light blade flickered up and entered the beast's torso as cleanly as if it were a sheath.

The wolf growled and twisted its head away from Avahn, and Dval struck thrice more, slashing now.

The wolf growled and backed away, leaving the entrance open to the starlight.

Outside, the creature snarled ferociously and jumped about, like a hart struck by an arrow.

Other wolves yapped at it, and Dval waited for it to come back, for a wounded wolf was more dangerous than a bear.

But it raced about erratically, then gave a lonely howl just outside the carriage, a howl that made the wood paneling shiver. The beast couldn't have been more than ten feet away. Dval could hear it panting louder and louder, as if it were growing more fatigued by the moment.

Dval's head was bleeding, along with his shoulder, and he could hardly stand, but he remained on his feet, fixed his eyes on the opening overhead.

The pack leader is dying, he thought. But that seemed too ... hopeful.

He waited for it to leap into the carriage again, but instead he heard it get up, panting heavily, and wander toward the woods.

We all hide from death.

For many long minutes, Dval stood waiting.

He felt he could stand no longer and began to float in and out of consciousness.

If they come for me, he thought, *I will be standing still.*

So he held his striking pose, as dawn came. Nuthatches chirruped outside in the forest, and mourning doves called. Flies began to buzz inside the carriage, spinning, spinning, in lazy circles, and Dval's head spun with them.

He waited, a monument.

I am stone. He told himself. *I am stone.*

The final attack came in the later afternoon. Dval must have fallen asleep on his feet. He wasn't aware of a scuffle on the carriage or even a shadow filling the opening above him. All he felt was a tug as he was jerked from the carriage by his topknot.

He swatted with his sword in vain. A giant had grabbed him, and now held him dangling with one hand, while he wrested the sword away with the other.

Dval would have preferred to face more wolves.

The giant hurled Dval to the ground. He rolled and struggled to rise, but the giant slammed one huge foot onto Dval's ribs, pinning him. "Stinkende theif!" the creature boomed in a voice more guttural than a bull's.

It was a hill giant, nearly nine feet tall, from the land of Toom. He was as burly as a great bear, and had to weigh a thousand pounds. No matter how Dval squirmed, he could not wrest free. Dval squinted up into the impossible sunlight. The giant's hair was as blue-black as ink, and he wore rat skulls braided into his beard. He stank of rum and sweat and unnamable nastiness.

Dval closed his eyes, blinded by the sun. Other Mystarrians surrounded him, men with drawn swords. Dval smelled of woods and crisp mountain air. These men stank of ale and grease and cities.

Some shouted at him, and one ripped the stolen ring from Dval's finger while another man, with tears in his eyes, salvaged the duskin sword, taking the relic in both hands.

Dval did not understand all of the accusations leveled against him, but one man drew his sword and strode forward, intent on taking Dval's head.

Dval gritted his teeth and bared his neck. He stared into his executioner's eyes as befitted a man who was no coward. The soldier raised his tall sword high, brought the blade down.

"Stobben!" the girl shouted.

The sword veered and bit into the ground near Dval's head.

Dval looked up to see a knight in fishmail help the girl from the carriage, while six others circled Dval, eager for the kill. They forced him to sit on the ground in the sunlight, where his skin would burn and his eyes could not see.

They pulled the bodies of the wolves that he'd slain together, and laid them side-by-side. The pelt of a dire wolf was valuable. Few men had ever killed five at a time.

Avahn found her mother's body downhill. Wolves had mauled it and pulled it into the shadows under the oaks. Only a bit of blue dress identified the corpse.

One of her father's guards covered it with a forest-green cloak and tried to pull Avahn away, but she stayed rooted, let the tears flow long and hard while flies buzzed about.

The soldiers kept the Inkarran boy on his knees in the sun. In the bright light, she could see his hair like braided silver, running down his neck. The wool earrings were as crimson as blood. Many bites and scratches marred his smooth skin.

She begged them to let him go, but Captain Adelheim said, "He's more than Inkarran. He's Woguld. They're all under a death sentence. Only your father can stay the boy's execution."

"He saved my life," she said.

"He was robbing corpses, and he would have killed you," Captain Adelheim said.

"But he didn't," she said vehemently.

One of the men mourned, speaking of her guard, "Sir Hawkins had grit in 'im. Can't believe he'd just die in a fall. He was too much of a man for it. The kid likely bashed 'is skull with a rock!"

Sir Bandolan the giant sang of the boy in that grumbling, nonsensical way of his:

Wicked he be.

Evil he does.

Why, oh why?

Because, because!

"Right, lads," another of Adelheim's men agreed. "Let's bugger him up." He kicked the boy, knocking him over, and others cheered.

Avahn stared hard at Captain Adelheim. He had a fair complexion with a red beard and piercing blue eyes. His frame and features were flawless. Silently she begged for compassion, but when he just shrugged, she whirled and slugged Dval's attacker in the gut.

The soldiers all roared in laughter. "Careful there, Pwyrthen," one said, "or the princess might drop her aim a bit."

The soldiers backed away, then, leaving the boy to gasp on the ground like a landed trout.

Avahn got one of her mother's riding cloaks and put it over him, then settled at his side, prepared to beg her father for the boy's life. She feared it would be in vain. For two hundred years they'd fought the Woguld.

Seeking to distract their attention from the boy, she asked Captain Adelheim, "Did you see the men from the gray ships?"

His expression became grave in an instant, and the words seemed to wound him like an arrow. Softly, in a voice husky with alarm, he said, "It wasn't men on those ships. There were monsters that came off them, things like reavers, with black leathery skin, and philia hanging like worms off their head plates. But they stood up on two legs, like giants."

She tried to picture such a creature, but her imagination

failed. Captain Adelheim continued, speaking softly, as if afraid to admit this. "Three years ago, your father sent out an expedition to the ends of the earth searching for new territories. Legend said that there was a land beyond the Carrol Sea, and there have been hints of fertile plains and rivers filled with gold. But no ships that sailed ever returned. So your father's scouts went, and they too never returned. Now, I think we know why. Now, *we're* the ones that have been discovered."

"So the creatures landed?" she asked. "They're the ones who set the fires?"

"Their ships never beached," Captain Adelheim said. "The creatures just stepped off them, into the water, and walked on the bottom of the sea until they reached the shore. Yes, they set fires. But none of those beasts will ever return home." He paused. "We call them *toths*."

"Toths," Avahn repeated. *Fangs.*

Avahn had never seen a reaver, only their skulls. She could not imagine what a toth might look like.

The night fighting wolves had seemed terrible, but Avahn knew in some deep part of her, that it was only the beginning.

At midday, the king of Mystarria came—a plump man with sandy brown hair and a dark crown carved from oak, and robes of royal blue. He rode in with thirty men, circled Dval, studied him.

The king's face was pale and drawn. He glared at Dval, and though he spoke to others, he growled with subdued rage.

In the hills above them, Dval heard a woodpecker tapping. *Peck peck. Peck, peck, peck, peck.*

It was Woguld warrior speak, made by tapping a sandstone pebble against a tree: *We are here.*

The king and his men did not seem to notice.

Instead, the Mystarrians argued.

King Harrill was filled with grief at the death of his wife, and he strode over the field of wreckage like an angry badger, like a storm in the brewing. His eyes were bloodshot and glazed from lack of sleep, blazing like meteors. He'd been fighting all night, and now he paced restlessly, moving one direction first, then changing in an instant.

He went to the body of his wife, looked down at her remains, as if to fix them in his memory. The wolves had been at her, had clawed open her torso, eaten her liver, ripped off her face.

As he gazed down, he seemed to collapse in on himself by degrees, as if every breath hit him like a blow. At first his face was hard with grief, then pale with shock, until at last his expression went blank and only loss was left in his eyes.

Avahn watched him, but she could do nothing for him, for she felt the loss as keenly as he.

"My love," he said at last, taking his wife's hand and kissing it. "Until we meet again."

Suddenly there was a snarl at the edge of the woods.

Avahn whirled to see a wolf, the huge leader of the pack, come limping from the shadows. Crimson blood matted the fur on its chest, poured down its right leg to its paw.

It lunged, blurring across the clearing. Knights shouted in warning, and Sir Adelheim's sword came ringing from its sheath.

The wolf raced toward her father and leapt, a heavy growl escaping its throat.

Any common man would have fallen beneath its attack like

a helpless doe. But her father was a runelord, with endowments of grace and brawn.

He did not cry out in terror or back away from the fight. Instead he ducked from the attack and leapt at the wolf, mailed fist swinging.

With three endowment of brawn, he slugged the beast. The air cracked as he hit, slamming into the wolf's skull. Bits of bone and blood flew in an arc, and something wet spattered Avahn's face.

The giant wolf fell, its body a dead weight, and it did not move any longer.

King Harrill stared down at it for a long moment, as if trying to understand where it had come from, why it had attacked.

Finally he growled and whirled on Dval, raging as if the wolf were the boy's fault, and shouted. "Why is that ... bastard still alive?"

"He saved my life," Avahn answered reasonably, stepping forward, so that she stood between her father and Dval.

"More than likely," her father argued, "he's the one who caused the wreck. They do it all the time—spook our horses at sunset, steal our crops in the night, murder travelers in their sleep. They're barbarians, not even human."

He shoved past Avahn, went to Dval, pulled his own battle-axe, and raised it high.

The boy, dazed and forlorn, did not cry out in fear. Instead, he spit at the king's feet.

"No!" Avahn warned Dval, for she knew better than to test her father's wrath.

The boy raised his chin and offered his neck, glaring.

The king withheld the blow for a moment, then shook his head in admiration. "Oh, this one has spirit," the king laughed. "I like him. I like him a lot, but I'm still going to kill him."

Avahn shouted at her father, "Da, I *trust* him. We can trust him."

"He's a barbarian," her father argued.

She stepped in front of the boy. "You train your knights for years, never knowing if their hearts will remain true in the fog of battle. This boy's heart is true."

The king jutted his chin toward her, and the giant Sir Bandolan grabbed Avahn's shoulder, pulled her from harm's way.

Her father drew back his axe again, prepared to take the killing blow.

In that moment, time seemed to slow and the world went quiet. King Harrill hesitated.

Up in the forest above, a woodpecker pecked, and in the distance a squirrel called from an oak tree.

The king stopped, peered uphill curiously.

"Hear that?" the king whispered to his men. He grew wary. His eyes danced left and right, as if he were thinking faster than a water strider could dance above a pool. He whirled and searched uphill to where green oaks spread over the dead grasses, casting deep shadows.

He shouted, "Come on, you bastards! I hear you up there. May you all taste my wrath this day!"

There was no answer from the silent woods for a long moment.

Suddenly a single archer stepped out from behind a tree. As a warlord of the Woguld, he wore a crimson breechcloth. A white silk cape flowed over his shoulders like a waterfall. His silver "sunmask" was a face like an elk's, with broad antlers and black glass-covered eyes to guard against bright light. The blue tattoos of the warrior's family tree wound around his calves, naming his ancestors and their deeds. He was glorious to look upon, regal and perfect.

He stood with his great bow, red as blood, its wings flaring wide, and nocked an arrow.

The king laughed and rubbed forefinger against thumb, the sign for "trade." He pointed to Dval.

Avahn did not know whether her father was offering to buy the boy, or to spare his life for a price.

To Dval, it was the worst of insults. The folk of the Woguld did not trade in slaves. Every man served his clan. The warlord above them was his uncle, and Dval felt certain he would order his men to waylay these barbarians.

Instead, his uncle drew the bow and fired.

As the arrow leapt forward, Dval thought, *He will kill their king!* Yet even as the thought came, he realized the arrow was winging toward him.

A flash to his side, a heavy thud—and Dval went flying from harm's way, his face skidding into the leaves. Avahn had shoved him, thrown him to the ground as the arrow whistled past.

Now she sat, holding her arm. Blood flowed from between her fingers, down her shoulder. His uncle's arrow had lightly kissed her flesh.

Dval's uncle called out, "Dval, what kind of fool are you? Do we not have enough enemies? You must save one?" Always that tone. "The friend of my enemy," his uncle roared, "*is* my enemy!"

His uncle spat, turned, and strode into the stark shadows under the trees.

For a second, Dval knew the sorrow of one who has been dispossessed.

Yet Dval watched his uncle, and did not know who was

more a barbarian—his uncle, the northerners around him, or Dval himself.

Perhaps we are all barbarians, Dval thought, *struggling to be human.*

Only one person seemed truly human—Avahn, who crouched stoically, holding her wound.

After that, no one threatened to kill Dval. Apparently now that he was cast out from the Woguld, his death sentence was rescinded. By trying to kill him, his uncle had saved his life.

The soldiers gathered their dead in silence and rode down from the mountains into the forbidden realm.

Avahn took Dval's hand. Together they rode down to the sprawling cities of Mystarria, to her home at the Courts of Tide, where the war fires of the Toth still burned.

Dᴀᴠɪᴅ Fᴀʀʟᴀɴᴅ—Dᴀᴠᴇ Wᴏʟᴠᴇʀᴛᴏɴ—was a prolific author, mentor, instructor, and family man. As a writer, he is best known for his Star Wars novel *The Courtship of Princess Leia* and his epic fantasy Runelords series. His other novels include *On My Way to Paradise* and *Nightingale*. A Grand Prize winner himself in the Writers of the Future contest, he eventually became an instructor and coordinating judge for the contest. He ran numerous intensive writing workshops, co-founded the Superstars Writing Seminars, created the Apex Writers Group, and never stopped helping aspiring writers.

Dave passed away in January 2022 and is survived by his wife, Mary, two daughters, three sons, and numerous grand-children.

Additional Copyright Information

About the Editor

Lisa Mangum has worked in publishing since 1997. She has been the Managing Editor for Shadow Mountain since 2014 and has worked with several *New York Times* bestselling authors. While fiction is her first love, she also has experience working with nonfiction projects.

Lisa is also the author of four national best-selling YA novels (The Hourglass Door trilogy and *After Hello*), several short stories and novellas, and a nonfiction book about the craft of writing based on the TV show *Supernatural*. She has edited several anthologies about various magical creatures, pirates, and food for WordFire Press. She regularly teaches at writing conferences, including hosting a writing weekend in Capitol Reef National Park through UVU. She lives in Taylorsville, Utah, with her husband, Tracy.

If You Liked ...

If you liked *Of Wizards and Wolves*, you might also enjoy:

Monsters, Movies & Mayhem
Edited by Kevin J. Anderson

Unmasked: Tales of Risk and Revelation
Edited by Kevin J. Anderson

War of the Worlds: Global Dispatch
Edited by Kevin J. Anderson

Other WordFire Press Titles
Edited by Lisa Mangum

One Horn to Rule Them All

A Game of Horns

Dragon Writers

Undercurrents

X Marks the Spot

Hold Your Fire

Eat, Drink, and Be Wary

Our list of other WordFire Press authors and titles is always growing. To find out more and to shop our selection of titles, visit us at:
wordfirepress.com

facebook.com/WordfireIncWordfirePress

twitter.com/WordFirePress

instagram.com/WordFirePress

bookbub.com/profile/4109784512